## A DREAM COME TRUE

Jack grasped Patricia in a one-armed embrace. "Got you," he said and leaned in to steal a kiss.

It was supposed to be a light-hearted touching of lips, a teasing Christmas mistletoe kiss, but when Patricia clutched his shoulder and leaned into him, he deepened it . . . deepened it still more when he heard a faint moan and felt her pressing closer.

When the kiss ended, they stared at each other in astonishment, neither quite certain what he or she felt, let alone what the other might feel.

"How do I feel?" he asked. His devil-grin appeared. "As if I would like to try that again."

"You would?"

"Don't pretend you didn't enjoy it," he retorted, his eyes narrowing, "or that I will not indulge you in as many such kisses as you like."

"Only if I likewise indulge you," she whispered.

# BOOK YOUR PLACE ON OUR WEBSITE AND MAKE THE READING CONNECTION!

We've created a customized website just for our very special readers, where you can get the inside scoop on everything that's going on with Zebra, Pinnacle and Kensington books.

When you come online, you'll have the exciting opportunity to:

- View covers of upcoming books
- Read sample chapters
- Learn about our future publishing schedule (listed by publication month *and author*)
- Find out when your favorite authors will be visiting a city near you
- Search for and order backlist books from our online catalog
- Check out author bios and background information
- Send e-mail to your favorite authors
- Meet the Kensington staff online
- Join us in weekly chats with authors, readers and other guests
- Get writing guidelines
- AND MUCH MORE!

**Visit our website at
http://www.zebrabooks.com**

# THE CHRISTMAS GIFT

## Jeanne Savery

**ZEBRA BOOKS**
Kensington Publishing Corp.
http://www.zebrabooks.com

ZEBRA BOOKS are published by

Kensington Publishing Corp.
850 Third Avenue
New York, NY 10022

All Kensington titles, imprints, and distributed lines are available at special quantity discounts for bulk purchases for sales promotions, premiums, fund raising, educational, or institutional use.

Special book excerpts or customized printings can also be created to fit specific needs. For details, write or phone the office of the Kensington Special Sales Manager: Kensington Publishing Corp., 850 Third Avenue, New York, NY 10022, attn: Special Sales Department. Phone: 1-800-221-2647.

Zebra and the Z logo Reg. U.S. Pat. & TM Off.

First Printing: October, 2000
10 9 8 7 6 5 4 3 2 1

Printed in the United States of America

## Books by Jeanne Savery

*The Widow and the Rake*

*A Reformed Rake*

*A Christmas Treasure*

*A Lady's Deception*

*Cupid's Challenge*

*Lady Stephanie*

*A Timeless Love*

*A Lady's Lesson*

*Lord Galveston and the Ghost*

*A Lady's Proposal*

*The Widowed Miss Mordaunt*

*A Love for Lydia*

*Taming Lord Renwick*

*Lady Serena's Surrender*

*The Christmas Gift*

Published by Zebra Books

# Prologue

Jack Princeton looked up from his bed at a fellow officer who was about to return to their regiment. The pity in his visitor's solemn face was unmistakable. Jack's lips tightened and the man flushed.

"Well, Princeton, I've things to do before I'm off." His tone was half apologetic, half embarrassed arrogance. "My new uniform to pick up, you know. And boots. Just wanted to say how glad I am you're recovering—"

*Recovering,* thought Jack. *Ha.*

"—so now I've said it and I'm off." He glanced at the other visitor waiting in the sickroom, an enlisted man who had been wounded in the same battle as Jack. "Good luck to you, too, Black," said the officer in a more condescending tone. He slapped his hat on his head and strode out.

Alone with his second visitor, Lieutenant Jack Princeton attempted to put aside his foul mood. The war damaged sergeant stood awkwardly at the end of his bed. He was obviously uncomfortable in the well-appointed bedroom. Absently, Jack rubbed his leg where his wound had nearly healed. It crossed his mind that he was far better off than the sergeant who had only one hand. The man was unlikely to find work, would be forced to go begging for his food. But—the man had two good legs. *He could ride.* Bitterness pierced Jack.

Jack's leg would *never* heal. Not properly. He'd be a cripple. *He* would never ride again. The knowledge lay like a weight across his chest.

*I'd be better off dead,* he thought.

"Wanted to say thankee," mumbled the grizzled soldier, drawing Jack from the self-pitying thoughts into which he'd so easily fallen. "Wanted to tell 'ee I knew 'ee saved m'miserable life and that I 'preciated it."

Appreciated it? When he must live the rest of his life maimed, useless? And why the sergeant thought Jack had done anything more than he'd have done for any of his men. . . .

"Wanted to say that if there was something I could do for you . . ."

*Do something?*

For the first time since he'd begun to recover from the infection and fever which nearly did for him, Jack's mind worked at the speed which helped make him an excellent officer. "Perhaps there is." Jack's eyes narrowed. One brow drooped in an odd fashion, while one corner of his mouth tipped up toward it.

The monkey expression brought a grin to the face of Jack's old sergeant. Bill Black had seen that devilish look on Crazy Jack's face often enough. And it always meant devilment.

*But*—grizzled brows snapped together—*what scheme can the lieutenant plot when the poor fellow cannot even get himself up from his bed?*

"Yes," mused Jack, "there *is* something you may do—and it may save *my* life in return."

Ignoring Black's astonishment, Jack pondered whether Sergeant Black was the man who always worked hard, was always careful of detail, and *always* followed an order to the last crossed *t* and dotted *i*. Jack was nearly certain he was.

"If you've not got a position—" Jack eyed the man's clean but shabby clothes, the rundown boots which had been lovingly, if futilely, polished. "—I'm in need of a man."

The sergeant's eyes widened. "Me, sir? But—" He waved

his empty wrist in the air, wondering if, somehow, Crazy Jack had overlooked it. "—you see, I can't perform m'duties as I should. Maybe . . ."

"You'll do." Jack's ever-simmering bitterness surfaced again. "We'll be a pair, will we not? You with one hand—me with one working leg?"

Black ignored the flippant comment. "Ye be serious, sir?"

Jack nodded. "Oh yes." His jaw clenched. "As serious as if the devil were in it."

Black ignored that, too. He drew in a deep breath. "Then, if you think I can do for you, o'course I will." The glint in his eye faded and he scowled. "Anything I *can* do, that is."

"Don't fret it. My needs are simple and you'll do very well."

Jack didn't care a jot if Black could not do all a man's valet should do. Pressed cravats and polished boots were unimportant. He needed the man for other reasons. Things another man might *not* do for him. Black was trained to follow orders. And, following them, they could engineer an escape from the suffocating care Jack received here in his friend's house!

When first brought home from the Peninsula by Rolly Templeton, a less severely wounded officer, Jack had been too ill to care what was done with him. He'd been so sick that he'd been unaware Rolly's elder sister had involved herself in his nursing. Besides, since he'd expected to die, who cared for him had made not an iota of difference.

Now, on his way to some sort of recovery, he *did* care. A lot. The blasted woman *hovered*. She seemed to think he could do *nothing* for himself merely because one leg would never again function as it should.

Jack remembered Miss Templeton's horror a few days previously when she'd come in with his luncheon tray and discovered him maneuvering himself toward a chair by the window. She'd screeched, startling him, and he'd stumbled, fallen. He scowled at the recollection.

"Sir?" asked Black, unsettled by the frown. He sighed. "If you've changed your mind, sir, I understand, sir."

"Nothing of the sort. I said I need you and I do." Once again Jack forced his bitter thoughts aside and returned to the problem of how to use this windfall. This gift from providence.

He and Black settled the terms of their arrangement. Then Jack swore softly. He hadn't so much as a Portuguese escudo to give the fellow! Black needed clothing suitable to his new position as general factotum and nursemaid to Jack's crippled self. He himself needed clothes and new boots, to say nothing of more personal items.

He glanced around the room. "That looks to be a writing case on the desk there, Black. Bring it to me."

The sergeant did so, setting it gently on Jack's lap. He stood by as Jack opened it, seeking paper, pen, and ink.

What Jack had not thought to find was a half-finished letter which Miss Templeton had begun to a friend. Nor had he expected to see his own name appearing far too often to miss. . . . *I love Lieutenant Princeton,* she wrote. *I've hopes he feels the same. We will marry . . .* For a long astonished moment Jack stared at the words which seemed to leap off the page. Then guilt that he'd read from her private letter diminished as he fought back the new fear her sentiments roused in him.

"Oh, yes," he muttered. *"More* than time I escape!"

He took paper and a pencil and, his words slashing across the page, wrote a note to his solicitor. He told his new employee where to take it, that he'd be given money. Then Jack gave orders as to how Black was to use that money, telling him where to order boots, a hat, and linens. That was followed by another spate of orders detailing what would be necessary for a journey.

"Our new boots will be a week or more in the making. Arrange all else during that time. Then, when everything I've ordered is done, you return here. While you do that—"

Once again a touch of bitterness colored Jack's tone.

"—I'll contrive tactics for getting me out of here without a cursed scene!"

Black returned the writing case to the desktop. As the man carefully placed the box exactly where he'd found it, he heard Jack mutter, "On top of all else, I could not bear a scene."

# One

The two men on horseback stared at the derelict buildings snuggled into the far hillside. Although the stabling appeared to be in reasonably good shape, a tree had fallen across a smaller outbuilding, crushing the roof. Ivy, turned red and brown by recent frosts, clung to the gray stone house, covering walls and windows alike with untrimmed vines. Worse, many of the windows gaped black with no glass or, here and there, were covered by planks. Slates had fallen from a section of a roof onto which a chimney had collapsed. Finally, the grounds were overgrown, the hedges ragged for want of clipping. In short, the property had been long abandoned.

"We were wrong," said the first man.

"No one could live there," agreed the second.

"So where is he?"

"Your guess is better than mine."

"I was so certain."

The bare headed man chuckled. "But, Alex, you always *are!*" Wendover slapped his hat against his thigh in emphasis.

Lord Alex Merwin shook his fist at Lord Anthony Wendover, the Earl of Hendred's heir, and friend from school days.

Wendover didn't notice. He stared, a vertical line appearing between his eyes. "Or perhaps you were *not* wrong?"

Merwin's head snapped back, his eyes narrowed. "What do you see?"

"There. Rising over the east wing. From the back. Isn't that smoke?"

Merwin shaded his eyes. Finally he perceived a faint gray smudge against the sere slope beyond the building. "I believe it is." On the words, he caught up his reins and kicked his mount into motion. "Let's go," he called over his shoulder. "If Jack is living in that wreck of a house, he's not only lost the use of one leg, but lost his mind as well!"

The horses forded a burbling stream and cantered over dry grass up the long slope, clattering onto cobblestones between which weeds grew. The men pulled up to stare at the run-down house and a girl gaping up at them. Obviously frightened out of whatever wits she had, the chit picked up her skirts and ran through a back door open to the chilly breeze.

Merwin noticed a calloused bare heel, a dirty ankle.

"Didn't mean to frighten her," said Wendover.

"At least we know *someone* lives here."

A man appeared. Not the one for whom they searched, but one dressed as an upper servant, his attire in strong contrast to badly weathered skin and—

Merwin's brows snapped into a Mephistophelian vee.

Both men could not help but notice the loss of one of the servant's hands.

"What may I do for yer?" he asked in the careful tone of one making an attempt at correct speech.

"We are in search of a friend, Lieutenant Jack Princeton," said Merwin.

The servant eyed them from under shaggy brows. "Friends, hmm?"

Wendover saw the face of the frightened child-woman peering through a window. He smiled at her and, instantly, she disappeared. His mouth tightened. He truly disliked that they unnerved the chit.

Merwin continued, "If Jack is here, will you inform him of our arrival?"

"Inform him *who* has come?" asked the man.

"Oh." Merwin felt the heat of mild embarrassment. Of course this man would not know them! "This is Lord Wendover and I am Lord Merwin. We are very worried about our friend."

"Why do you suspicion he's here?" asked the man. He pushed his hat back with the arm stubbed off at the wrist.

"His brother owns this—" Merwin's brows formed a disparaging vee. "—lodge?" He'd heard rumors that Lord George Princeton had rowed up the River Tick, that he'd soon find lodging in debtors' prison. But the decay of this, a prized family possession, suggested things had gone farther, and for longer, than he'd known.

"Look, you, whoever you are—" Wendover was also inspecting the lodge. "—if Jack *is* here, he cannot remain. Winter will come upon us in no time and this place is uninhabitable! I wouldn't house a dog here."

The servant turned a sardonic eye on Wendover. "Oh, it ain't so bad. We had it worse in Spain. Often and often."

*"We?"* Merwin's eyes narrowed. "You and Jack?" The man cast a wary look over his shoulder and his lordship sighed. As he swung his leg over his horse's back, he said, "Come along, Tony. We'll see for ourselves."

"Don't bother," said a new and grating voice.

There, leaning against the doorjamb, was their friend. And he scowled at them.

"Don't dismount," Jack added sharply as Alex lowered himself to the ground. "Get back up, Alex, and on your way," he ordered. "I don't need you. I don't want you. Either of you. Just go."

Merwin looked at Wendover, who frowned at him and shrugged. Merwin grimaced. "Not exactly the most hospitable offer I've ever had." He turned back. "You could at least give us a meal before sending us off all those miles to that wretched inn in Ilton."

"Inn?" Wendover's expression was one of overdone outrage. *"Inn?* You call that thieves den an *inn?* Jack, if you care for us at all, don't make us go back there for the night. We'll be murdered in our beds!"

"Yes, but at least you'd *have* a bed," said Jack. He didn't move, except to glance at the sky. "Besides, if you waste no time, you could not only make it to Ilton, but collect your traps and go on to the Golden Fleece in Thirsk."

"But I'm hungry." Wendover dismounted. "Jack, you wouldn't send us away without feeding us. I know you wouldn't!"

Jack compressed his lips and scowled. "Damn you! The both of you!"

It was the husky whiskey voice they remembered, but the tone was wrong. All wrong. Where was the jest always found on Jack's lips? Where was the laughter that had drawn one into good humor, even if at one's expense? Still, it was Jack's voice, a well-loved voice. . . .

"Could you not leave well enough alone?"

The bitterness grated on Wendover. He cast a glance up at the lodge's structure, along the row of broken windows, the lost slates. *Leave well enough alone?* "Well enough?" Wendover repeated both his thoughts and Jack's words. "You consider this *well enough?"*

"We're working on it," said Jack defensively. He *looked* as if he'd been working. He wore no coat and his shirt, torn at one elbow, gaped over his chest.

"Been trying to winterproof a few rooms," offered the servant, his arms crossed over his chest, his eyes narrowing thoughtfully.

"Trying?" asked Merwin, his voice sharp.

"That's enough, Black," ordered Jack. "Disappear if you cannot keep your jaw under lock and key!"

"I'll keep m'mummer dubbed," grumbled the servant and moved away, but only a few steps.

A comfortably well-padded woman, her dark hair showing white threads at the temples, appeared behind Jack.

"Sir," she said, "it's only stew, but there's plenty. More than enough for friends. And I just pulled that meat pie from the oven. The one you shot the birds for. It'll go down a treat with my home brew . . . Sir?" she finished, alarmed by the glare Jack shot her way. Apprehensive, she wrapped her arms in her apron and stepped back. "Oh, dear, I didn't mean . . ."

Jack groaned and threw up his hands. "To the devil with all of you. All right," he said, staring at Merwin. "But I warn you." His glance flashed toward Wendover. "You'll not like the accommodations." Limping badly, holding the wall to steady himself, Lieutenant Jack Princeton shoved past the woman and disappeared into the house.

"I'll just put up your horses," said the man Jack had called Black.

Wendover cast an involuntary glance to where the man's coat sleeve covered the end of his wrist.

"You'd be surprised how well I manage," said the servant, a sardonic glint in his eyes. "Your prads won't suffer. Hester—" He spoke to the plump woman. "—you settle the lieutenant's friends in the kitchen. He's talked about them. Lots. They'll understand we can't put 'em in proper salons and dining rooms with fancy bits and pieces."

She blushed rosily. " 'Tain't right, though."

"Lots 'taint right. 'Tain't right Crazy Jack living like this, not a gentleman and an officer like him," retorted Black. He turned to Merwin and Wendover. "You go on in," he said more civilly and gathered up their reins.

Even Merwin, who was not so very tall, ducked under the low lintel of the house into the cozy stone-floored room beyond. They were in time to see the shy girl whisk the tail of her dirty skirts into a room to one side. Very likely a pantry or scullery. When she peeked back into the room, Wendover once again tried smiling at her and, again, she disappeared.

"Leave her be, Tony." Jack had appeared when they were not looking, leaning against the doorjamb. He'd put on a coat, but not bothered with a cravat, and the ties, although they closed his shirt, dangled. "The child was badly treated and not all there. I promised her mother she'd be safe here. See that she is."

Wendover's pale skin took on a rosy tint. "Don't mean her harm, Jack. Just wish she didn't think I might!"

Jack grinned. It would have been the slightly wicked grin they remembered—if there were not a sardonic twist to it neither man had seen before. *"You* know it. *I* know it. But *she* doesn't know it. And she wouldn't understand if you explained. So, if you really want to make her happy, ignore her."

The words, too, were not right. Where once they would have been a light-hearted gibe, now they had a bite, spoken in the tone of an order. Merwin and Wendover glanced at each other and, both together, rolled their eyes to the ceiling. Jack, meanwhile, moved nearer, half-sat on a worktable.

It occurred to Merwin that Jack hated for anyone to see him limp, and he promised himself he would have a word about it with Wendover as soon as they had a moment together. Alex put the thought aside and asked, "Jack what do you think you are doing here in the wilds of Yorkshire, living in a building about to collapse around your ears."

"Fixing it so it won't collapse," was Jack's prompt retort.

"Your brother should be shot for letting it get into such a state," scolded Wendover. He recalled delightful parties, long days out with a gun and longer nights at cards. But they'd all been younger then. "A man has responsibilities . . ."

"Yes. I do," interrupted Jack.

"You . . . ?"

"I bought it from George."

"Before you'd seen it." Merwin didn't make a question of it.

Jack sneered. "Now how," he asked sarcastically, "did you come to that conclusion!"

"Because if you'd seen it," said Merwin promptly, "you'd have known it wasn't worth ten pence."

"Actually," said Jack, looking at his nails, "that's about all I paid for it."

"You *had* seen it?" asked Wendover.

"Oh yes. I came up early this summer. Then I had inquiries made and discovered how far up Queer Street my dear brother has traveled. You would not believe how far. Anyway, I caught him at a moment when he needed a few pounds rather badly, and offered him a few more than needed, thereby, saving one small piece of the estate." Bitter lines settled around his eyes. "He will lose it all before he's done."

"I hope this was his to sell you," said Merwin, with almost as much bite in his voice as in Jack's.

Jack's old monkey smile twisted his face and both friends heard true humor when he chuckled. "George forgot he owned it or it would have been long gone. Everything entailed which he cannot sell is mortgaged to the hilt. The blood suckers will have their paws on any profits for decades. Maybe forever." Again his quick, sharp grin resembled the old one. But it faded, and Jack shrugged. "I've my work cut out just putting *this* place back in order. But the structure is sound. All it needs is a bit of this and that."

"And the money to do it."

"There is that, of course," agreed Jack, neither admitting nor denying he'd the necessary funds. "Tell me how you guessed where to find me," he said, changing the subject.

Merwin told how they had worried and wondered and fretted, finally remembered Jack's brother and this lodge as the woman called Hester scrubbed an already shining table and set it. Merwin admitted it had not occurred to them that Jack would have bought it.

"It and the hunting and fishing rights. I'll do quite nicely here."

"You expect to *live* in this Godforsaken place?" asked Wendover, appalled. Lord Tony Wendover loved society and all that went with it.

"A Godforsaken place for a Godforsaken man. Seems fitting," said Jack, the sneer returning to voice and features.

His friends winced at the acid note. Merwin was beginning to get a glimmer of just how deep Jack's bitterness ran, but Wendover did not. "You've no neighbors," he objected. He got no more than a sardonic glance for his objection. "You've no one to talk to," he persisted. When Jack only compressed his lips, he added, "No company, no one with whom to play cards or go hunting or to flirt and dance—" He broke off, embarrassed at mentioning something Jack would never again do. "—or, like I said, talk to," he finished a trifle awkwardly.

"And no one—" The words burst from Jack, weakly derisive. "—to *pity* me or pretend I'm *a whole man!*"

"Do you think we like you less because your leg didn't heal properly?" asked Merwin softly.

Two spots of color appeared on Jack's cheeks. He rubbed his leg. "No, of course not," he said quietly. He looked up and met Merwin's eyes. "But can you tell me with complete honesty that you do not pity me?"

"I am sorry," said Merwin with great care, "that you may no longer indulge your love of riding as you once did. But I do *not* pity you. You are *alive,* Jack, when so many others are *dead.* And there are, whether or no you are yet willing to admit it, other things in life than riding."

A defiant Jack held Merwin's steady gaze. Then his eyes dropped. "For others, maybe," Jack muttered. He looked into some distant place the others could not see. "For me," he said, "riding was life itself."

Luckily, Hester called them to the table just then, interrupting what might have become a divisive argument.

What he might have said next would, Merwin feared, have cut Jack deeply. But the response was prevented by the call to dine and, remembering that Jack would prefer they not watch his awkward progress, Merwin took Wendover's shoulder and turned him away, walking him around the far end of the table. As he'd expected, Jack was seated by the time they reached their own chairs.

The next few days were the most uncomfortable Lord Tony Wendover had ever experienced. Not only was he expected to sleep on the floor, no more than a few thin blankets padding it, but, almost worse, he discovered that if he wished to eat, he must first bring in the meat and fish from which a meal would be prepared! It was outside of enough. No wonder Jack had become so sardonic, so severe.

Wendover said as much to Merwin as they brushed down their horses, heated from a ride into town. They had purchased a few provisions needed in the kitchen, and a small keg of nails from the blacksmith before returning to Jack's lodge.

Jack had told them that, since it appeared they meant to stay, they could make themselves useful. Merwin was certain Jack's biting tone covered the embarrassment he felt at making such a demand of them.

He also thought the errands he and Wendover ran in Ripon, the nearest town of any size, had saved Jack the even greater mortification of showing himself before the town folk. Jack, as Merwin had guessed, hated anyone seeing his ungainly stride.

Merwin moved around his mount, slipping on frost-slicked cobblestones, saving himself from a fall by grasping his horse's mane. "Tony, he cannot be allowed to stay here. He wants to hide from the world, but it will not do."

"But if he won't go, what *can* we do?"

"If we conclude we cannot convince him, then——" Merwin straightened and shook the curry brush at the heavens. "——blast and bedamned to it, Tony, we'll kidnap him!"

" 'n I'll help if'n you tell me what to do," said Bill Black from the other side of a nearby hedge. Jack's man pushed through the long, untrimmed bushes to stand before them.

He removed his hat. "The lieutenant ain't himself," he said, his untidy brows brought together in a worried looking frown. "Not at all himself. But you know that, seen'n as how you're his friends and all. And staying here and broodin' like he does, 'tain't doing him one bit of good, either."

"I appreciate your offer of help, but he will have your job if he finds you've betrayed him," warned Merwin, his narrow face set in stern lines.

Black nodded. "So be it. Just so long as Crazy Jack is all right. My job ain't—*isn't*—worth a farthing compared to *his* suffering."

"You feel *that* strongly?" asked Wendover, laying his arms across his horse's withers and staring, wonderingly, across the back of his horse.

"He saved my life. But even before that, I'd have done most anything for Lieutenant Jack Princeton. So would have any of us. He wasn't like some officers. A real come-on, Crazy Jack," he finished, his pride in Jack evident.

"A . . . come on?"

Black grinned at Wendover, revealing a broken tooth. "Lots were the go-on sort. No one liked a go-on officer."

Wendover's mouth tightened, spreading into a slight smile. His eyes narrowed, twinkling. "I see. What you mean to say is that he *led* you into battle rather than *following* after you, is that not correct?"

Black nodded. "A real come-on officer. The very best, *he* was." The man sobered. "And he still is if he'd only see it. The same good man. Why, when we came here, even the kitchen was a wreck—with no decent place for Hester and the girl. Those were his first orders: We had to fix their room before all else, and the kitchen second."

Wendover frowned. "But where did *he* sleep?"

"In the haymow. The barn roof stayed whole and the hay was pretty well dry. We had it champion." Black cast them a sardonic look. "Fact is, it still is a better place to sleep than in there!" He gestured toward the house behind them and then back at the stable. He pushed back his hat in that way he had. "You think it disloyal of me," he continued, "suggesting I help you get him away from this, but what you said, it's true. He can't stay here this winter. We do the best we can, but we don't have enough firewood ready and if'n we get snowed in, which ain't unlikely, we might not get out to shoot our dinner." The man, made loquacious by the strength of his emotions, added, "Much better if he goes away 'til spring. Maybe then, with all next summer to work, we could have the place ready for next winter?"

Wendover shook his head at the thought of living here, alone, lonely. Tony Wendover liked people far too well to understand how one survived without company.

Merwin, however, had a far better understanding of Jack's current state of mind. He nodded. "I'll use that argument when the time comes. Black, I suspect we *will* need your help getting him away. At least my guess is he will refuse to come voluntarily."

"Likely not," agreed Black, a trifle morosely. "You'll need a carriage for him, too. You tell me and I'll go for it."

"We've one waiting for us in Ilton, but thank you for reminding me to bring it here. We'll make our plans and then consult with you to see if we've forgotten anything." His words were a dismissal. Black marched toward the house, where they could hear Jack pounding away at some repair.

As he finished grooming his gelding, Merwin worked out a few more details of the plan which had been burgeoning in his mind from the moment he woke, stiff and sore, after their very first night at the lodge.

"Alex," said Wendover, "were you serious? We'll *kidnap* him?"

"Not if you can come up with a better plan!"

*"Me?"*

"I have tried but can think of no other way of managing the trick. Assuming he refuses to come. And I cannot imagine

Black's Crazy Jack acting tamely, doing the sensible thing, can you?"

Wendover sighed. "No. And if *you* cannot come up with another means of rescuing him, then I know I cannot. So, Alex, what do we do?"

# *Two*

Patricia Haydon moved gracefully to Merwin Hall's salon window and stared down the long drive. It was the third time in the past hour she had watched for signs of an approaching carriage. Returning to her needlework, she berated herself for a fool. When her cousin, Alex Merwin, had asked if he and Wendover could bring Jack Princeton and his valet to Merwin Hall, Patricia could hardly have refused. It was his home! So, after all these years, she would see Jack again.

But Jack Princeton was no longer a boy verging on manhood. He would be nothing like the puckish creature with a touch of the devil she recalled from that long ago summer, when her cousin's friends had allowed her, in the young male's disgustingly arrogant fashion, to join their activities.

She had met the boys fondly known as the Six when she spent the summer before her marriage at the Merwin estate. The six boys had gathered for a month before going off to University. They included her cousin Lord Alex Merwin, Lord Anthony Wendover, Lord Jason Renwick, Ian McMurrey, Miles Seward . . . and of course . . . Jack Princeton. The Six had remained friends, sometimes losing touch, but always thought of themselves as the Six.

She would never forget that summer. Despite their superior attitudes, it had been fun. *Jack* had been fun. Best of all, he alone had not seemed to see her as an unwelcome female, but as just another member of the group who rode like demons across the fens, fished until their skin burned, or played cricket and lawn tennis. After her disastrous Season, it had been a relief, a return to childhood. Pure heaven and Jack Princeton—her good angel!

*I suppose it is not surprising I developed an infatuation for a boy who showed signs of the man he'd become.*

A born leader, he had been fearless, but, with it, careful for others less able or less daring. He seemed to know intuitively just how far each of his friends should go, and watched that they were no more than challenged to do their best. And he had treated her in the same casually careful way.

He was lightning. Endless energy. Always on the move.

He was laughter and jests and a flashing smile, teeth white in a sun gilded face.

*And,* Patricia scolded herself when she found herself once again moving toward the window, *he is no longer sixteen going on seventeen and I no longer barely eighteen, unhappy, doing my best to forget my wedding, scheduled for early in the fall. A marriage giving me into the hands of a good man, a kind man, a rich man . . . and, oh! such a boring man.*

Raising her eyes toward heaven, Patricia apologized to her dead husband. He *had* been good and kind. And he had left her comfortably well off. But comfortable, he'd also left her with more than mere disinterest in ever putting herself under another yoke with yet another good, kind, perhaps wealthy, but more than likely boring man!

*So instead,* she continued her scold, *you daydream of a boy who no longer exists. A boy who grew up and went to war, a man among men. A man who nearly died. He cannot possibly be the same,* she told herself. *That boy has disappeared forever.*

Still, when she finally heard the long awaited sound of carriage horses trotting up the Merwin Hall drive, Patricia moved quickly toward the front door.

Colliers, Merwin's butler, ordered the doors thrown open

and the footmen out to unload the carriage. Patricia put aside thoughts of the past, allowed a footman to drape a shawl over her shoulders, and strode forward to stand in the shadow just beyond the entry.

Her heartbeat increased. *How idiotic of it,* she thought, but her eyes never left the carriage.

Her cousin, Lord Alex Merwin, dismounted and waved to her as he moved to the carriage door which, waving aside a footman, he himself opened. Lord Wendover descended, casting Alex a look. Then, noticing Patricia, Wendover strolled in his usual languid fashion up the shallow steps to greet her.

"Terrible journey," he said, once he'd said all that was polite.

"The roads are always worse to the north," she responded. Her eyes remained on the carriage from which an upper servant hopped down and turned back. "You *have* brought him, have you not?" she whispered.

An expression of long-suffering crossed Wendover's usually pleasant features. "Oh yes." He raised his quizzing glass with which he'd been fiddling and pointed it toward the carriage. "We have him. *He* is the reason travel was difficult, not the roads. Although," he added politely, "there is enough to complain about there as well."

A fluent series of curses drifted from the carriage.

"I see," she said, her tone dry as dust.

Princeton's husky voice was deeper than she recalled, but had the same fascinating and unforgettable rasp. Another round of oaths—and she laughed.

Wendover smiled wryly at her contralto chuckle. "That's the problem, you see. Jack has not stopped swearing since he woke up."

"Woke up?" Patricia cast a curious glance toward Wendover, but immediately turned back.

"We dosed him with laudanum," he confided, "and kidnapped him."

Patricia blinked at that. Again her heart betrayed her when a dark-haired, wiry man appeared. He hooked a cross-handed grip over the roof, twisted, and lowered his legs to the ground, dropping one hand to his servant's shoulder. He found his balance, but not without difficulty, if the pained expression crossing the valet's face was any indication.

"All right, Jack?" asked Merwin.

"No." The word had a clipped and surly sound.

"Leg paining you?"

"Enough to notice." Jack's reply was sharp, the words bitten off. *"Why the devil did you do it, Alex? Why couldn't you leave well enough alone?"*

"We've been over and over this," said Merwin impatiently. "You could not possibly have remained in that ruin all winter. And what of the women? Did you wish your maid and cook to suffer along with you?"

All he got was a glare from Jack.

Less astringently, Merwin said, "Far better they spend the winter with my sister's old governess, Jack. And maybe *next* winter it will do. Once you've had a summer to make repairs and get in necessities." Still the same glaring response. "Blast it, Jack! Don't play the fool. You know I am right."

"We put up with worse in Portugal. Often."

"Put up with. That is the point, is it not? You no longer have to *put up with anything.*"

Jack sighed. "Well, just remember, you promised me the countryside lacks company. I'll not be made a laughing stock . . ." As he spoke, Jack hopped around, his leg dragging. His gaze fell on Patricia and he twisted back, grabbing a handful of Alex's coat. *"You promised."*

"Promised . . . ?" Alex looked around, frowning. "Oh. But Jack, it is only Patricia. You remember my cousin, do you not? She is the widowed Mrs. Haydon now, and she is not company." Jack glowered. "Damn it Jack, she *lives* here."

Red spots appeared, barely apparent through Jack's weathered skin, and his jaw clenched. He turned further, grasping the doorframe. "I'm going home."

"Hell and damnation! I'll knock you on the head and carry you in if you don't stop acting the biggest fool in Christendom!" When Jack bent to enter the carriage, Merwin added, "It is your *behavior* which makes you the laughing stock you dread you will be named. Not your *limp!*"

Jack straightened, rigid with outrage. "Tell her to go away."

Patricia, concern fighting with horror, heard her cousin growl a low response. She waited his approach. "Alex?"

"Jack limps," he said. "Badly. He hates it. He hates anyone watching him move. Please go in and join us later?" A touch of humor lightened his tone. "Perhaps once he has come to the green salon before dinner?"

Patricia cast a glance toward the man standing beside the carriage. His scowl deepened. "I see how it is with him." She spoke clearly, a touch of acid in her voice. "You are right, of course, that it is his nasty disposition which will cause him difficulties, and not an ugly gait."

"Shrew," said Jack. He too spoke in normal tones, the word lacking any emotional significance.

Patricia hid a smile. "I'll see his things are put away properly. His room," she said, "is on this floor, by the way. When I received your letter, Alex, I had a bedroom and sitting room made out of the lady parlor and sewing room. Your not-so-tame bear—" A touch of acid returned to her speech. "—will not find himself required to climb stairs."

"Or perhaps it is an angel?" she heard Jack exclaim. "Ah! But a *red headed* angel? Is it possible?"

As she entered the house, Patricia had to strain to hear Jack's final question. As he spoke, his tone softened, was different. Slightly apologetic, perhaps? Slightly fervent, holding just a hint of his old humor? And perhaps, by losing her temper, she had learned something?

Jack was acting like a hurt child, a child who needed understanding. However, like a child, *he must not be allowed to act the brat!* Was it possible Jack Princeton would respond more favorably if she did *not* baby him?

Having settled in her mind how she would treat Jack Princeton when next they met, she went to the suite prepared for him in order to check, for the fifth time, or was it the sixth?, that all was ready.

When assured by Black that he needed nothing, Patricia climbed the stairs to her own suite in a thoughtful mood. The valet lacked a hand. She had ignored his condition, but was amazed at what the man could do. One-handed, he'd deftly unpacked Jack's belongings. Quickly and neatly. Patricia had never before dealt with someone maimed in such a way and, if she had ever thought about it, would have assumed a one-handed man pretty useless. How wrong she'd have been!

Once in her room, Patricia went directly to the fireplace where a small coal fire burned all day from first frost to last. She held out her hands to the blaze and considered Jack. The wounded man resented his lameness. Patricia judged he also hid deep dejection under simmering rage. She guessed he was disheartened and that he grieved for all he'd never do again.

But just exactly what were the things he could no longer do? She wondered if he had made any attempt to find out. If not, she must suggest he experiment, make him try, get him to see that a failure here and there was not the end of his world.

Still . . . could he be reached? Yes. He could be. There had been his last teasing comment before she'd come in the house. He was *not* so far fallen into despair that he could not be scolded or cajoled into proper behavior. And she was just the one to scold, was she not? Had he not called her a shrew?

"The gray or the green gown?" asked Patricia's maid from the doorway to her dressing room.

Patricia swung around and looked at the two dresses Milly held up. She pressed her lips tightly together. Her plump and bustling abigail raised first the gray and then the green. Patricia shook her head.

Her maid's eyes widened. "You don't mean to change?" asked Milly, shocked to the core.

"Oh yes. I'll dress for dinner."

Patricia recalled her last visit to London, her consternation at just how far fashion had altered since her previous visit two years earlier. She had made quick forays into the shops and another to her modiste. And then, home again, she had felt uncomfortable in her new finery and ordered that Milly put the gowns away.

Still—for *company?*

Patricia put aside a mental picture of Jack and told herself, *I'll do it because Lord Wendover is here. He, after all, is an arbiter of fashion, knowledgeable about all the latest fripperies, and, I have noticed, a trifle severe with those who fail to dress their best!*

"Perhaps—" She paused, still a trifle hesitant. "—the brown?"

"What brown?" Milly frowned, her thick brows drawing together. Then her eyes sparkled and a grin spread across her middle-aged features. *"Brown.* You mean a London gown? A new one? You will wear one of your *mistakes?"*

"Did I call them that? I suppose I did. Yes, bring out the chestnut-brown with the ecru lace. I will wear it in honor of our company."

"You will bring the men to their knees," said Milly complaisantly. "They will stare to see you so beautiful."

The maid disappeared into the dressing room and Patricia, her mood lightened by such foolishness, called, "You would say I am not to be thought beautiful unless gowned extravagantly, drawing attention from my face?"

Milly returned instantly. "That's nonsense and you know it," she scolded. "But a man likes to see beauty nicely wrapped up. And when you go down—" She pasted on an expression of innocence which *might* have fooled someone less percipient than her mistress. "—I'll bundle up your old things and give them away, shall I?"

Patricia mimicked both her maid's words and scolding tone. *"That's nonsense and you know it,"* she said. Her lips twitched. "A very good try, however."

Milly's chin rose a notch. "You wear your clothes 'til they fall to bits."

"And then you mend them," teased Patricia, "and I wear them a bit longer." She sobered. "Don't reproach me, Milly. I am not a pinchpenny where money is needed. I am merely careful."

Her maid sighed because there was no answering that. Her mistress was the most generous of ladies when a need arose. Just think of how she helped Widow Remmy and her children, paying the rent each year for the cottage and all? And then there was the time old Farmer Jones broke his leg, his sons all gone off to war. Didn't she hire a man out of her own pocket until he was able to manage? And Vicar never went away, his pockets empty, did he?

No, Mrs. Haydon was not a pinchpenny. It was just that she refused to spend her pennies on herself! Which was a shame. Mrs. Haydon was a lady who paid for dressing, as the saying went. Her tall figure was designed for the new styles. And to see her in a riding habit! Now *there* was a pleasant sight. Like a princess, she was.

A princess who deserved a prince! Milly's thoughts strayed along that path as she brushed her lady's hair. *Now that nice Lord Anthony Wendover would do her very well,* she mused. *Oh, very well indeed!*

Lord Wendover was just the sort of man to whom Milly would like to see her mistress wed. A man who spent all of each Season in London and the rest visiting great houses here and there. She had heard he was even invited to visit Prince George's Pavilion in Brighton! Now *there* would be a sight worth seeing . . . her mistress dressed for a musical evening at the Pavilion . . . or perhaps a *soirée?*

*Ah!* thought Milly, *she'd wear lace and jewels and her hair'd be piled high, with one of them little crown-like things adorning it. Tiara. That is what they call it, don't they?*

"Here now, Milly! What are you doing?"

Milly looked at the elaborate hair style she'd begun to contrive. Her rosy cheeks flushed an unbecoming red. "Sorry. Must have been thinking of something else."

"So you must. We are not readying me for presentation in the queen's drawing room!"

Milly bit back a tart response to the effect that she'd love to do just that and, instead, forced herself to pay attention to her brush, comb, and hairpins.

Some half an hour later Patricia stood before the cheval glass and reassured herself that she looked as well as could be expected of a woman long past her glory years. She noted tiny lines near her eyes and leaned close, peering at them.

*The beginning of the end,* she thought glumly.

"Why," she muttered, "do creases on a man's face merely make him look distinguished or handsome or some such thing, when the very same lines on a woman's face are aging?"

"Nonsense. Proper lines add character to a handsome woman," said Milly. "Don't you go worrying your head about a line or two, Mrs. Haydon. You'll turn heads long and long."

"You are a loyal thing, Milly, if you truly mean it!"

"I mean it. You'll see."

But, staring at her strange new look, Patricia felt uncomfortable with the style. "What I see," she muttered softly, "is an old ewe dressed as a lamb."

For half a moment she debated changing into her old green gown, but then put the thought aside. Everyone was allowed a bit of foolishness once in a great while. Her idiotic nostalgia for the past, the youthful emotions shadowing corners of her mind and heart for a boy who no longer existed, well those things would be her foolishness for this decade.

And, while she suffered through the nonsense of this long delayed infatuation, she would do what she could, in whatever way it must be done, to make life more tolerable for Jack Princeton.

"Merely doing a good deed. And *not* because I am idiotically in lo . . ."

Patricia bit off her words and Milly, straightening the dressing table, cast a sharp look toward her mistress's back as Mrs. Haydon exited the room.

"In lo . . ." repeated Milly. "Now what," she asked herself, "did Mrs. Haydon mean by that? In . . . *love?* Could it be? And with Lord Wendover, perhaps?" Milly's eyes widened. "Ah, they will wed and we will go into society as we should. Yes we will!"

The maid did a little jig before returning to her tidying.

And while Milly jigged, Patricia scolded herself, giving herself one more stern lecture about the utter stupidity of remaining in love with a memory.

# *Three*

Jack chose a seat to the side of the fireplace. One that faced the door. By choice, he had arrived in the salon early. As the first to enter the room, no one was there to watch him limp. The bitter thought crossed his mind that, if he had a real choice, he would go directly to the dining room and take his seat before anyone arrived.

He rubbed his thigh which ached abominably. No matter how well he supported it, the bouncing had jarred his bad leg unbearably. Not that it was as bad as the times he and Black traveled to and from London. Those two journeys, endured before his leg was fully healed, were true nightmares.

Still, the nightmare had, at the time, been more desirable than remaining in London. He could not allow Lady Anne to dream that, someday, he would wed her. How, he wondered, had he missed the signs? Why had he not noticed how she felt *before* that accidental perusing of her letter when, *after,* he was forced to admit how it was with her.

He had felt penned in by her, imprisoned, overly cosseted by her care of him. But, grateful for her earlier nursing, he had hidden his feelings. Gratitude. Was that why he hadn't noticed when Lady Anne's behavior changed from that of a caring nurse to something warmer?

Perhaps. But that was the past. That was over. Never again need he meet Lady Anne Templeton, so he should no longer feel the horror which crept up on him whenever it occurred to him he might have been trapped into marriage with her, might have been forced to suffer her overly solicitous care for the rest of his life. He shuddered. Still, it had not happened. He need not catch her pitying looks, the too-careful offers of help, or her apparent certainty that he would need such help forever.

Or would he? Not from Lady Anne, of course, but another woman's pity? Was it not possible Merwin's cousin was another nurse-maid?

Jack scowled. Tricksy Minxy, as he'd tagged Patricia all those years ago, had become a tall, handsome woman as he'd seen before she'd entered the house. And he'd noticed no extra delicacy in her treatment of him, pretended or real, no shrinking from his ugliness. Still, she was a female. Would she not wish to cosset, coddle, comfort, and care for him?

Jack grimaced, recalling the lecture given to Hester when he brought her and her daughter to his lodge. He had been forced to make it an order that she not run to his aid on every and all occasions, that she allow him to attempt anything he chose to do, at any time, without interference.

Jack scowled at how difficult it had been to convince her. Did *all* females believe a maimed man must be treated as a helpless half-wit? Jack was still scowling when the door opened. His eyes narrowed slightly. Why was it not Alex? Or even Tony?

"Good evening, Lieutenant," said Mrs. Haydon.

Jack ignored her greeting. Nor did he rise, as courtesy demanded. He would rather be rude than see pity for his awkwardness. "Alex tells me condolences are due you," he growled.

"A year or two ago I'd have welcomed them," she replied, "but I've been a widow too long to feel any need of condolences."

"You must feel *some* need," he replied with only a touch of acid. "If only because you are stuck here in the country."

Patricia's brows moved. One lowered, the other climbing high, a mild version of his oft seen expression. "You do not like the country?" she asked.

"Of course I do. I am a man. I have observed that women do *not*."

"Do we not? How interesting." Patricia adopted a look of surprised wonder. "I'd not noticed I dislike it . . . I must immediately decide what I am to do." She allowed her eyes to widen. "My goodness, here I have been unhappy all this time and never known it!"

Much against his will, Jack laughed. "Still the same brat you always were, are you not?"

"Am I? I hadn't noticed that, either," she retorted with more bite.

Jack sobered. "I apologize. That was outside of enough."

"Yes it was."

Her quick response roused Jack's temper which, ever since his early convalescence, always simmered near the surface. He nearly made a truly unforgivable response when the door opened again and Colliers, the butler, entered. He was surprised by how difficult it was to bite back the harsh words hovering on his tongue. Jack was shocked that he'd let himself become so undisciplined.

Colliers carried a tray on which rested a dusty bottle and stemmed glasses. Patricia hurriedly removed a book and a stray glove from the table by the fireplace. She stood aside to allow Colliers to put down the tray and handed him the items once his hands were free. Her glance contained a mild rebuke, and two spots of color appeared on the butler's high cheekbones. He bowed slightly, a silent apology acknowledging that he had not, earlier, seen that everything was in proper order.

Jack, watching, nodded. Mrs. Haydon had handled that well. She expressed displeasure over work sloppily done, but without putting up the man's back, which verbally berating him in the presence of another would have done. Jack thought of the best officers he knew, and wondered if any of them would have handled the situation in a better fashion. He decided it was unlikely. Despite himself, he felt a touch of admiration for Patricia Haydon.

"Will you have sherry?" she asked, touching the bottle with one slender finger. "It appears that, in your honor, Alex has had one of the few remaining bottles from his grandfather's day brought up."

"Then it would be better for us to await his presence, would it not?" said Jack caustically and instantly felt regret that he'd spoken more tartly than the circumstance required.

*Damn this leg! Will I never react to others in a normal manner? Will I always bite off everyone's head merely because I can no longer act like a normal man myself?* Jack sighed.

Just then, the door opened. Lord Wendover entered. "Good evening, my lord," she said, turning her back on the rudesby seated by the fire.

"A very good evening to you, Mrs. Haydon." Lord Tony Wendover looked beyond her. "I see you are down in good time, Jack."

"Yes I am, am I not? Perhaps—" Even as he spoke, he wished he'd learn to hold his tongue. "—because it is unnecessary for me to primp and preen? As it is for you?" He cast Wendover a quick smile to soften his words and Wendover, bless him, grinned.

"You suggest I have become a fop? My dear Jack, you really must spend a little time in London. You've not the least notion how a true dandy must attire himself these days!"

"No I don't, do I?" Again there was a caustic shade to his words and a faint touch of strain around his eyes.

"And why should you?" his lordship continued in a thoughtful tone. "You were busy with far more important things, while men such as myself toddled off to a snider to order a new coat or up Bond Street to peruse the latest caricatures or into a club of an afternoon or off to dinners and balls in the evening. . . . *Far* more important. Unless—"

Lord Alex Merwin entered and Wendover pointed his glass at him.

"—you were, as is our friend here, in the government, making speeches and making decisions, and voting more taxes to support the war."

"You pay no taxes, Tony," said Alex, his tone mild.

"Do I not? Then what do you call what I pay for my carriages? And the window tax on my little bijou cottage on the Thames? Or . . ."

Merwin raised a hand in defeat. "Very well. I was wrong." He moved to the table by which Patricia remained. "Sherry anyone? Patricia?"

"I'd appreciate it, Alex."

"And I," said Wendover. "Especially if that is what I think it is. Jack, you always had an excellent palate." Merwin handed him a glass. "You just tell me what you think of Alex's prize sherry!"

Jack took a small sip. He sniffed the aroma, then held it up to the light, all the while rolling the drop of liquor over his tongue. He shrugged.

"You mean to say it isn't special?" asked Wendover, outraged.

"Well it is—" Jack looked faintly apologetic, but his eyes had a twinkle to them. "—and it isn't."

Patricia, who had also felt irritated, stared at Jack. Suddenly she relaxed, her contralto laughter bursting into bloom, drawing eyes and smiles from the men. "Lord Wendover," she said when she could speak, "I believe you have been taken for a flat. . . . As they say," she added quickly, lightly flushing for her use of cant language.

Wendover's frown deepened and he too stared at Jack, his temper wavering between chagrin and humor. He allowed humor to win. "I should have remembered," he said. "You always were able to take a rise from me. But what do you really mean, it is and it isn't?"

"From what I recall of the sherry I drank before joining the army, back when we were all much younger and on the town, this *is* special. But compared to some of the very best I've been privileged to drink in Portugal—" Again he shrugged. "—I'd say it comes near the top, but not right up there."

"I hear a tale," suggested Merwin quietly.

Jack grinned that odd half-grin. "An elderly aristocrat lived much of the year in the mountains close to where my regiment was quartered each winter. He liked to entertain and when he discovered someone truly appreciative of good wine, my humble self for instance, he brought out his best. His sherry was excellent but his port—" Jack kissed his fingers in a theatrical manner. "—was superb." A dreamy look settled over his features. "His port," he purred, "was nectar for the gods."

"Ares, perhaps, since you were men at war? I can almost see you licking your lips," said Merwin. "Sorry that this is my poor best," he apologized, overly somberly.

"Don't let me spoil it for you, Alex," said Jack, coming out of his reverie and sitting straighter. "It is very good. As you well know."

Wendover stared at Merwin whose lips twitched once and settled. But his eyes twinkled. "Aha!" said Wendover, pointing. "Finally."

"Finally what?" asked Jack.

"Finally someone has sent *you* up in return! Congratulations, Alex." Wendover moved to shake his friend's hand.

Even Jack laughed. He could, it seemed, still laugh at himself. The revelation surprised him.

Colliers, standing in the doorway, cleared his throat. "Dinner," he said when he had Lord Merwin's attention, "is served." He retreated.

Merwin glanced toward Jack who, rigid, was suddenly

cold stone sober. His lordship looked from Jack to Patricia, who had finished her wine, set aside the glass, and was gathering up her fan and reticule. Quickly, he moved to her side and offered his arm. She stared at him in surprise. He caught her gaze and held it, attempting to get across his message.

Patricia blinked. What, she wondered, was Alex trying to convey to her? That she was to take his arm was obvious. She did so and was immediately led from the room. "How polite of you, Alex," she murmured.

"Am I not?" He chuckled. "I know we are not normally so formal, but it was the only thing I could think to do to get you out of there." He turned away from the dining room. "Now if you will not take this amiss, we will also spend a trifling amount of time together, just ourselves alone, which is also unusual. We will stroll down this hallway all the way to the end—"

They spoke of this and that until they reached it.

"—And now we will turn and stroll back the way we came."

"And now," he said when they reached the front hall, "we have dawdled quite long enough that we may take ourselves in to our places at the table."

"Is this because of Jack?" Patricia pinched her cousin's arm. "His limp?" Merwin nodded and her tone took on an acid bite. "Does he truly think everyone should pander to his vanity forever and ever—and never ever stay around to see him move?"

Merwin's brows eased into a characteristic vee shape. "You feel it is wrong to accommodate him in this fashion?"

Patricia, instead of making an instant response, thought for a moment. "I don't know. I must consider the situation more thoroughly."

"Let me know what you decide, but now, shall we go in?"

"Yes. Definitely." They swept into the dining room. "I mean to be quite unfashionable," said Patricia as they entered, "and stuff myself. There is quail *and* trout, both favorites of mine." She smiled at Lord Wendover. "You must promise to tell no one what a guy I make of myself. I love to eat, however unfashionable that makes me, and, besides, I am hungry. It is somewhat later than I usually have my dinner when here alone."

Before his lordship could assure her that his lips were sealed, Jack spoke sharply. "Don't change anything because of me."

Patricia's smile faded and she turned a narrow-eyed look his way. For a moment she stared at him. And then away. Ignoring his comment, she asked Wendover if he had made plans for Christmas which was less than two months off.

It was, although she didn't notice it herself, the most perfect of iciest cuts-direct. It tied knots in Jack's stomach. He found himself picking at the excellent food, far more silent than usual. Why had he done his best to rub Patricia Haydon up the wrong way? Why did he strike out at her at every turn?

But it was obvious, was it not? Strike first. Hit hardest. That way one need not worry about when one will be pounced upon—as if the Patricia he remembered were the sort who pounced!

Very, very softly, Jack Princeton swore a few of his favorite oaths.

The week following that first dinner continued in much the same way. Except that when Jack spoke without thinking, Patricia retaliated, refusing to ignore either simple rudeness or acid comment. Toward the end of that long miserable week, although she had some trouble convincing herself of the truth of it, suspicion jelled into certainty. Jack Princeton, she decided, was actually looking forward to their battles!

"This will not do," she told her cousin when she found him alone at his desk in his library.

Merwin sat back. He pulled the barbs of an old-fashioned

quill pen through his fingers. "What will not do?" he asked, studying her intently.

"Jack Princeton is impossible. In truth, there is some reason for him to feel embittered. *That* I understand. But, Alex, if he is allowed to go on in this fashion much longer, the bitterness will become a permanent part of him—rather than merely a stage in his readjustment." She pointed a long, slim finger at her cousin. "Alex," she said, her tone stern, *"something* must be done."

"You never come to me merely to complain, so I presume you've a scheme."

"Well, I do." Patricia frowned slightly and paced to the window where she turned and faced him. "I do," she admitted, "but it is so out of the way, so lacking in propriety, I hesitate to mention it."

He laughed. "Come, Cousin, surely there is nothing you cannot say to me?"

Patricia blushed. "I hope so. The problem is that my scheme requires that you beg for help. From a friend."

"That is it?"

She nodded, looking guilty.

"You think I am too proud to ask for help? Especially when it is for Jack's sake?"

Patricia, who was pacing, swung around, horrified. "No. Of course not. You must not think such a thing!"

He smiled. "I do not. What I think is that you are overly agitated, and that you have yet to explain why."

"Well, how would you feel if a friend wrote you and made the very odd suggestion that *you* must make up a party of friends for over Christmas and, still worse, that you are, without fail, to invite the worst of all possible curmudgeons to attend along with more favored guests?"

Merwin laughed. "Very heated, Patricia. Just who is *the* host who is to invite *our* particular curmudgeon? And why?"

"Oh, I am so glad you understand what I would ask of you!" Patricia approached the desk. "It is Lord Renwick.

He, too, is Lieutenant Princeton's friend, is he not? And he has recovered from *his* injury, has he not? At least you speak of him as if, although blind, he lives a perfectly normal, happy, and interesting life. And do you not agree that blindness," she continued when she'd drawn breath, "is a far worse handicap to overcome than that the lieutenant suffers? Might it not help Princeton to observe what can be accomplished if only one will try?"

Merwin's hands stilled and then, once again, he ran the quill gently through his fingers. "Patricia," he said, "have I ever mentioned how much I admire you?"

She flushed and cast him a wary look. "Alex?"

He grinned. "I *admire* you, Patricia. I have not," he continued gently, "fallen in love with you."

The flush deepened for her mistake. "No, of course not. But having escaped my father by way of marriage, and then escaping the burden of a husband when the poor man had the goodness to die, you are well aware I swore I'd not put myself under the foot of still another man. Your words induced a sudden irrational fear that I must find a new home for myself, and frankly Alex, I am very well suited right here."

"Patricia, you have a home under my roof for so long as you wish it."

"Or until you wed," she said absently, failing to notice that Alex looked a trifle uncomfortable at her qualification. "Alex," she went on, *"will* you write Lord Renwick? I think he could help Jack. Lieutenant Princeton, I should say."

"I believe," said Merwin carefully, "that *Mr.* Princeton is the correct form. Jack told us he sold out."

"Did he? His man calls him lieutenant, you see, so I rather thought he was still an officer."

"An odd fellow, his man Black," mused Merwin. "I believe he'd run an errand into hell and back if Jack asked it of him. And yet, without his help, it would have been next to impossible to have gotten Jack away from that ruin of a lodge in which he had every intention of spending the winter."

"Was it so very bad?"

"You cannot imagine."

"Hiding himself away!" Patricia bit her lip, her gaze intent. "Alex, you must not allow it. He will only grow worse until he is of no use to anyone, especially himself!"

"I agree. I will write Renwick immediately. Since I've not had word of it, I doubt he's planned a party. He will, however, if I ask it of him."

"Especially if you explain *why.*"

"I will do so in only the most general of terms. There is no need to prejudice his wife against Jack before she ever sees him! A small party, I think. Only a handful of guests beyond ourselves . . ."

His words trailed off and his frown deepened. Patricia, knowing he was composing a letter in his mind, went softly from the room, closing the door gently so as not to disturb him. She discovered Lord Wendover wandering toward her down the wide hall, stopping here and there to study one of Alex's private collection of paintings by contemporary artists. The one he stared at as she approached had been bought quite recently from Constable, who was deep into developing a style quite different from that of other painters.

"Do you like it?" she asked, startling him.

"Like it? I have studied it twice since Alex bought it and cannot make up my mind. The technique is so odd, so different from that to which one is accustomed, you see."

"Come here, across the hall," suggested Patricia, who had also spent time studying the oil.

"Over there?" He cast her a confused look.

"Look at it from a little distance, my lord."

Wendover joined her against the far wall. His eyes widened and his mouth dropped open. "Why, it almost looks real. A misty, moisty morning, that pup half-trained and excited by the scents . . . and the boy. Why, you can almost see the . . . the . . ."

"The future?" asked Patricia. "The man in him who will emerge as the boy grows up?"

"Exactly. Thank you."

"You are very welcome. And now I must see to my duties." She curtsied and moved away.

After one more long look at the painting, his lordship continued down the hall. He knocked at his friend's door, entering when permission was given.

"Alex . . ." he began, but stopped when his friend raised his hand and continued writing. Wendover moved to the window.

"Now," said Alex some few minutes later. He wiped his pen and lay it aside. "What may I do for you?"

"Nothing for me."

"It is Jack, I suppose. You, too, are worried about him?"

"Me *too?*" Wendover frowned. "You would say *you* are worried?"

"I am, of course, but I refer to my cousin. Patricia came here to suggest that something be done before Jack turns into an irredeemable grump."

"It is that acid tongue of his that frets me," confided his friend. "I think he could flay a man at ten paces when he gets it going—and then he gives you that apologetic look and you forgive him and forget about it—" Wendover grimaced. "—until the next time!"

"I know exactly what you mean. I find it distressing, but that silent apology gives me hope. I think he isn't liking himself very well, and it is on that we must work."

"But what can we do?"

"I've already set a plan in motion."

"Thank goodness!" Wendover thoughtfully eyed his friend. "But what?"

Merwin picked up the sealed and franked letter centered

on his desk. "This. Renwick has yet to give it the slightest consideration, but—" Merwin grinned a quick grin. "—although he doesn't yet know it, he is about to arrange a Christmas house party."

"*And,*" crowed Wendover, "Jack Princeton will be one of the guests. Yes?" Wendover understood without explanation. All of it. And instantly.

*Dear Jason,*

*You will find this letter an impertinence, but bear with me. As you know, Jack Princeton is at Merwin Hall. Tony and I do our poor best to entertain him, but he continues difficult.*

*My cousin, Patricia Haydon, thinks a visit to you would be good for Jack. She suggests that seeing how you, Jase, coped with a far more difficult problem will provide Jack with encouragement to come to terms with his plight, which is less wretched than the blindness you face with such fortitude!*

*En fin, I beg that you hold a house party over the Christmas holidays to which you invite Jack. I suggest you ask only a few guests: Jack is overly conscious of his limp and is reluctant to move when there is anyone to see him.*

*Forgive my rudeness, old friend. It is outside of enough that I make such a request of you. Still, something must be done and we, his friends, are the only ones who will do it.*

*Yours, etc.*
*Alex Merwin*

"What do you mean, we are to attend a house party at Jase's?"

Jack's roar could be heard throughout the house. Patricia, scanning the week's menus, heard it as far away as the house-keeper's room, well beyond the baize covered door at the back of the front hall. She looked up, her eyes meeting Mrs. Basset's.

"I wonder. Should I add my mite to the argument?" murmured Patricia, touching her chin with the paper on which the menus were written.

Although she spoke more to herself than to the house-keeper, the usually placid Mrs. Basset responded. Tartly. "You just tell that awful man he can take himself off and make some other household miserable!"

"He troubles the *staff?*" asked Patricia, startled.

"He threw a boot at little Janey only the other morning merely because she came in to brush out his grate after he was up. What the man was about, being up at that hour, no one knows, do they?" said the housekeeper, finding that particular thoughtlessness intolerable. "And he *will* go about swearing at anyone for no reason at all, won't he? And people don't like it, do they?"

"I'll have a word with him," said Patricia, a glint in her eye. *It is one thing for him to play the rudesby to me,* she thought, *but it is outrageous that he behaves badly toward Alex's servants.*

She stalked toward the voices coming from beyond the baize covered door but, reaching it, hesitated. Inwardly she cringed. She had not heard such language since . . . well . . . since *never.* And in a gentleman's house, too!

Stirring her temper, deliberately rousing it very nearly out of control, Patricia gave the door a shove and strode like a Valkyrie into the midst of the shouting match. The male voices were so loud she covered her ears, threw back her head and used a trick she'd learned as a child, never forgetting the way of it—although it was rare indeed that she allowed others to know she possessed the talent.

She whistled shrilly.

Instant silence.

*"Enough!"* she shouted. *"Bloody well enough!"*

More silence.

Blessed silence.

"Bloody well?" repeated Jack mildly.

Patricia ignored not only her cousin's efforts to stifle chuckles but her own embarrassment when she noticed Wendover's shocked expression. "You *gentlemen*," she said, "are making spectacles of yourselves."

Wendover and her cousin instantly murmured apologies but, unappeased, she crossed her arms. "Lieutenant Princeton, you have been allowed to behave like a spoiled brat for far too long, allowed to act the infant by people who should know better."

Her glare matched Jack's glower. But, although he glowered, it was also true that Jack's ears burned red. He shot a quick glance toward his friends and rubbed the back of his neck.

"Do not tell me you have *not*," she continued, noting his embarrassment. "Even *you* know you have behaved badly. As, I suspect, you *have* done ever since you realized you were left permanently lame by your wound. Well, *I*, at least, *have had enough.* I will put up with it no longer. Lord Renwick has invited you for a visit. You will accept his invitation gracefully and you will attend his party." She pushed her finger firmly into his chest. *"And you will not argue the point."*

"Why?" he asked blandly. "Because you'll put up with my childish behavior no longer?"

*"Yes."*

The red in his ears invaded his cheeks. "I see. I am no longer welcome at Merwin Hall."

"Untrue," she snapped, crossing her arms. "You are my cousin's guest. It is not my place to dismiss you. But *I* will not remain if *you* mean to do so." She tapped her foot.

"My presence forces you to leave your home. I see." Jack's

eyes narrowed and *he* crossed *his* arms. "Well, I have come to look forward to our little battles, Mrs. Haydon."

*So,* she thought, *I was right about that!*

"I will follow," he added, "wherever you go."

Patricia's anger fell from her and the starch washed out of her. She blinked rapidly several times. Once again she ignored the fact her cousin fought back laughter and that Wendover gasped.

"What," she asked, "can you mean?"

"A life lacking your tart tongue would be unbearably boring." Jack shrugged. "That is all."

Patricia recovered. "I could bear one lacking yours," she retaliated. "Is that not what I said?"

Jack nodded. "Perhaps there is a compromise. I will promise to be less, er, tart if you will promise to continue barking at me even when I have not pricked you into it."

"You, Jack Princeton, are mad!"

He smiled that odd grin of his. Only one side of his mouth rose while his brow arched in his devilment expression. "The men called me Crazy Jack so perhaps I am. But not so deranged that I will give up my only certain source of entertainment!"

Patricia frowned at Jack before glancing at her cousin. "What should I do?" she asked.

He smiled. "Jase's invitation includes you, Patricia. Perhaps," he suggested gently, "we should all go?"

*Dear Lady Anne,*

*I am writing a few friends, informing them of my movements. You will be surprised to learn that I am to leave Merwin Hall for the holidays. At least I am. Surprised, I mean. No, I will not be in London at Lady Merwin's. I am, to my dismay, joining a house party at Lord Renwick's Tiger's Lair.*

*You will not know that my cousin has had guests the last few weeks. Lord Wendover, whom you know, is one, of course, but there is also another old friend, an officer who was badly wounded in the Peninsula. He has recovered his health in that the wound healed, but his temperament has not.*

*I remember Lieutenant Princeton from when he was a lad. His present state of bitterness is so unlike him that I know he can learn to deal with his lameness and return to his normal, cheerful nature.*

*I wish to let you know that I will be elsewhere until after Twelfth Day, and to wish you all the best in this holiday season.*

> Your servant,
> Patricia Haydon

"House party. Tiger's Lair."

Lady Anne Templeton paced the width of the small salon at the back of her father's London home.

"Tiger's Lair. House party."

She paced some more.

"How, how, how?" she asked herself for the hundredth time. "How can I too attend the party at Lord Renwick's?"

Earlier, when she'd demanded her father get her an invitation to Lord Renwick's party, he'd cast her a look of astonishment. And he had, with a firmness previously unknown to her, refused to do her bidding.

"How, how, how? Who, who, who?"

Lady Anne paced.

And paced.

And paced . . .

. . . until called to join her mother in the blue salon where several ladies were enjoying Lady Templeton's weekly at home.

*Dear Harriet,*

*It has come to my Ears that you are to attend A House party at Tiger's Lair. I write you in Utter Desperation. Please <u>please</u> ask me to join your Party! It is imperative that I get Myself to that Gathering. You cannot Possibly know how Important it is to Me.*

*Dear Harry, you will recall the desperate Secret that I revealed to you only last spring. It is no Better with me, except now I have Learned that the Object of my Tender Emotions will be among the Renwicks' guests, and He needs me. I know he Needs me.*
<u>*Do not Fail me in this. You are my only Hope.*</u>

*Your servant in all things,*
*Lady Anne Templeton*

*P.S. I know you will not allow your Brother's silly Infatuation to Interfere in doing what is Best for all of Us.*

*Sincerely, A.*

# Four

When the carriage reached Lord Renwick's estate, Jack was once again in pain and utterly exhausted. Knowing his limp would be particularly bad, and appalled by the number of steps to the front entrance, Jack pulled his hat low over his brow, crossed his arms, and flatly refused to remove from the carriage. When Patricia chided him, he clenched his jaw.

Then he sighed in defeat. "It is beyond me." He turned to her. "Mrs. Haydon, I am not pretending. Truly. If you will *permit*—" He spoke with something of his old bite. "—I will ride around to the stables where I may enter the house through a back door. A door which does *not* require climbing stairs."

Patricia glanced at her cousin. Lord Merwin nodded. She shrugged. "Very well. Since you assure me you are acting sensibly and not from false pride, I will allow you this small sop to your vanity. But what do you mean to do once you are inside? Will you sleep by the fire in the drawing room and dress in the breakfast room?"

*Her* tart words lightened Jack's foul mood and brought that special grin to his face. Since he had ceased to be so rude to Patricia, that familiar devilish look, well-known from their youth, reappeared more often.

Only now and again, but far more often than previously.

"Will you think I cheated—" For once *both* his brows arched high. "—if I admit that I wrote Jase, explained my problem, and asked if a room could be made up for me on the ground floor?"

"No," retorted Patricia. "I will think you have begun to use your noggin for something other than a place to keep your hat. You have begun to find ways to solve problems . . . which is good." His self-satisfied smirk caused Patricia's eyes to narrow. "On the other hand, the time has come when you should practice on the stairs. I know you can, because, as you recall, I found you in the old picture gallery only a week ago—and I will not believe you were *carried* there."

Both Jack's mood and expression instantly cooled. "No one carried me."

"So?"

He eyed her, a trifle pensive, then shook his head. "No, I will not explain."

Patricia blinked. Then she chuckled. "I am to figure it out for myself?"

"If you can, *then,*" said Jack, making a rash promise, "I will learn to climb stairs. If you cannot, I will continue to go up and down in that particular fashion." He sat back in the carriage, his face shadowed. "But only when I must."

"Ha!" she called as she stepped down from the carriage. Before it pulled away, she cried, "You think I cannot unravel your little mystery!"

Patricia thrived on challenges and here was one she could solve if she only put her mind to it. She *would* solve it. It was stupid, Jack's refusal to accept his limitations and his still more dim-witted refusal to test them!

Patricia watched the carriage until it turned the corner of the house, and then climbed to the front door. She nodded to Renwick's butler but was no more than absent-mindedly polite when led to her room by her hostess, Lady Renwick. The two exchanged polite greetings. Patricia was still mulling over the question of how Jack had climbed those stairs when Lady Renwick left.

*"How did he do it?"* she asked her reflection. Removing

her hat, she saw her hair had become matted, curled by the day's humidity. "I detest hats," she muttered as her maid appeared. "All hats."

"Nonsense. That bonnet is excessively flattering, as you well know!"

"Milly, you are impertinent."

"How is it impertinent to say that the hat suits you?"

Patricia chuckled. "I don't know why I put up with you. See what you can do for this hair and then I'll change my gown. Travel gowns are *not* flattering and this one is crushed as well."

"Travel gowns can," contradicted her maid, "be as flattering as one liked. If," she hinted, "one only took the time for fittings and . . ."

"Enough," interrupted Patricia.

Milly sighed loudly before she set to work repairing the damage to Patricia's difficult hair. Then she helped her from the heavy skirts and padded top of the gown worn whenever Patricia had to endure winter travel. It was sadly out of fashion and Milly, who would have preferred to see her mistress dressed right up to the knocker at all times, found it distressing.

The afternoon gown pleased the maid far better. The high waist and slim skirt showed her tall mistress to advantage. Still better, the color of the lightweight twill, an odd orangy-yellow, brought out chestnut lights in hair which, too often, appeared a trifle carroty in color.

"Just the thing," said the maid as she adjusted the last golden ribbon. "You will outshine that sickly blonde who is acclaimed such a beauty!"

"Milly! Sickly blonde indeed!" But, curious, Patricia felt forced to inquire as to whom was meant.

Milly retied a bow that was not quite right. "Lady Anne. The one you visit in London? She came with Miss Bladney and Lord Bladney."

"Harriet and Baron Bladney are here? But their father

died a mere six months ago, did he not? I am surprised to hear they joined the party."

"As to that," said Milly carefully, "Miss Harriet's maid told me her mistress did not wish to come. It was at Lady Anne's urging that they did so."

Memory stirred. Was not Baron Bladney, in his quiet fashion, wooing Lady Anne? For several years now? Patricia wondered that he persisted. Still, there was some tale of the three growing up together, the Bladney and Templeton homes nearly on top of each other. The Templetons, she knew, had moved to London only when his lordship became so enamored with politics he could bear to live nowhere else!

"Miss Harriet's maid said Lady Anne has come only to trap our lieutenant," added Milly, leaning to twitch a fold of the gown into place. Because she was bent down, Milly missed her mistress's startled look, quickly followed by a strange, closed expression.

Patricia Haydon was surprised to discover that she disliked the notion that Lady Anne Templeton was bent on pursuing Lieutenant Jack Princeton!

As Patricia descended the stairs, she recalled the problem of how Jack had managed to reach the Merwin portrait gallery. *Surely,* she thought, *it is not so simple as grasping the banister firmly and hopping up and then, later, hopping down again. Jack would not have worn such an odd expression if it had been no more than that.*

She put the mystery to the back of her mind and joined the others. As the day wore on, she forgot it altogether in her growing dislike of Lady Anne's infatuation with Jack. She watched her old friend's dealings with the lieutenant, and itched to tell Lady Anne that she went about her work in quite the wrong way. For Jack's sake, of course. *Not* to promote Lady Anne's plans.

Anne fussed and twittered. She ran errands whether Jack asked for help or not. And the silly girl *hovered*. Patricia noticed more than one occasion when her friend's behavior drove Jack very near to exploding. Patricia didn't know whether to laugh or cry, upon observing that Jack managed to remain polite.

*If it were me hovering over him,* she thought, a touch bitterly, *he'd be ranting and raving, and asking me what I meant by it.*

*Why* was he so polite? Did he not wish to hurt Anne's feelings because he returned them—or, conversely, did it mean he treated her as a stranger with whom he did not feel at ease?

*And,* Patricia questioned herself, *why do I care?*

"I don't," she muttered.

"Excuse me?"

Patricia turned on her heel, only now noticing the gentleman beside her. She flushed slightly. "Oh dear. Was I talking to myself again?" She wondered how much she'd said aloud. "It is a very bad habit and I must break myself of it."

Patricia recalled a story about her hostess, Lady Renwick, whose mother married to disoblige her family. Only when her grandfather died did Lady Renwick come to know the oddity of an uncle, the present Earl Hayworth. "How are you, my lord?" she asked the earl.

"Very well indeed. You are admiring my cravat, are you not?" Lord Hayworth preened in an exaggerated fashion, his eyes twinkling, a tiny smile hovering around his lips.

"Hmm . . ." Patricia looked at the article in question. "Blue, my lord?"

"Such a pretty conceit, is it not? To match my eyes, you see."

"It does *not,* however, match your coat," said Patricia in an overly thoughtful tone. She cast him a glance full of meaning.

"Ah! You will not be fooled!" Lord Hayworth chuckled. "I like you."

"Did you wish to fool me?"

"Not at all," he responded. "It is a test. Those who conclude, no matter how outrageous my absurdities, that I an an ass can be dismissed as dullards. It never occurs to mos that I enjoy teasing them. But you, my dear, were not bamboozled for so much as a moment, I think?"

"Your eyes laugh. I could see there was a jest. I merely had to guess what it might be."

"Which you did. But you have yet to explain what it is you *don't*."

"I don't?"

"That is exactly what you said, aloud but to yourself which I rudely questioned," said Lord Hayworth gently.

"Hmm." Patricia frowned, her gaze drifting around the room, eventually settling on the corner where Lady Anne was insisting that she must insert a pillow behind Jack's back. Patricia grinned.

"You have seen something to amuse you?" asked his lordship. "Besides my good self, of course?" She cast him a quick look and he laughed. "May I, too, know the joke?"

"It amuses *me*," said Patricia, "but perhaps no one else would see the humor. For instance, Lieutenant Princeton is most particularly *unamused*."

Lord Hayworth followed the direction of her gaze. "Ah yes. Very diverting." Then, muttering, he contradicted himself. "Poor fellow. Perhaps if I . . ."

Patricia was first startled and then amused when his lordship, his words trailing off, wandered toward Lord Bladney. Bladney seemed to do no more than tolerate his lordship, but something among the words prattled into his ear must have reached him—because when Lord Hayworth again appeared to lose interest in his companion, strolling off in still another of his odd perambulations—Bladney turned his eyes to Lady Anne and Lieutenant Princeton, his brow gradually blackening.

Patricia, watching, saw exactly when Lord Bladney reached a solution to some inner dilemma. She observed his determined approach to where Jack, usually the epitome of curmudgeonly behavior, still managed to tolerate Lady Anne's presence. Once there, his lordship pulled a chair around and seated himself facing Jack. He asked the lieutenant a question.

Within minutes Bladney and Princeton were so deep in discussion that it appeared as if the rest of the room had ceased to exist for them. Lady Anne, frowning, inserted a word or two, was ignored, and, with one or two disconsolate glances over her shoulder, wandered off to join her friend, Miss Harriet Bladney.

Satisfied that Jack was no longer harassed and was, in fact, enjoying himself, Patricia took herself in a different direction, seating herself with Lady Renwick and her host's aunt, Lady Blackburne. She greeted the older woman and then turned to her hostess.

"Thank you for inviting me," she said. "I fear I was not at all polite when we first arrived and I apologize. Will you forgive me?"

"I saw you were deep in a brown study, as they say," said Lady Renwick. "I did not allow it to overset me."

"You are generous." Patricia glanced around. "I have yet to greet your husband. He is not here?"

"Just before your carriage arrived, word came of a problem with the roof of a tenant's barn. Jason felt he must go and Lord Wendover, who arrived some little time before you, accompanied him. But they have been gone long enough, and I grow a trifle concerned." Faint lines appeared across Lady Renwick's forehead. "The problem must be more serious than we thought."

Patricia, who never understood why anyone suffered needlessly, asked, "Could you not send a groom after them to discover the situation?"

Lady Renwick colored, glanced at Lady Blackburne, and then smiled ruefully. "It is difficult . . ."

Patricia recalled that Lord Renwick was blind and, despite his acceptance of it, perhaps a trifle touchy. Having come to know Jack, she felt she'd some understanding of Lady Renwick's particular difficulty. "Men," said Patricia in a disgusted tone. "They have such a ridiculous sense of pride, do they not? I see it getting in the way of common sense at every turn."

Her ladyship smiled. "Exactly. My poor Jase would instantly assume I fear he cannot handle the problem. It would never occur to him I might be no more than curious. Not in a million years. But what particular man's pride has been setting up *your* back?" she finished, her eyes twinkling.

"Lieutenant Princeton, of course," Patricia promptly responded. "He is ridiculously sensitive and hates for anyone to watch him move in the awkward fashion he must adopt. It is a bad limp and he *is* awkward. Still, no one blames *him* for it, so why can he *not* accept it?"

"I noticed he doesn't use so much as a cane," said Lady Blackburne, speaking for the first time. "I would think a cane or a crutch would be no end of help."

"A crutch!" Patricia's eyes narrowed, recalling an incident when Jack threw one at his valet's head when the man had dared offer it to him. "He would not use one earlier, but perhaps he will reconsider? If approached properly?" Her voice dropped to a mutter. "How would one best go about it?"

Without a by-your-leave, she rose and left the room. Only when she had asked a footman to find the lieutenant's valet did she realize how rude was her behavior. She sighed. It appeared that apologizing to her hostess was to become a habit. And, this time, to Lady Blackburne as well!

"That crutch!" exclaimed Jack's man. Black had come, hat in hand, to the room where Patricia awaited him. "See if *you* can get him to use it!" he exclaimed.

"I mean to." Patricia pursed her lips, thinking. "Why does he not use it?"

"Nonsense, that's why. He thinks if he lets himself use it,

it is admitting he will never get better, that his leg will never heal properly."

"Will it?"

A distressed look crossed Bill Black's face. He shook his head. "No. Oh, the leg will become stronger as it gets used, but it'll never be as good as it was. Too much muscle was lost to the infection, you see." Without thinking, he added, "A great bit of flesh is gone and there are puckers. He hates the looks of it."

"Is it so very awful?"

"Not really. Not once you get used to it." The man gave her a sudden pleading look. "You won't say I told you, will you?"

"Of course not. But it is past time that he accepts he must use a crutch. Did you bring the one I saw, or must another be made for him?"

"I brung it. He will have my head for washing when he finds out."

"Very likely. Unless I can persuade him to use it."

Black looked skeptical.

Patricia's eyes narrowed. "You think I cannot?"

"I'll be as surprised as a pig on ice if'n you *do*." When Black heard himself, the crudeness, his ears turned red. He was relieved when Mrs. Haydon burst into laughter rather than anger at his thoughtlessly cheeky retort.

"We shall make a little wager," she said.

"Wager?" asked Black tentatively, certain it was improper to make wagers with a proper lady.

"Hmm. I give myself three days to convince him. If I do not, then I owe you . . ." Patricia, also realizing the impropriety, looked as perplexed as she felt. "Oh, dear," she said. "It is a problem, is it not? What the wager will involve, I mean?"

Black grinned. "Sixpence, Missus. It's about all I can afford if I lose. And—" He sobered. "—I hope I *do*. Lose, that is."

Patricia returned to the salon just after the entrance of the missing host and Lord Wendover. Stalking in a majestic fashion at Lord Renwick's side was a huge beast. She stopped, shocked, although she had, of course, heard of the creature's existence. Renwick's pet was so much larger than she'd ever thought a tiger would be. And so oddly colored. Instead of the tawny gold and ebony stripes one saw in pictures, this one was nearly white, with only faint gray stripes running through the lush fur. Patricia could not help staring.

"This way, Jase," she heard Wendover say. "They are in the far corner talking to Bladney."

The men moved in that direction and Patricia followed their progress with her eyes. She watched Jack struggle to his feet and reach to grasp the hand held out to him. The men were soon involved in a deep discussion, so Patricia joined the women.

"So! You still have no notion of the problem?" she asked Lady Renwick, mischievously. "With the barn, I mean?"

Lady Renwick chuckled. "They do not appear to feel it is important enough to discuss, do they?" She glanced toward the corner. "At least not with *me*. Now," she continued, changing the subject, "I have been explaining our plans and was just telling Miss Bladney that we will . . ." She broke off at the sound of a faint scream, and turning toward the door, observed Lady Anne, white of face, rigid of posture, staring at the tiger. "Oh, dear," muttered her ladyship. "I do hope Lady Anne gets over this ridiculous habit of panicking every time she catches sight of Sahib!"

The tiger, curious about the odd sound and odder stance of the woman who had just returned to the room, took a step toward Lady Anne. She instantly fainted.

"Jase, call Sahib to order," said Lady Renwick as she hurried to the fallen woman's side. A gentle word from his master and Sahib subsided, merely staring toward the women. A pair of footmen were called to carry Lady Anne to her room, Lord Bladney and Miss Harriet at her side.

Once the room was calm again, Lady Renwick turned to Patricia. "And you?" she challenged. "Are you afraid of Sahib as well?"

"I think one would be a fool if one did not find it a trifle wearing, having a wild beast in one's drawing room. On the other hand, I assume that, since you *do* allow him in, he is under control?"

"We believe so—" Lady Renwick flashed a quick teasing smile. "—but it is always best, we feel, to introduce new people to his notice. So he knows they are friends?" Lady Renwick drew in a deep breath and let it out with a sound of exasperation. "Anne has refused to approach within yards of him. I feel it is a great mistake." She smiled at Patricia. "Now that I have insulted you in advance if you will *not,* will *you* come with me?"

"How can I do other?"

"What can you mean?"

"I refuse to find myself spoken of as you speak of Anne. Since you oh-so-kindly indicate you will consider me as cowardly as she is if I do not, I will put aside my silly fears and allow the introduction!"

Lady Renwick smiled. "I do like you. I thought I would. Come along now."

Sahib rose to his feet as they approached. He produced a wide-mouthed but silent roar and moved toward Lady Renwick, who put a hand on the animal's head. The beast jounced her hand until she indulged him with a scratch around his ears and then Sahib looked up at her, moved his gaze to Patricia, and back to Lady Renwick.

"Friend, Sahib," said her ladyship in a firm tone.

"You are quite beautiful, Sahib," said Patricia when the animal shifted more toward her. "Exceedingly beautiful. I'm certain there must be a tale about you . . . ?"

"Someday I will tell it to you," said Lord Renwick, who had risen from his chair, orienting himself by their voices before approaching. "Welcome to Sahib's Lair, Mrs. Haydon. We are very happy to have you here."

"I am happy to be here," said Patricia never taking her eyes from Sahib's. "He watches me. He doesn't seem to have accepted me," she added.

"Sahib, are you frightening Mrs. Haydon?" asked Lord Renwick.

The beast twisted toward his master, turned back to Patricia, and then gave that silent roar again. He moved closer. Half frightened, half curious, Patricia put her hand on his head. In a few moments she relaxed and tentatively scratched him. Then, when she felt rather than heard a rumbling coming from the beast, she put both hands onto his fur and scratched vigorously. A bit later he moved again, leaning into her and very nearly knocking her over.

"He's wonderful," she breathed.

"You are very brave," said Jack, grinning at her. "I have yet to touch him."

"He is purring. At least I *think* that noise must be an odd sort of purring," said Patricia doubtfully. She raised her gaze to meet Jack's. Her eyes glowed nearly as brightly as Sahib's. "It is quite something, is it not?"

"Quite something," Jack murmured in reply.

But Merwin, watching the scene, was uncertain whether Jack referred to the tiger or to his cousin. For the first time, it crossed his mind that the bickering with which the two indulged themselves might actually be something other than mere antagonism. Could it be unwanted attraction? Was there a match there?

Merwin concluded it possible, but unlikely—unless Jack accepted his lameness, accepted he was as good a man as ever was. Jack would never allow himself to burden another, as he would think it. And perhaps he would continue to think that way, even if he managed to accept he was lame.

*So. Forget the notion,* thought Merwin, *put it from your mind.*

It was irrelevant that he believed a second marriage would be good for his cousin. *Especially* if he himself were to wed, as he must, in the not too distant future. Far better for all if Patricia had, by then, a home of her own. Merwin wondered how he might promote what seemed to him an excellent match. Merwin joined the others in teasing his cousin for her sudden and obvious infatuation with the Renwick's white tiger. The infatuation appeared mutual since Sahib refused to leave her side. Or perhaps it was her talented fingers which found just the proper places for scratching which he refused to give up?

Whatever it was, the two seemed perfectly content in their mutual admiration.

# *Five*

"Go away," growled Jack. He glared at Patricia, who peered around the entrance to the gazebo. "Can a man be allowed no peace?"

"She is preparing to ride out with Lord and Miss Bladney."

Jack rolled his eyes. "You would say I need not fear your presence is a harbinger of Lady Anne's?"

Patricia chuckled. She leaned the crutch against the bare rose stems alongside the wall and stepped into the bower. "If you truly wish to hide, may I suggest you wear something other than that blue coat? I'd not have known where to find you had I not seen it through the stems."

"I'll remember," he growled. He plucked at his coat sleeve. "I didn't like this blue when my tailor recommended it, but the demned fellow insisted he must sew up one or two things in something other than brown or black, which I prefer."

Ignoring the curse word, Patricia said, "I believe that particular blue is called Bath blue and a favorite of Prinney. Or is it Brummell's preferred color?" She put her finger to her chin and appeared to study the problem seriously, drawing a grin from Jack.

"I have missed that," he said.

"Missed what?"

"Your talent for making one laugh."

"Ah! You would say I am a clown and should humbly beg Grimaldi to take me as an apprentice?"

"Not a clown. It isn't that sort of humor." Jack frowned. Then he cast her one of his sardonic smiles. "It is the ability to make one aware of one's foibles, to feel free to laugh at oneself with none of the sarcasm or sneering tone which all too many use when making pointed remarks to another."

Patricia choked back a chuckle, half humor and half outrage. "You would say I am a nasty, carping sort, with the advantage of knowing how to sweeten my nagging?"

"Something of the sort," he agreed, nodding in a judicious manner.

Spots of color appeared on Patricia's cheeks. "I apologize."

"For nagging?"

"Not at all," she retorted promptly. "Not for *that*. But for hiding it and making it appear as something other than nagging. *You*, dear soul that you are—" She spoke with overdone sternness to conceal her feelings. "—need a great deal of nagging—" She shook her finger at him. "—and I would not like for you to think it unimportant jesting which you needn't take seriously."

"Ah." His one brow arched and the other drooped. "And about *what*, my dear Patricia, do you mean to nag me today?"

As she had ignored his swearing, she now ignored his improper use of her name. They eyed each other. "You saw me coming." It was a statement, not a question.

"I saw you coming, and the thing hidden by the wall," he agreed, speaking more quietly than she'd have expected.

"Blast." She scowled pensively. *"Now* how do I convince you?"

He grimaced. "I admit I was more than a trifle angry when I saw what you carried."

"So you did *not* fear that Lady Anne might follow in my footsteps?"

"I know she means to ride. She apologized with great

fervor for abandoning me," he said with more than a touch of sarcasm, "explaining in that careful way of hers that she was one who needed a certain amount of exercise and I must not feel bad that I could not join them."

He made no effort to hide his bitterness. Patricia spoke slowly. "I think the thing you resent most about your situation is that you can no longer ride."

"I wonder how you guessed!"

"Oh, it was not difficult," she retorted in a bantering tone, but her mind was not on their conversation. She was searching it for the whisper of a notion which teased her, drawing her attention but not quite revealing itself. She ceased striving to regain the lost memory and turned. "But that is not the issue, is it? The problem is to make possible anything and everything you *can* manage."

"And you think that blasted crutch will make life easier for me?"

"I do."

He stared at nothing at all. "I think it merely means I must give up all hope."

She nodded. "That is what Black said you'd say."

"He spoke of this? I'll have his guts for garters," he growled.

"Perhaps so, but I do not think you should tell *me* so. At least not in that particular manner," said Patricia primly.

He slid her a glance. "Or that I will chop him up for dog meat?"

"No. Perhaps . . . that you will roast his toes in the coals and feed them to the chickens?" she asked with mock seriousness.

Jack laughed. "You do it again. You draw me from my bad mood and insist I look at the bright side. Well, Miss Sunny Day, why should I accept that damn crutch? Why should I accept that I will never again walk as a normal man?"

"Because you won't?"

Jack stiffened. The starch washed out of him and he slumped. His fingers around the seat on either side of his thighs gripped the board so hard the knuckles turned a greasy yellow.

Patricia touched the one nearest her. Then lay her hand over his. He turned his up, grasping her fingers, holding them with a trifle too much strength and, seeming to realize it, released her.

Very slowly he relaxed. "You should take up boxing, my dear," he said, his voice thin.

She nodded. "I was once told I've an exceedingly sneaky left, that it can come out of nowhere to level a man." She tipped him a worried look. "Have I that right?"

His laugh had a wry note to it. "I don't know if it was a left or a right, Patricia, but it flattened me." He drew in a deep breath, let it out slowly. "You would say I have again acted like a spoiled child, wanting the moon when I can have no more than a lamp?"

"You can have so much more than you've yet allowed yourself, Jack." She bit her lip, awaiting his reaction. "The whole blessed chandelier, at the very least."

"You truly believe that, do you not?"

"I do." She was surprised by the mildness of his tone and waited to see what he'd say next.

"But—" A deep shuddering breath escaped him and his voice changed. "—I'll never ride."

The bitterness was back . . . multiplied.

"Perhaps not," she finally responded, "but are there not other things you enjoy?"

"I must merely accept that I need help, is that it?"

"Not necessarily. Would you require aid fishing, for instance? Or hunting? Perhaps you need a bearer, which before you did not, but is that so very wrong? At least you can afford a man to carry your guns. Many cannot."

"Those who *cannot* could not afford the guns," he said

dryly. "I hunted while we lived in Yorkshire. Black and █
supplied most of the meat we ate. It was necessary."

"In other words, it was work? Rather than fun, I mean?"
she asked. "Necessity rather than diversion?"

He laughed sourly. "I suppose it was not *all* necessity." He
glanced at her. "Have you guessed how I climbed the stairs?"

"Since I doubt it was merely that you hopped from step
to step—"

He shook his head.

"—I have not guessed." She cast him a sidelong glance.
*"Yet."*

He nodded. "Why the crutch?" he asked after a moment.

"Because you will find moving less onerous and less awkward."

"You responded promptly enough."

"It is only good sense, is it not?"

"I suppose." He stared morosely out over the rose beds
beyond the gazebo. Beside him, Patricia shivered. He turned.
"You are chilled. I just saw the Bladneys and Lady Anne
turn into the lane. They should be gone half an hour at the
very least. Will you stay and watch me make a fool of myself? Mild exercise will warm you, and if it does not, then
laughing at my attempts will surely do so?" He pushed himself to his feet.

Rising, Patricia smiled widely. It had no touch of gloating.
She felt only pride in the courage this man showed in suggesting she watch him learn to use the hated crutch. "Do
lets," she encouraged. "And this evening you can surprise
everyone when they see how deft you are."

"You have more faith in me than I have in myself," he
said, staring into her glowing face.

"More faith?"

"I cannot believe it will be so easy. So—" A muscle
jumped in his jaw. "—if I am to make a fool of myself when
we join the others before dinner, we'd best begin."

He hopped to the entrance, then out, turning, and lifting

the crutch from where it leaned against the rose stems. He glared at it. Then he sighed.

*"A cripple,"* he growled. *"A bloody useless cripple."*

Patricia held her breath as he placed the crutch under his arm, settled himself, and, bearing his weight down, took his first step. No more than a quarter hour later Jack had become proficient with it. And he seemed to enjoy himself as he swung along the path.

Patricia, laughing helplessly at his wry comments on his progress, was forced to trot to keep up.

The riding party returned as they approached the front drive. Jack looked at the horses, lost his concentration, and set the end of the crutch on a patch of wet ice.

The inevitable occurred.

Jack landed hard on his good hip with a muffled cry which was half-pain and half-outraged *amour-propre*. He glared at Patricia who stood over him, her expression one of mixed concern and suppressed laughter. He looked at the crutch, grasped it, and threw it like a lance, neither knowing or caring where it landed.

Lady Anne appeared at his side, kneeling, ignoring the wet cold path. "My dear Lieutenant Princeton, how could you possibly put yourself in such danger? Why take such terrible chances? Oh dear! How did you harm yourself? How badly are you hurt?"

"I am unhurt," Jack managed to insert into the running babble of questions. "Stop that!" he added when her ladyship tugged at his arm. As if she had even a quarter of the strength needed to lift him! "Patricia, since this is all your fault, it is up to you to get Black. He knows how to deal with me. Will you stop that?" he finished, turning toward Lady Anne, pulling his arm from her grasp.

"Well!" she said. "There is no reason to be rude when I merely wish to help you. Is it really Mrs. Haydon's fault you lie here? Helpless and very likely far more hurt than you are willing to admit?" She turned to stare after Patricia who was halfway to the house. "How dare she?" ranted Lady Anne. "How can she behave so cruelly? How can she think of allowing you to do things she must know you cannot do."

Jack thought back over the time before his fall. He had actually begun to admit, at least to himself, that he enjoyed getting around with the help of the crutch. *He had enjoyed it.*

"She is a fool," raged Lady Anne, her words tumbling over each other. "A dangerous woman who would . . ."

Jack caught her ladyship's arm and held it a trifle too firmly. "Patricia Haydon is the very dearest friend I have. Never again insult my friend."

Jerking free, Lady Anne covered her mouth with the back of her wrist. She rose to her feet, her eyes staring painfully into Jack's steady gaze. "Ohhhhh . . ." she wailed and turned away.

Lord Bladney, his face a mask, put his arm about her and walked off, his head tipped toward her, soft words and gentle pats encouraging her.

Miss Bladney, hands on her hips, stared after them. "Well done, Lieutenant," she said softly. "Once or twice more and perhaps she will fall into my brother's hands, ripe for the plucking, just as he wishes. *Why* he wishes it, I will never understand, but do—" She turned and stared down at Jack, a smile in her eyes. "—continue to push Anne away from you. Particularly when my brother is there to catch her!"

"I had noticed he comes to my rescue whenever Lady Anne is her most irritating, but I had not guessed the reason for it."

"How could you? I suspect he does it more because he feels he must protect her from herself than to save you annoyance. He loves her, you see, and is the sort of fool who would actually harm his own cause by aiding her to attain her heart's desire which, or so she thinks, is you."

"I have come to think that Lady Anne has a need to be needed," said Jack slowly. "Perhaps your brother could develop some particular need where she is concerned?"

"I will suggest it. Ah! Here comes your rescue party."

"If you would do me a favor, Miss Bladney, you will retrieve my crutch. I allowed my temper to get away from me and I am sorry for it . . ."

She nodded and, as Black and Lord Merwin approached, she moved gracefully to where the crutch had slid half under one of the rose bushes which had been planted for their scent when Jason, newly blind, had returned from India. Only the harshness of this particular winter had left them leafless and barren so long before Christmas.

Lord Merwin and Black lifted Jack to his feet. Black groaned when he saw the condition of Jack's trousers and the back of his coat. "It'll take something to clean *that,*" he growled.

Jack, taking the crutch from Miss Bladney, told his man to stifle it. "You haven't enough to keep you busy in any case. Why are you staring?"

Black's eyes goggled. "You . . . You're using *that?*"

Jack glanced at the crutch. His chin rose a notch, two splotches of color marring his cheekbones. "What of it?" he asked somewhat belligerently.

"Nothing, I guess." Black breathed a lugubrious sigh. "I gotta find Mrs. Haydon."

"Why?"

"I owe her sixpence, that's why. Thought it couldn't be done. Thought you'd never use the blasted thing. Tried hard enough, m'self, didn't I? But would you? No. Never. Got tired of having the blasted thing thrown at m'head, I did." Black looked around. Merwin grinned broadly. Miss Bladney wore a shocked expression. And Jack gazed at him with overdone patience. "Well," growled Black, "you'd get tired of it, too!"

"I think I would," said Merwin soothingly. "And very likely a lot more quickly than you did. In fact, it is very likely I would have bashed him over the head with it when he persisted in being so stupidly stubborn about using it."

"*I* think he has been very brave to try it at all." All eyes turned toward her and Miss Bladney blushed. "It must be very difficult, I think."

Jack had managed to control most of his irritation at what he knew was friendly teasing. He nodded. "Oh yes. Very difficult," he said, only mildly sarcastic. "I think it took me all of five minutes to master it. The biggest problem, I find, is that it is uncomfortable under the shoulder. Black, as punishment for your impertinence, you will contrive a padding for the top."

"Yes sir," said a subdued Black. "Sorry sir."

"You spoke no more than the truth. I *was* foolishly stubborn about it. I admit it. Mrs. Haydon has done me a service, jollying me into using it. And now, if we have finished putting me through all sorts of emotional and physical contortions, I think I would like to go to my room and get out of these clothes, which are cold, wet, and miserably uncomfortable." He glanced toward Black. "And you needn't say we were far more uncomfortable in the Peninsula, because I know that, too."

"Right you are, sir. Not in the Peninsula now, sir. No need to be uncomfortable, sir."

"You can stop with the *sirs* as well. I sold out, remember?"

"Yes . . . sir."

"I said stop!"

"Well, I don't know what to say to you if I don't say *sir.*" The defiance faded and Black, a touch of belligerence in his tone, added, " 'Sides, you'll be my lieutenant forever. Makes no odds you sold out."

"I think he has you there, Jack."

Jack raised his eyes to the heavens. "To the devil with it!—" He cast a startled look toward Miss Bladney when she gasped softly. "—Oh blast and . . . !" He stopped again and drew in a deep breath. "Pardon me!"

She nodded, smiling. "Of course. You have been having

a most irksome time of it, have you not? I must go in and change from my riding clothes. I will see you all when we meet for dinner." She nodded goodbye and walked off.

"Now," said Jack when she had gone some distance. "Once again we shall endeavor—" He scowled. "—and I'll tell you this! There better be no more ice in my path!"

He settled the crutch under his arm and went into the odd swinging walk he had found worked best. Within minutes he reached a side door to the house which had no steps. He looked back and was somewhat surprised to find Lord Merwin trailing him, way in the rear.

"What took you so long?" he asked when Merwin sauntered up to the door.

"I'm damned if I'll run after you," he said. "You will outpace us all with that thing, Jack."

Jack felt something inside his chest unknot. "Odd."

"What is odd?"

Suppressing a grin, Jack said, "It never occurred to me there might be *advantages* to being lame! Just think of the races I can win."

After half a moment's startled silence, Merwin burst into laughter. Jack grinned in response and, in a better frame of mind, went on to his room.

*Perhaps,* he thought, *I am learning to tease myself out of my moods?*

A day or so passed with few problems other than what might be expected. Lady Anne continued to faint whenever she unexpectedly met up with Sahib. Once the novelty of his improved mobility palled, Jack returned to a state of quiet desperation. And Patricia still could not think how Jack had managed the stairs.

Of course, there was an additional problem, that Lady Anne was no longer on speaking terms with Patricia. This caused her hostess some trifling difficulty with regard to the seating arrangements at the dinner table. But for the most part, all went as smoothly as it could with such an odd collection of guests, and Lady Renwick refused to descend into utter despair over the state of her party.

One evening, Jack sat with his friends in the salon, listening to a conversation in which Merwin and Renwick discussed the news of Napoleon's terrible defeat in the vicinity of Smolensk in Russia. "According to the newspaper," said Merwin, "both Tower and Park guns were fired in celebration."

"Surely it is the end. The number of men reported lost in that battle! Even if it is exaggerated, he will, at that rate, soon find he is without the arms to defend even the *old* borders of France!" said Renwick.

"Besides, such a loss will surely have repercussions in the morale of the remaining troops, do you not agree, Jack?"

"No. He is a leader men follow, willy-nilly," said Jack, "In my humble opinion, if he doesn't return immediately, it is the *climate* in Russia which will do for him, rather than a battle. He has no understanding of their winters or he would never have attempted it."

*"You* do?" asked Merwin.

"Only what I have read, of course," said Jack, "but, years ago, you too perused the diary of that man who was a fur trader in Russia, did you not, Alex? I recall giving it to you when I finished it."

Merwin looked startled. "Oh, but surely the harshness was exaggerated!"

"I don't think so. It is merely difficult for someone who has never experienced it to accept that people would continue to reside where the weather is so inclement."

"Like someone who has never been there accepting the existence of the unbelievable heat in India," inserted Renwick, nodding agreement.

"It is true, however, that Nappy," continued Princeton, "will find he has made his first serious error, attempting the

Russian campaign. And now may we please change the subject? I find it depressing, knowing I will not be there when the final battle is fought! Cards, perhaps?" he suggested.

Silence followed. Jack looked around, confused.

"Jack . . ." began Wendover.

"Surely you do not think . . ." said Bladney at the same moment.

Renwick cleared his throat, interrupting his friends' unfinished attempts to explain. "Jack, if you can invent a way whereby I may play again, I would appreciate it very much indeed."

"Play again? What do you mean?"

*"He doesn't know!"* said Wendover, his astonishment obvious. "How can he not know?"

"He was in Spain. Did anyone write to him?" asked Renwick, his hand drifting to Sahib's head.

Jack, looking from one to another, realized he had missed something important. "Know what?"

"Why, Jack . . ." Merwin glanced toward Jason.

"Jase is . . ." began Wendover. He looked embarrassed and was unable to continue.

Renwick chuckled softly. "Is it so hard to say? I realize you had difficulty accepting my fate, but it is fact and must be faced. And, Jack, I do not know how you have not guessed." Silence followed until Jack growled in rising irritation. "I am blind," said Renwick quickly.

"No," Jack said, simply and firmly.

"No?"

"I have seen you move all about the house. You never hesitate. You eat your dinner with never a problem. You—" He shrugged. "—do not act in any way like a blind man."

"Thank you."

"It is true he has overcome most of his problems."

"Stop it! You have plotted some nonsense to make me feel better."

"Jack . . ."

"I have heard him," Jack continued, "discussing the book he writes. How—" Jack rose to his feet, leaning on his hands on the table and glared. "—can a blind man write a book?"

"With the help of a loving wife who acts as my eyes," said Renwick in a reasonable tone. He leaned back in his chair and his hand closed over Sahib's nape when the big cat rose to his feet, growling softly. "Down. All is well," he said softly. After a moment Sahib subsided. "Jack, relax, will you? Sahib always appears to want to come to my defense when he feels I am threatened. It worries me. I cannot promise he will not, someday, actually do so! I might not be able to control him."

"You are truly blind?"

"Yes. A gun exploded. When I was in India. I stood too close. The powder burns destroyed the vision in my right eye and very nearly all of it in the left. With the left I can see very bright light, but that is all."

"And you . . ." Jack shook his head. He drew in a deep breath. "You have accepted it? You overcame it?"

"Not easily! Do not think I adjusted all at once. Or even soon. I was a very bitter man when I arrived home, and for a long time after. Ask my aunt!"

"But you *have* managed . . . Blind, you are not . . ." Jack stopped in mid-sentence for the second time and then, gruffly, excused himself. In his agitation, he forgot the crutch and limped in his old hop-slide way across the room.

In the hall he discovered new arrivals. Abruptly he halted, waiting for Ian McMurrey to approach him.

Grinning, Ian reached for him. "Jack! You came." He drew his wife forward. "Lady Serena and I were unsure if you could be convinced."

"Ah! I recall," said Jack, forcing a lightness he did not feel. "You, my lady, were my savior at Rolly's wedding! Which I foolishly attended long before I was well enough to so much as leave my bed! How do you do?"

Lady Serena McMurrey smiled. "We were glad to see you that day, but we did worry about you."

"The day tired me, but it did me good, too."

"Lady Anne fretted, I know."

"Lady Anne frets over trifles," he said, a touch of bite back in his voice.

Lady Renwick came from the salon, having been informed by her butler of the McMurreys' arrival. "My dear Lady Serena! How good of you to come."

"We could not stay away," said her ladyship.

"But in this weather! To have come so far in your condition!" She glanced at the men, noted Jack's quick glance toward Lady Serena's waist and added, "Ah! Once again my tongue runs away with me. I should not have mentioned such a delicate subject in mixed company, of course. Now, Serena, do come along with me." Lady Renwick led Lady Serena toward the stairs. "I have put you and Ian in the suite just at the top where you will be comfortable. I am certain you must wish something warm in the way of refreshment and then a lie down." Her foot on the bottom step, she turned. "Excuse us, gentlemen."

"You look ever so much better than the last time I saw you," said McMurrey once the women were gone. "Have you any notion how much you worried us all when you disappeared in that odd fashion?"

Jack grimaced. "At the time I felt I'd no choice. Not if I were to escape at all."

"Escape?"

"You cannot know what it was like, living in Lord Freeman's house with Lady Anne worrying about every little thing. Worse, I discovered accidentally she believed she had developed a *tendre* for me! I dared not stay lest she manage to compromise herself and force me into parson's mousetrap."

"Would it have been so very bad?" asked McMurrey. "I find I rather enjoy that particular trap!" He grinned.

Jack didn't laugh as his friend expected. If anything, he became still more grim. "She would have smothered me, Ian. I would have murdered her before a ten month had passed." He grimaced. "Or myself. More likely myself, I suppose."

"Driven to suicide." McMurrey nodded. "I see how it might be. Except, according to what Merwin wrote me, you have also, and more than once, he said, offered to murder Mrs. Haydon. Your years as a soldier, Jack, have made you excessively bloodthirsty!"

This time Jack grinned broadly. "I might have threatened mayhem, but I would never harm a hair of Mrs. Haydon's impertinent red head. She is, although you must never tell her so, my good angel." When some further explanation seemed necessary, he added, "She has the amazing ability of making me laugh, Ian."

"Laughter is, I think, important."

"I have discovered it is not just important, but necessary. When I can laugh at myself, I find I can overcome far more of my difficulties than I ever dreamed possible. Ian . . ." He paused, a grim look appearing about his eyes. "Ian," he repeated, "I have made an utter fool of myself. I did not know of Jase's blindness!"

"So?"

"He has made such a life for himself that one might not know his problem exists and I—" The grim look deepened. "—have been acting like a spoiled brat, as Mrs. Haydon tells me often and often, about a problem which is *far* less important. A fool and an idiot and an utter *coward*."

McMurrey gripped Jack's shoulder. "Jack, Jason did *none* of what he accomplished easily or instantly. He was so depressed when he returned that he lived in England for *two years* before he allowed any of us to know he'd come back from India! He suffered black moods of deep despair, and I have sometimes wondered if he might not, eventually, have . . . have done himself an injury if it were not for Lady

Renwick. She came, in the first instance, to help with his writing and for no other reason." He grinned conspiratorially. "I am told Sahib played a large role in their affairs. He took a hand—" He grinned. "—or should one say paw? in my problem with Lady Serena, as well."

Jack stared at nothing in particular for so long that his friend wondered if he should say more. He decided that perhaps he *should,* but not *instantly.* It appeared that Jack had more than enough about which he must think. So instead of something in the way of the mild lecture he had in mind, he said, "I must change from my travel clothes. If things have not altered, there will be a tea tray in less than an hour. I will see you then."

"Hmm? Oh. No, I think not. I am tired and mean to retire early. We can talk in the morning," said Jack. He settled his crutch which Lady Renwick had brought him, concentrated on placing it *just so,* and moved carefully toward the Renwick's private part of the house.

For a moment McMurrey wondered about that, but then it occurred to him that Jack would not care to climb stairs if he could avoid it, and that the Renwicks must have provided him with a room on the ground floor for that reason. Lady Renwick descended the stairs just then and McMurrey turned to her. "My lady wife?" he asked, his concern shifting from his friend to Serena.

"She is fine. Perfectly healthy and looking forward to motherhood. And you, Ian? Are *you* fine?" teased her ladyship.

"You see before you a very worried man," he said, his tone light, but he obviously meant every word. "One cannot help but be anxious."

"I think you need not. Choose your midwife carefully. Find one who has a history of little trouble with childbed fever and all will be well. It has always seemed to me that some have the problem and some do not, but why the difference I cannot tell you." A twinkle appeared in her eyes and a half smile on her lips. "You do have *one* problem, of course. A serious problem."

McMurrey quirked a brow.

"The impossible problem, Ian, of choosing a godfather for the babe! Each and every one of your friends, the instant they know she is breeding, will vie for that honored position."

McMurrey grinned. "Hmm. I'd not considered that . . . I wonder. Can a babe have multiple godfathers?"

Lady Renwick adopted a look which suggested she was much struck. "Now that *would* be the best solution, would it not? We must discover if it is permitted. Or perhaps the Six could draw lots to be godfather in proper order?"

He chuckled. "I must go up to her," he said. "I will join the party in time for the tea tray, but I cannot promise Lady Serena will come down."

"She has already asked me to apologize to the others. I am to tell them she will greet everyone at breakfast."

Lady Renwick smiled and moved toward the salon as McMurrey, taking the steps two at a time, disappeared above stairs.

Later that evening, in the privacy of their room, Lady Renwick said to her husband, "It is the oddest party, Jase."

"Hmm?" He removed his coat before moving to the window. He opened it to the chilly air and allowed Sahib, hooked to a long leash, to jump out. The cat would not be gone long.

"Never before," said his wife from behind him, "have I held a party at which the guests seem so prone to disappearing. Lady Anne spends far too much time in her room and only in part, I think, because of Sahib. Lieutenant Princeton is, as we expected, a trifle moody, and may be excused, to a degree at least, for his abrupt absences. But now I fear Lady Serena will be another who takes herself off more often than one might expect of a normally polite companion."

"Lady Serena?"

"She is in an interesting way, Jase."

He turned, grinning, and groped for her. She moved into his embrace and he pressed a hand to her waist. "As are you?" he asked softly.

Lady Renwick felt herself blushing. "Jase! How did you guess, when I have only just begun to believe it may be so?"

"I may be blind," he said with mock sternness, "but I am quite capable of counting!"

The blush felt hotter still. "Bother! This having one bedroom makes it very difficult to have any sort of secret from one's husband!"

"Hmm." He nuzzled that especially sensitive point where her shoulder met her neck. "Do you wish separate rooms, Eustacia?"

"Never," she said fervently, and reached to undo the bone buttons running down his vest.

Jack, in a room several doors down the hall, would have been shocked by the depth of emotion running between the two as his friend made passionate love to his wife.

He would have been deeply jealous as well.

# Six

In the middle of the night Patricia Haydon sat straight up in bed and said, "That's it! That is what I could not remember!"

She felt a smile tip her lips as she lay back. Almost immediately she drifted back to sleep, waking the next morning with the oddest feeling she was forgetting something important. Patricia sipped her morning tea and mused about what it might be. Setting aside the empty cup, she got up, put on her robe, and moved to her window.

Her bare toes curled into the chill of the waxed floor. The rose bushes wore caps of new snow. An opening in a wooded area beyond the lawn revealed a small portion of a formal ride and, just at that moment, several horses crossed her line of sight, disappearing quickly. The men of the party had gone for a ride before breakfast.

Except Jack, of course.

"That's it!"

"Did you say something, Mrs. Haydon?"

"What?"

Milly turned from where she'd just laid out a fresh chemise. She held stockings in her hand which she meant to check for snags before laying them down as well. "Did you say something to me?"

"Did I speak out loud?" Patricia wrinkled her nose. "I truly must rid myself of that bad habit!" She sighed. "It is merely that I have remembered something I wished to recall," she said dismissively. "I'll wear the green day gown, please. And did we bring my old brown shawl? The soft one?"

Patricia was soon ready to go downstairs. She wondered if Lady Renwick would have the information she needed, or if she should apply to Lord Renwick. Or perhaps Lord Wendover? He seemed far more interested in *things* than the other men and would, perhaps, know where she might inquire about what she wanted.

As she reached the hall, she decided she was acting foolishly. Her wisest and most discreet course would be to consult her cousin. So, later that morning, she tracked Lord Merwin to a quiet room at the back of the house where he wrote letters. It took little time to recount her memory and only a few more words to explain what she wanted.

"But Patricia," he said, shocked, "you cannot buy such a thing for a man. Certainly not for one who is unrelated to you!"

She frowned.

"On the other hand," continued Merwin, his fingers tracing the length of the quill pen, "there is no reason whatsoever that *I* should not."

"It will be expensive," she warned.

"Yes. Very likely more than usual, since it will be wanted quickly. I'll wish to have it for Boxing Day giving, will I not?"

Patricia was sorry that she was the inadvertent cause of such expense to someone else. "Would it, perhaps, come better from all of you?"

"From the Six?" Merwin frowned. "Or four, actually, since Jack can hardly give something to himself and heaven knows where Seward is to be found."

Patricia had a fleeting memory of a wild-eyed youth who could never be still, who had such an ear he was an incredible mimic that he could actually converse with the Merwins' oldest retainer whose ancient tongue was so thick with the local dialect he was incomprehensible even to some of his grandchildren. "Did you not tell me he once took a trip up the Nile disguised as an Egyptian?"

Merwin nodded. "By now Miles's curiosity will have led him into even more remarkable adventures. I do wish he'd come home."

"He cannot stay away forever, surely. Something will bring him back. But, Alex, what of my notion?" Patricia drew the conversation back to her suggestion, and her cousin obliging wrote down the description she gave him of the item she had in mind. "Do you think it will work?" she asked anxiously.

"His leg has healed as much as it ever will. It lacks strength and is unlikely to return to its original condition. I see no reason, however, why your notion will not solve the problem." He frowned. "I do wonder if we can keep Jack from attempting more than is wise. If he were to get into difficulties through some rash and unthinking action or experiment, he might cause himself still more damage."

Patricia stared over her cousin's shoulder. Through the window, beyond a courtyard, were the stables. She saw Jack standing within the protection of a wall, out of the wind. He stared hungrily toward a groom who washed down the legs of a horse the man had just exercised. There was a hopeless longing in Jack's stance that tore at her heart. She firmed her jaw and looked back at her cousin.

"I think," she said, "he would prefer to chance that, rather than to never again sit on the back of a horse."

Something in her voice drew Merwin. He turned and also watched Jack. "I am forced to agree." His lips compressed and his eyes narrowed. Finally he laid aside his pen. "I will discuss it with Ian. He is the sensitive one. If he agrees, I will go forward." He rose to his feet. "Patricia," he said, really looking at her, "have you been so foolish as to fall in love with Jack?"

"Love?" Patricia felt heat in her cheeks and covered them

with her palms. "I don't know. How *does* one know? I only know I cannot bear for him to be so unhappy. I cannot stand to see him waste his life on fruitless yearnings. And—" Her eyes danced. "—perhaps the most telling, I absolutely detest for Lady Anne to come anywhere near him."

Merwin grinned. "Yes, jealousy is an excellent indicator. On the other hand, in this particular case, it might be merely that you know how she frets him and how she would, if she could, make him continue to live unhappily in that useless existence you cannot abide."

"So. We still do not know if I am or am not in love."

She sighed dramatically to mask her ridiculous emotions. Because Patricia Haydon knew very well that she had done the most idiotic thing of her life when she'd fallen deeply in love with the man who was not in the least like the boy who had been her first love! Or perhaps she was wrong. Perhaps the man was *very* like the boy, but so very much *more* as well?

Merwin patted her on her shoulder as he went by her and Patricia suspected she had not fooled her cousin one jot or tittle.

She hoped he'd the sense to keep the knowledge to himself.

Unlike Patricia's difficulty locating Lord Merwin, Lord Hayworth had no trouble whatsoever finding Lady Blackburne. She worked that morning in the conservatory. The gently falling snow melted and ran in rivulets down the glass ceiling and walls of the room which was warmed by the fire in a large porcelain stove. He found her standing at a table, her hands grimy from potting soil.

Lord Hayworth picked up a pinch of dirt and sniffed it. "A very good mix, I think," he mused and hoped the overly warm room would not wilt his extra high shirt points.

She glanced at him, blinked at his bright yellow shirt and green cravat, but ignored them after that one involuntary response. Even when, from the corner of her eye, she noticed the tops to his low boots had yellow trim to match, she made no comment about his odd choice of garments. "What would *you* know about potting soil?" she asked.

"What do *I* know?" he asked. "About soil? Very little. But I know *you* are exceedingly knowledgeable. If you use this mix, then it is the best."

"Palaverer."

"Nonsense." When she merely compressed her lips, he added, "It is false modesty to suggest I merely flatter you."

She cast him a glance from the side of her eyes, but returned instantly to watching her hands as they gently removed a fern from the pot it currently occupied.

"I never indulge," he added provocatively, "in false coin."

"Never?"

He grinned. "Well, *hardly* ever." When she made no response, he added, "And never with you. I want honesty between us, Lucy."

Lady Blackburne stilled. "If you wish honesty," she said tartly, "then allow me to inform you that I detest the name Lucy."

"Cilly, then?" he mused. "I'd think that worse."

"If you insist on an abbreviation of my perfectly good name, then you must call me Luce as Jason does."

"Luce. Excellent. It fits you."

She cast him an exasperated glance. "You think me *loose,* Lord Hayworth?"

Two spots of color appeared high on his cheekbones and, turning aside, Lady Blackburne hid a smile.

"Of course not—" He was very close to blustering. "—I did not think of such a thing at all. It is the sound of it. The implication of lucidity," he added a bit wildly. "The lucidness of your character and temperament," he said more urgently. "Or perhaps—" He'd cast her a quick glance, caught a hint of her smile. "—*the loosening* of a lady's corset strings?" he finished without the least change in tone.

"Oh! *You dare* say such a thing to me!" She spun around

to face him, watched his eyebrows climb and noted just the least little bit of movement at one corner of his mouth. She bit her lip.

"My dear," he said after a moment in which they eyed each other, "we grow no younger, and I did mention that small unimportant question of honesty. I have, on more than one occasion, been excessively tempted to try if I could manage those strings."

Lady Blackburne flushed. She glanced at him, looked away and, determined she would not allow him to overset her, returned to her plant, finishing the work in silence.

"You must know I meant within honorable wedlock." He spoke gently.

Still she said nothing, busying herself by pushing spilled dirt into a neat pile. She searched for a trowel which she used, along with the side of her hand, to pick up the soil and sprinkle it in the fern's pot.

"Have I placed myself entirely beyond the pale?" he asked gently.

"No."

"An exceedingly crude proposal, I know, but can you not give me a hint of hope?"

The rigidity went from her spine and she leaned on hands placed flat on the tabletop. "I have been a widow so very long."

"Yes. Too long. Far too long."

"I am older than you."

"Not much." He pushed his tongue into his cheek. "Five years, maybe?"

This time her glance held a touch of outrage. *"Three."*

He snapped his fingers. "Three. A mere nothing."

*"Is* it nothing?" Lady Blackburne picked up a towel and wiped her hands, paying careful attention to each finger, thereby keeping her head bowed.

"Will you not look at me?"

Her hands stilled. Slowly, she raised her eyes to meet his.

"My dear Luce, I have been in love with you almost from

our first meeting. I would like," he said, "to share my life with you." He smiled at her wide-eyed look. "I might even manage to exchange my current wardrobe for one less startling. If it would please you."

She shook her head. "The *ton* would say I nagged you to do so."

He smiled. "I would not care."

"But I would. No, you must go on as you always have—" She stiffened. "—not that I have accepted your kind offer. I . . ." She looked flustered.

". . . need time to think," he finished for her. He nodded. "For my sake, do you feel you might manage to do such thinking rather hurriedly?"

Lady Blackburne frowned. "There are problems. I am needed here."

*"I* need you."

Another startled look was cast his way. "You . . ."

". . . need *you.*" He nodded. "I am lonely, Luce. I need you for a friend as well as lover."

"I am too old!"

"I thought we settled that," he said only a trifle crossly.

"No. I mean I am unlikely to give you an heir."

"Is that all?" He snapped his fingers. "I have an heir, my dear. He is a commonsensical fellow whom, I promise you, you will like. If I had ever felt the need of another, I'd have wed years ago."

Lady Blackburne laid aside the towel and faced him. "I have enjoyed our association, my lord," she said carefully, "but I do not know if I have those feelings which a woman should have for the man she weds."

Very gently he reached for her. Still more gently he tugged her near. He looked into her bemused face and smiled. Tenderly.

"Shall we discover?" he asked, his voice caressing.

The snow continued to fall gently but persistently against the warm glass of the well-heated conservatory. An interesting and enlightening interlude followed, although Lord Hayworth, determined on the honorable course, remained ignorant of whether he could or could not manage the bothersome corset strings.

In still another part of the house, Lord Bladney discovered Lady Anne hunched over her sewing, working candles on either side, since the gray day did not provide near enough natural light.

"I've a splinter in my finger," said his lordship plaintively. He could not believe how much effort it had taken to acquire the splinter.

Lady Anne looked up. He held the offending finger for her inspection. One could see the change in her as she set aside her embroidery and took his hand, moving the finger into better light. She picked up her needle and he winced as she dug at the splinter. Once it was out, he managed to thank her politely.

"I had thought to go riding," he said, watching her wind her handkerchief around the mangled spot on his finger, "but it is snowing. This has been a miserable winter, has it not?"

"Oh. The *weather*. Horatio, can you not converse on something more interesting than the weather?"

"Certainly." His brows arched. "But perhaps you would prefer to suggest a topic?"

Giving her old friend a challenging look, she asked him what he thought of the latest vote in the House of Commons for the enclosure of still more land. Lord Bladney recalled that Lady Anne's father thought the process had gone much too far already and very nearly erred by agreeing. At the last moment he changed his mind and spoke as he truly felt.

"But, Horry, so many people—" She shifted in her seat and pointed to a nearby chair. "—have already left the land. They move, in droves, into the manufacturing cities where they are *miserable*."

Lord Horatio Bladney, wondering if he had finally found the way back to Lady Anne's good graces, settled himself for a discussion of politics. It was unusual, talking politics with a woman, but it occurred to him that she had often managed to hang about her father and other older gentlemen when they discussed such things.

Was she truly interested? Housebound by the snow as they were, he not only learned the surprising depths of her political interests, but how much she had learned over the years.

"You make me wonder if there is something I might do," he said musingly, as it neared time to dress for dinner.

"Of course there is. You should choose a good man for that seat you control, and back him. *And* see that he votes as he should."

Lord Bladney reminded himself that his sister believed Lady Anne was one who needed to be needed. "I don't think I'd know how to go about it."

"Nonsense. It is simple." Then she bit her lip, casting him a worried look. "It would be expensive, however."

"I am not a poor man, Annie."

She drew in a sharp breath. "Annie," she breathed. "No one has called me Annie . . . oh, forever it seems."

"Do you like it?" he asked softly.

"Yes."

"Then that is what I will call you."

Fearing to push his luck too hard, Lord Bladney returned to their discussion, asking her if she recalled someone, a neighbor from before she'd moved to London, whom he might promote. "Someone," he finished, "who could be groomed to stand for the seat."

They talked until the bell rang, warning them they must retire to their rooms and dress for dinner. And finally, once again, they spoke of the weather when they noticed it was again snowing.

\* \* \*

Ian McMurrey sat with his host in Jason's library, perusing the latest pages of Lord Renwick's manuscript. This chapter concerned travel within India and included Jase's journey up into the highlands north and east of Calcutta, reminding Ian that it was on the occasion of that visit, during a hunt for a man-eating tigress, that a gun exploded and his friend lost the use of his eyes.

"Jase, it just occurred to me that I have seen neither hide nor hair of your princely ward." Ian referred to the young Indian prince who had been sent to Jase for schooling. "Did your patience run out or did you finally give in to your temper and wring the lad's neck?"

Renwick chuckled. "Actually the boy goes on in a much better way. You would, I think, be amazed by the change in him. But, as you've noticed, he is not here."

"Ah! You forbore to strangle him, but merely sent him home?"

Jason sobered. "It was Bahadur. Prince Ravi's man? He never recovered from that illness after he saved me from the river—"

"When you dove in to save Lady Renwick, you mean?"

"—and the cold weather was bad for him." finished Jason, ignoring Ian's reference to that fool-hardy but successful rescue. "Ian, I am not supposed to mention this, but, since the subject has arisen, I can restrain myself no longer. Ian, Miles is back in England." He frowned. "Well, in a manner of speaking."

"Miles! And he has not looked any of us up?"

"He is the same old Miles, Ian. Impulsive and always involved in something. He was commanded to Brighton for an audience with Prinney when he recalled my estate was only a few dozen miles out of his way." Jason smiled and shook his head. "He made a, hmm, slight detour."

"But why were you not to mention it?"

"Because he means to return. Assuming he is free to do so. He hopes to surprise everyone by arriving when all are here, but he isn't certain he can manage it, so he didn't wish to rouse anyone's expectations."

"I see. Jase, does Miles's appearance have something to do with Prince Ravi's absence?"

Renwick nodded. "Miles arrived as I considered arranging for the boy and his entourage to winter in Naples. Miles had a better plan. I haven't a notion what he did because, when I asked, he shrugged it off, but it seems he was rewarded for some service to the Portuguese Royal family with a small estate in the south of Portugal. It is staffed, in part, with wounded servicemen, so English is spoken. And it is warm. He also owns a pirate ship . . ."

"You," interrupted McMurrey, "will not convince me Miles has become a pirate!"

Lord Renwick grinned. "No. He won it, and just incidentally his life as well, playing at dice with the pirate who captured him."

McMurrey shook his head. "That sounds like Miles all right." Ian stared out into the heavy snow obscuring his view of the gardens. "It will be good to see Miles again."

"Assuming we do . . ."


Jack was in his room when the dressing bell rang, reading a book he'd found in Renwick's library. It was Captain Charles Pasley's *Military Policy and Institutions of the British Empire* which had not come his way although he had heard others discuss it.

Jack chose to read because it was an excuse to slip away from company which would be thrown together by the bad weather. He could not believe how tiring he found company after so many years away from society. While in the army, he had forgotten the behavior expected of one in a salon. For those who lived their lives in society it was habitual, but he needed to watch himself carefully lest he insult someone by not observing some nicety which, after years at war, seemed not only unimportant but even slightly ridiculous.

Even among his friends there were conventions the other men obeyed without thinking, but which he had to work to recall. Then too, so much of their conversation turned on people he no longer knew and activities in which he could no longer join.

When they did not tire him for one reason, they bored him to tears for another. Or left him enduring feelings of jealousy, exasperated by self-loathing that he'd sunk to jealousy in the first place!

Therefore he was grateful to discover that the book was not only thoughtful and interesting but well-written. He was surprised to discover how much time had passed when Black arrived to help him into evening wear.

"Company tonight," said Black in an off-handed manner.

"Oh?"

The tension, which his afternoon with the book had reduced, flowed back into him.

"Just a few local people for dinner and cards."

"Jase no longer plays cards."

"Don't suppose he does, but should everyone else be forbidden to, just 'cause he can't? As well say no one should ride 'cause *you* can't."

"Ouch."

"Well, if the shoe fits. . . ."

"Why are you so cross?" asked Jack. "That maid you have your eye on refuse to look your way?"

"Isn't a maid," growled Black. He added, "She's an undercook."

Jack chuckled. "You'll turn her head."

"Don't know that I will. She's got *her* eye on his lordship's coachy and I don't think he's adverse to the attention." Black gnashed his teeth.

"Ah well, there are other fish in the sea."

"Aye," said the man sourly. Black glanced up from the

boot he was rubbing furiously. "And hens in the coop as well. And you'd say that all cats are the same in the dark?" Black scowled. "That makes me feel better?"

But Jack had had enough. "So don't be so particular about those boots. I don't need boots in the evening, just slippers. And finish dressing me or I'll not go in to dinner on time!"

Black nodded. "But very likely the guests will arrive late. If they come at all. Which is doubtful."

"If people have been invited, why would their arrival be doubtful?"

Black cast him a startled look. "Ain't you looked out your window?"

"I've been reading."

"Been snowin' all day, that's all, and snow's piling up pretty deep out there. And *that's* why no one may come."

"I suppose I'll be labeled a curmudgeon if I say I hope they've all got the sense they were born with and stay home!"

"Likely you will," muttered Black, still in a foul mood due to the snubbing he'd received from the undercook during the servants' dinner an hour previously.

# Seven

The invited guests, prudent souls that they were, did not come. Which was wise, since it continued to snow all that night. When everyone woke the next morning, the meadow beyond the ha-ha dividing the lawn from pasture land stretched a pristine white as far as the trunks of the copper beeches lining Lord Renwick's property. Only to the back, where the servants worked, had anyone marked it.

The guests straggled into breakfast in ragged groups of twos and threes. When all were served, Lady Renwick cleared her throat. "We've a surprise," she said. "My lord ordered out the old sleigh. Anyone who wishes may join us this morning when we take it out."

"Bells?" asked Lord Hayworth urgently, his fork suspended midway between plate and mouth.

"Bells, my lord?" asked a confused Lady Renwick.

*"Bells.* We must have bells."

Her ladyship's bewilderment was not eased.

"On the harness," explained his lordship. "You surely know if there are bells." He folded his arms and frowned in an ostentatiously dramatic fashion. "I'll not go if there are no bells."

Lady Anne found this humorous and giggled. Lord Renwick laid a hand on Sahib's head when the beast heard her and made as if to rise. Lady Anne was seated as far from the tiger as possible, but she continued to be nervous of the creature. It was better if Sahib remained out of sight.

"I've a vague recollection of bells," said Lord Renwick. "It is a long time since I last rode in it, but what is a sleigh without bells?"

Lord Hayworth pretended to relax. "Since there are bells, I will come. Lady Blackburne? You will accompany me?"

He had been on edge since she had told him she would not make a decision concerning a marriage between them until the house party ended, but Lord Hayworth was very nearly certain her response would be positive and could not help but feel a mild possessiveness whenever his gaze rested on her. Which was often.

"Please?" he added softly when she frowned slightly.

Lady Anne would not decide whether or not to go until she heard Lieutenant Princeton's decision. Then, when he said it would be fun, Lady Anne trotted off to collect extra scarves, a fur lined travel rug, and hot bricks wrapped in flannel. With a footman lugging her hoard, Lady Anne left the house the instant the horses pulled the sleigh up to the door.

The sleigh had a huge, old-fashioned body set high off the ground with room for eight comfortably, or ten if one crowded in a bit. There was also a seat for the driver built out on a perch in front, on which there was room for still another passenger. Lady Anne stared. How was she to guess just where Jack Princeton would sit? As she dithered, Lady Renwick appeared, followed by Lady Blackburne and Lord Hayworth.

"Aha!" said Lord Hayworth. "You have thought of hot bricks for the ladies. What an excellent notion, Lady Anne!"

Lady Renwick and Lady Blackburne knew the bricks were for Jack, who would not appreciate the gesture, so they stifled giggles and asked politely if they each might have one. Lady Anne could do no other than give up two of her precious bricks. Lord Renwick, and Mr. McMurrey and his wife, Lady

Serena, were next to arrive and Lady Serena, at Lady Renwick's urging, also requested a brick. There were two left.

Lord Hayworth, winking at Lady Blackburne, said that left one for Mrs. Haydon and one for Lady Anne herself. He thought that if Lady Blackburne were to sit in the center of the front seat next to Lady Anne, they might share the travel rug while he and Lord Bladney, who appeared just then, sat on the outside to keep them warm and secure.

Lady Anne, panicking at the thought that all her careful planning had come to naught, stared at Lord Bladney with huge, begging eyes. For half a moment he considered giving in to her silent plea that he seat himself elsewhere, but then he remembered his plan and asked if she might loan him one of the scarves which he saw she had been thoughtful enough to provide in case someone was in need of one. He himself, he said, had forgotten that one would be helpful.

"I had a bit of a tickle in my throat this morning," he confided, a lie which he hoped would not be held against him. "It would be terrible to come down with a nasty quinsy just now, would it not? If I were to suffer a putrid sore throat, it would spoil the whole of Christmas for everyone, since all would worry they too might catch one," he finished earnestly.

Lady Anne moved closer. "Oh dear. Perhaps you should not come?"

"I believe the use of one of your scarves would prevent the worst and perhaps, when we return, you might be so kind as to see if Lady Renwick has, er, hmm—" Lord Bladney searched his mind, frantically. "—a black current cordial! That's the ticket! Just the thing to prevent a sore throat, do you not agree?"

Lady Anne allowed him to help her into the sleigh as they discussed the best means of preventing the hint of a sore throat from developing into something worse. Lord Bladney had some difficulty keeping up his end of the conversation but, by pretending to be interested in learning all the most modern methods, everything from the latest recipe for a cordial to the current practice of burning medicated pastilles, he managed to keep Lady Anne's attention focused on himself.

They were well on their way, Ian McMurrey holding the reins with Lady Serena up beside him, before Lady Anne realized she had forgotten all about Lieutenant Princeton's welfare in her concern for Lord Bladney's. She twisted in her seat at the sound of Jack's infectious laugh, only to see him looking at Patricia Haydon, amusement and perhaps something warmer in his eyes.

Silenced, Lady Anne turned back and could not be drawn into further conversation, no matter how Lord Bladney tried. He gave it up and, speaking across her, talked with Lady Blackburne and Lord Hayworth.

The snow was perfect for sleighing and McMurrey took them all the way into Chaley, where he pulled up near the inn. Since the inn yard had been swept free of snow much earlier that morning, the inn's groom was forced to come into the street to unharness the team. The horses must be rested, so McMurrey led the way into the establishment which soon provided refreshment for all.

The inn was cozy, the innkeeper had a light hand with a bowl of punch, and the ale was so good it was only after an excellent luncheon that the party reluctantly decided they must return to Tiger's Lair. Word went out to the stables and while the horses were reharnessed, everyone wrapped themselves up in their warm winter coats, preparing to depart. The couples drifted into the courtyard and on out to the street.

When Jack came out, using his crutch, of course, he was exceedingly wary of how and where he placed the thing. He was not about to find himself in the ignominious position in which he had once landed, due to an unnoticed patch of ice. But, because of his care, he was the last to arrive by the sleigh. He handed the crutch to the groom, and only as he prepared to climb in did he realize everyone had taken their places, leaving him to take the reins.

Jack froze. *Drive?* A *team?* He hadn't driven so much as a lowly gig for a great many years, and someone was fool enough to think he should start in again by driving four horses attached to a *sleigh?* Had someone lost his mind?

"Someone else . . ."

"Come on Jack," said McMurrey. "I drove over, Lord Hayworth does not wish to drive, and we know you were an excellent fiddler before you went into the army."

"Remember that race when you bribed the driver and took over that stagecoach, and those bucks driving that old-fashioned calash challenged you to a race?" Lord Renwick grinned wickedly. "We were on the road to Brighton, I think?"

Jack felt his cheeks glow. What *he* recalled was that he'd very nearly tipped the stagecoach into a ditch. "But . . ."

"You can do it, Jack," said Patricia, just as Lady Anne, who had been overly preoccupied with her bricks and her lap rugs, realized what was in progress. Her ladyship instantly protested it was too much, that Lieutenant Princeton would surely damage his wounded leg and that he must *not* drive.

Which, of course, was exactly the right way to go about convincing him he *should.*

Patricia, perched on the narrow driver's seat, folded her hands in her lap. She smiled down at him and, involuntarily, he smiled back. "We are ready, Jack, whenever you are," she said gently.

"Are you certain you don't wish the groom to take that seat and you crowd in behind?" asked Jack quietly after he'd pulled himself up beside her. "If I get into difficulties, he might be able to save us."

Serenely and in completely normal tones, Patricia told him not to act the dunce. ". . . You, Jack Princeton, are not a jackass," she continued. "You will do very well."

He drew in a sharp breath at her roughly phrased compliment. "I hope to God your faith is not misplaced," he said, his jaw set. He forced it to relax and clucked at the horses.

Slowly, warily, Jack recovered his expertise. What is more, he discovered he enjoyed it. But, later that night, he also discovered his good leg, which he'd rigidly braced against the mudguard, ached as badly as his bad leg ached back when it was nearly healed and he'd attempted too much.

The next day he was in the front hall, intent on going out to the stables when he discovered Patricia dressed for a walk. He asked if she'd care to accompany him which, to his surprise, she agreed to do. "Then hurry," he said in a whisper. "I think I hear Lady Anne coming this way from the breakfast room, and I'd much prefer to be elsewhere when she arrives!"

Patricia laughed at the wry look which accompanied his words, but knew that, despite his light tone, he was serious. They immediately moved out of the front hall, passing through the Renwicks' wing which ended in a door not too far from the stables. Once out in the cold winter air, Jack paused. "A narrow escape," he said. In a more hectoring tone he added, "You, Mrs. Haydon, must learn to move more quickly in dangerous situations. I feared your dawdling would make mice feet of our flight to freedom."

"It is not that I dawdled, Jack Princeton. It is that you've become too good with that crutch!"

"Have I now?" He grinned his devil grin, but it quickly faded. "Did I," he asked, "ever thank you for making me take up the use of it? What a coward I am, fearing to accept that I am crippled."

"I personally think it takes a great deal of courage to do so, even now." She spoke with quiet earnestness.

"Courage?"

"Yes, it takes courage to make such an admission. Especially when it is so important to you that you *not* be crippled."

"But it should not be," he retorted, moving on ahead of her at the swinging pace he'd developed.

"Not?" she asked, the one word all she could manage, since it took all her breath to keep up. "Stop!" she gasped. "Just for a moment. Please?"

Jack complied, giving her a wry look, but he forbore to tease. "When I discovered Jase was blind," he said, "I felt the complete fool for having been such a gudgeon about something so simple as a gimpy leg."

Patricia noticed he spoke without heat, that he truly seemed to have come to some sort of adjustment to his situation. "I believe, from something Lady Renwick said, that her husband's acceptance of his blindness was not easy either. We go along in life thinking good health will continue forever, so it is a dreadful shock to discover just how fragile we are."

"Is that what it was?" Jack asked. "Shock? I thought it merely a stubborn, perhaps selfish, desire to return to what was."

"That too, perhaps," she said.

Jack grimaced. "Insult me at your peril!" he said and set off.

He swung along the path and again Patricia hastened her steps to a brisk trot along with the occasional skip.

Once they reached the stables, Jack asked for Jase's coachman. They followed the man across the well-brushed court to the coach house, entering the huge, dusky room where they looked over Lord Renwick's vehicles. Among them was a neat gig which Jack studied.

"Is there a horse that will pull this?" asked Jack.

"Sweetsome goes it alone between a pair of shafts," said the coachy with such a broad burr to his words that Patricia had difficulty understanding him. "Maybe Firebug, who is a bit faster."

"Sweetsome will do very well. I am not, I fear, up to

either a fiery steed or one that behaves in the nasty way of a bug!"

The coachman smiled. "You'm want her put to the gig then?"

"Not just this instant," said Jack, "but later today?" He turned on his heel. "Mrs. Haydon? Will you chance life and limb once again and ride out with me?"

"Yes. Especially if you are willing to drive into Lewes. I packed so quickly for this visit, I managed to forget one or two things."

Patricia had "forgotten" the need to purchase Christmas gifts for her hosts, but what she really wished was to find something special for Jack. She would, of course, also acquire small gifts for the other houseguests. There was time, she thought, to embroider initials onto handkerchiefs for the men, and she recalled a book of herbals which Lady Anne would like. As to the others . . .

". . . Mrs. Haydon?" she heard and glanced at Jack, whose eyes twinkled.

"Yes."

"Have I your attention now?"

She felt her cheeks warming. "Yes."

"The jaunt you suggest might be a trifle more than I care to attempt my first time out with an unfamiliar horse. Could we postpone that for another day when we might leave earlier, and perhaps have a luncheon at the inn before returning? I too have a few trifling items I should purchase." He smiled when she nodded. "But what about a drive this afternoon?"

"I will take my life in my hands and accompany you on one condition!"

He turned a wary look her way.

"That when we continue our walk, you slow down!"

He grinned. "Perhaps a crutch should be made for you so that you could learn to keep up with me." His eyebrow quirked in that special way it had.

Patricia laughed. "An excellent notion. We must do that."

Patricia spoke as if it were merely a jest but, even as she said the words, she wondered where she would find Lord Renwick's estate carpenter, a man who could provide her with one, making the jest complete.

"And have you discovered how I climbed those stairs?" he asked, a teasing glint in his eye.

She grimaced. "No I have not, and it is unkind of you to remind me." Patricia promised herself she would set her mind to the problem. She would *not* be beaten.

That afternoon, they discovered that the lanes near the Renwick estate were not in the best of shape for driving, snow and ice making them treacherous. Jack took it slowly. Still, he and Patricia explored more of the region than he'd intended, simply because their discussion of everything and anything was so interesting that neither wished to cut short their time together.

And, for the whole of that drive, neither Jack nor Patricia made one comment which could be considered by the other the least out of line. Neither made a jest which could not be enjoyed by both. And neither was particularly surprised by the other's range of knowledge or interests, but simply enjoyed the process of discovery.

It was, thought Patricia later upon their return, an exceedingly enlightening afternoon.

Jack, enduring one of Black's rough but efficacious massages, thought about how interesting Patricia Haydon was. She knew about horses, which was perhaps not too surprising when one remembered her years in Ireland, but she also knew far more on the subject of the war with Napoleon than any other woman with whom he'd discussed it, although he readily admitted he'd not spoken of it with many. For instance, she had read the Pasley volume which he was currently reading and she had followed the war in the newspapers and journals. She was not particularly interested in fashion, which surprised him, since the subject seemed to preoccupy most women to the exclusion of all else. She also knew a great deal more than he did about the modern literary world, both through extensive reading of newly published works, and by reading reviews and articles about books and authors in journals which published essays written from different points of view.

Black told Jack to roll over. He complied and continued thinking about Patricia Haydon. A surprising woman altogether, he eventually concluded.

"There," said Black crossly, covering Jack with a warm coverlet. "Don't know why you get so knotted up."

Jack rolled onto his back, pulled the comforter higher, and tucked one arm under his head. He watched Black lay out his clothes for the evening. "Perhaps because I worry I'll make a mess of things. Today it would have been disastrous if I'd had an accident while out with Mrs. Haydon. She might have been hurt. Badly."

*"You?* Have trouble with a *gig?"*

Jack felt his neck warm. "I feared I might."

"You worry too much."

"Maybe I do." Jack stared at the ceiling. "Very likely I do."

Black cast him a sharp look but decided to ignore the morose tone. At least Crazy Jack had found an occupation which he could both enjoy and feel fulfilled by. It was a big step in the right direction.

Perhaps it was, but that evening Jack took a step backward. Discovering that Lady Renwick planned to hold an evening party later in the week to which she meant to invite a large number of their closer neighbors, Jack went back to scowling and growling and, in general, acting the bore. He even snapped at Lady Anne when she attempted to place a pillow behind him, sending her off in tears.

"What bee have you in your bonnet now?" asked Merwin.

"A *party.* You promised there would be no society at your estate and what did I find? Mrs. Haydon. And then you talked me into coming here. Just a few old friends, you said, and look at the company, half of whom I'd never met! Now you all expect me to make an ass of myself before still more strangers. Dancing! Can you see me dancing?" His scowl blackened and he stared out a window.

"Actually, I can't."

Jack swung around. "Can't? Can't what?"

"Can't see you dancing, of course. But then I never *did* see you dancing. You always avoided it."

Jack's eyes widened.

Merwin observed him before adding, "Before you went into the army. You do remember, do you not?"

Jack burst into deep-throated laughter. "Tell your cousin she is wrong—and I am most definitely the jackass she once assured me I was not." The laughter faded and he sobered. "Still, it will not be the same, Alex. In the past I abstained from choice. Now no one will think it anything but necessity." He growled. "I hate it. The pity and the special kindness to the poor wounded soldier—it is not to be borne!"

"You'll survive," countered his friend, hardening his heart. Jack had come so far in a relatively short period of time—he would not allow him to slide back into self-pity.

Jack glanced at Merwin. He struggled to his feet and, with a general good night to everyone, left the room.

Lady Anne, seeing him go, instantly informed Patricia it was all her fault, allowing Jack to drive all afternoon, exhausting him. "I am certain you encouraged him. It would be just like you. Thoughtless and careless of anything but your own fancies. You are selfish, Patricia. Selfish and insensitive and not at all the sort to take care of an invalid."

"What invalid?" asked Patricia in a bland tone, knowingly baiting her old friend.

"Why, we speak of Lieutenant Princeton, of course."

"The lieutenant? An invalid? Nonsense."

"But his limp . . ."

"His leg healed, Lady Anne," said Patricia. "Long ago. What must be dealt with now is his tendency to fall into black moods and pity himself. He cannot be allowed to do so."

Lady Anne's eyes widened. She blinked several times rapidly. "But Patricia, he has every reason to feel sorry for himself."

"What an absolutely idiotic thing to say," Patricia retorted. Then, turning on her heel, she said an abrupt good night to Lady Renwick and she too went early to bed.

Patricia feared that, if she had remained anywhere near Lady Anne, she would say or do even more for which she would later feel the need to apologize.

# Eight

Late in the afternoon of the party, long before the early winter dark, the Renwicks' guests began arriving. The public rooms were soon comfortably full, the more elderly guests settled at card tables and the younger people gathered in the salons.

A violin player and his wife, who played the piano, provided music, and a lively reel was just beginning. Patricia Haydon, who had taken part in the country dance which preceded it, came into the hall with Lord Merwin who had been her partner. As she started toward the table holding a large punch bowl, she heard Jack laugh one of his wonderfully fascinating laughs. She turned on her heel.

And stared.

"Why that . . . that . . . that . . . !"

"Exceedingly inarticulate of you, Patricia," said Lord Merwin. "To what do you refer?"

"*Jack.* Look at him!"

"You had not noticed until just now? He has been surrounded by wide-eyed beauties all the evening. He is a hero, you see, wounded in the service of his country, and worthy of all due consideration."

Patricia blinked. Her cousin's words were quite out of character. "He is?" she asked cautiously.

"Well—" Merwin's teeth flashed white in a quick grin.

"—that is what one young lady told me. Very earnest she was. A Miss Turnbell, I believe."

"The mousy little dab in the pink gown?" asked Patricia rather unkindly. Almost immediately she felt guilty for speaking so tartly to her cousin.

"Definitely mousy." He lowered his voice. "She squeaks."

Patricia chuckled but her eyes never left Jack. *His* eyes flashed sparks as he said something up over his shoulder to one of the two young ladies leaning against his chair. There was a tinkling chorus of giggles from the four sitting on stools before him. One daringly put her hand on Jack's knee, removing it immediately once she had his attention.

Suddenly, Jack glanced up. His eyes met Patricia's and a sheepish grin spread across his face. He beckoned.

"Go to him, Patricia. I don't think it is that he wishes to be rescued, exactly. I suspect it is more that he wishes to point out that he prefers a more mature lady to mere children, before one or another of those sweet young things allows into her head the ridiculous notion that he might favor her. I will bring you your punch," he finished when she glanced toward Jack.

As Patricia approached, Jack gestured to the girls sitting before him to give him room. Struggling less than he had only a week or so previously, he rose to greet her. "Mrs. Haydon. Do you know my young friends?" he asked, speaking lightly but with a faint emphasis on the word "young." And then, quite suddenly, his eyes widened in faint alarm.

Patricia, suspecting he had realized he must now introduce them and had forgotten names, smiled. "I have met Miss Croydon, but I don't believe I've been introduced to the others. Miss Croydon, will you do the honors?" Patricia asked.

Miss Croydon did, and Patricia suggested they might all wish to go into the salons for a while, that she had heard a rumor that Lord Wendover and a guest who had traveled on the continent were to demonstrate that exciting and rather scandalous German dance, the waltz.

". . . It is not to be danced generally, of course," she finished. "Later, you may return to entertain Lieutenant Princeton. I am certain he appreciates the time you give him."

The girls, torn between hero-worship and the opportunity to actually see a performance of the shockingly fast waltz, decided they would depart until the demonstration was over and then return. "We will not desert you," said one with a flirtatious shake of her fan.

"Oh, dear," said Patricia when they'd gone off amid giggles and whispered confidences. "I did not think!" She adopted a chagrined expression. "They will be asked to dance, and will soon promise so many sets I fear you will not see them again. Should I have left well enough alone?"

"No. They were rather fun, but—" He cast Patricia a look equal in mortification to hers. "—so very *young*. Were we ever such children, Mrs. Haydon?"

"I suppose we must have been. Ah. Thank you, Alex." She took the cup he offered her and drank half of it. "I do so little dancing that after the least little exertion, I find I am much in need of this." She lifted the glass cup slightly and sipped again. "Well, Lieutenant, have you concluded that perhaps a party such as this is not quite such torture as you believed?"

"Listen carefully—because it may not happen again. Not ever. I—" His face took on an impish look and he spoke in a hushed and dramatic tone. "—admit it. *I was wrong.*"

Patricia smiled. "I will remind you of that the next time some new and untested situation comes your way."

They spoke, laughing and joking, for some little time. Then a lady of about her own age, to whom, earlier in the evening, Patricia had been introduced for the first time, politely and a trifle hesitantly asked if Mrs. Haydon would, sometime that evening, attend to her mother who wished to speak with her about her parents.

Jack made a shooing motion. "Go. You must not keep the lady waiting."

"Very well." Patricia rose to her feet and spoke to the diffident lady. "I will come with you now. You must introduce us, must you not?"

Her new acquaintance giggled shrilly. "Actually, my mother claims to have met you. It seems the two of you were introduced while you were lying in your cradle after your christening."

"Your mother will understand if I have forgotten?"

Again that rather irritating giggle.

Patricia wondered what she had become involved in the instant she discovered Mrs. Beacham had no particular desire to speak about Patricia's parents. Instead, the woman promptly and a trifle coyly introduced Patricia to her son.

The young man was a red-faced country gentleman interested in nothing but his acres and the glass in his hand which, every so often and without the least sign of embarrassment, he replenished from a flask kept in a pocket in the tail of his coat. Patricia realized quickly that his mother was determined to find her son a wife. She had obviously had difficulty doing so since she was well practiced in the art of keeping a likely candidate at her son's side!

It was nearly half an hour later before Patricia escaped and returned to the hall, where she discovered Jack surrounded by another group of hero worshiping young people. This time five young men hung on Jack's every word.

Patricia wondered what he spoke of to keep them so engrossed. She hoped it was *not* tales of daring-do and glory. War was not about glory but doing one's duty and, when necessary, dying with bravery. She would have words to say to him if she discovered he was filling the boys' silly heads with anything but the truth! She approached Jack's chair from the rear so he'd not realize she was there.

". . . so you see, you have to expect a great deal of discomfort if you join the army. It isn't all dirt and duty and dying, of course," said Jack, repeating, much to her embarrassment, Patricia's thoughts on the subject. "There is also a great sense of camaraderie you can find nowhere else. Friendships quickly become intense when you know they may be short-lived, one or the other of you catching it in the next battle. But we had balls of a sort and several of the men kept dogs for haring. The hares, by the way—" He grinned that quick mischievous grin. "—are a welcome addition to the stew pot which is often a trifle thin. Wellington is dead against raiding the countryside for supplies, you know!"

Patricia wandered off, her concern eased, and entered the makeshift ballroom. She discovered Lord Wendover and Lord Cowley's wife were only now to give their demonstration of the waltz. Was it, she wondered, truly as scandalous as she'd heard?

After a very few moments she decided it was. And she envied Lady Cowley immensely for daring to indulge! How free and exhilarating it must be to swing about the floor in that graceful manner. Patricia toyed with the notion of asking Lord Wendover to teach her the trick of it. Not tonight, of course. But perhaps sometime later during the party when they might have privacy for the lesson?

When the demonstration ended, she drifted back to the hall where she discovered several pairs of young people sitting on the stairs, laughing and talking and nibbling from a plate one young man held and offered to each. Had supper been served and she unaware? It seemed it had. Patricia went into the dining room where she too had a plate filled with this and that and carried it back to the hall where she approached Jack's crowd cautiously, not wanting to spill anything.

She excused herself to one young man who, realizing she had brought Jack's supper, cleared a path for her. One or two, noticing there was food available, took themselves off immediately, but the others continued to bombard Jack with questions.

"But the cavalry is the *most* important, it is not?" insisted one lad who had obviously asked the question more than once.

"It depends on the battle, of course," said Jack patiently. "You will understand we have little enough to do during a siege! But even in a battle where horses are important, one should not say they are *most* important. Where would we be if we didn't have the big guns to bombard the enemy and soften them up? And what would we do without the infantry? No, every part of the army is important." Again that quick grin. "Actually, the *most* important is the commissary! I recall once when it went astray and we had nothing but acorns to eat for two whole days."

One of the boys looked almost ill at the thought. Jack ignored him and added, "I'll even admit the navy is important. They are our transport and carry goods and whatnot. And occasionally, it is necessary to use them to take on another country's navy in battle. No one could fail to admit that Nelson did us a favor when he beat the French at Trafalgar!"

"Yes, but the cavalry, they . . ."

Frowning, Jack interrupted. "They are the *flashiest* of units with the *most spectacular* of uniforms, but they alone could never win a modern war." He spoke sternly without a trace of his usual humor. "If you mean to go into the army, any of you, remember that the whole army must work as a team. It is no good for someone to go off half-cocked attempting to run his own little battle. You must all work together."

He shifted in his chair. "Gentlemen, I find I am a little tired. Perhaps you should go see about your supper before it is eaten by someone else. Mrs. Haydon?" He looked up at her. "Will you keep me company for a bit and dine with me?"

The boys apologized, thanked Jack for talking to them, and said all that was proper to Mrs. Haydon. And the one who didn't wish to give up his belief that the only important part of the army was the cavalry was already arguing the point before they were out of hearing.

"You *look* tired," she said when the lads had gone.

He ignored her concern, which she had taken care to conceal as well as she could. "That youngster," he said, "will have a great deal to learn. Assuming his father relents and he attains his desire to serve in one of the cavalry regiments."

"I am glad you told them what it was *really* like and not merely tales of great battles and heroic deeds."

"We discussed this briefly the other day when we went driving. How could you think I would ever encourage false images of life in the army among the young?"

"I have insulted you. I am sorry."

Jack relaxed. "No, no. I must apologize. I had no reason to snap your head off. I told those lads I am tired, but I think I'd not realized just how tired until they took themselves off. Will the party disintegrate if I take my very important self off to my room so early in the evening?"

"There are so very many people, are there not? And you are not used to crowds. I know that when I force myself into London for part of a Season, it takes me days to feel comfortable with the pace—" She flashed a quick smile. "—and then, about the time I do, I'm off for home and must once again adapt to peace and quiet! Have you finished eating? I'll take the plate and find your crutch for you."

Patricia still held the empty plate when Lady Anne entered the hall. Her ladyship balanced two well-filled plates, her hands extended before her. She didn't see Mrs. Haydon until she had come very near Jack's chair.

"You!" She glanced at the single plate in Patricia's hand. "How like you. You bring your supper here and eat while Lieutenant Princeton must contain his own hunger."

"It is quite the other way around, Lady Anne," said Jack, giving Patricia a quick glance, both chagrined and apologetic. "She brought me my plate and I did not think to share it with her. Perhaps you would be so kind as to offer one of yours to her?"

Before Lady Anne could respond to this unwelcome suggestion, Jack struggled to his feet, accepted the crutch Patricia held for him, and, after a quick bow to the ladies, made a careful way toward the Renwicks' private hallway to the room where he was quartered.

Lady Anne glowered, her eyes never leaving Jack's back. When he disappeared, she thrust one of the plates at Patricia. "He has said you are to have it. Take it. I hope you choke on it." She set her second plate on a nearby table and moved, more quickly than caution suggested might be prudent, to the stairs. She then picked up her skirts and hurried up.

As Patricia thoughtfully nibbled on a lobster patty, Lord Bladney approached her. "Lady Anne left rather abruptly," he said softly. "Do you feel you can explain to me why?"

"It appears I am once again at fault."

Lord Bladney smiled. "And how, may I ask, are you at fault this time?"

"I brought Jack Princeton a plate of supper goodies some twenty minutes before she arrived with her offering. Jack had just told me he was tired and meant to go to his room. It is my guess that Lady Anne suspects me of deliberately interfering in one of her little plots to have Jack to herself for a bit."

"Ah. Then she is very likely more angry at me than at you. She allowed herself to be coaxed into one last country dance, you see, or she'd have been before you."

"This last dance?" When he nodded Patricia frowned. "But was it not the supper dance? Should she not be eating with you?"

Lord Bladney grinned. "Surely, Mrs. Haydon, you do not believe an old friend such as myself will be bothered by a little thing like my supper partner haring off to dine with another gentleman? Why, it is not possible I should object!"

"Is that what she told you?"

"In very nearly those words. I do not believe she considered herself to be haring off, of course."

Patricia smiled. She nodded toward the abandoned plate. "Then, my lord, since we have both been deserted, perhaps you would care to join me?"

Lord Bladney bowed, collected the plate, and led Patricia to a pair of chairs flanking a sideboard. He seated Patricia and pulled the second chair around so they could converse.

Which they did on all sorts of conventionally innocuous and, Patricia silently admitted, rather boring topics. It crossed her mind that Jack, for all his faults, never attempted to discuss the banal!

Very late that night Sahib growled softly. He got up and padded to the door. There he stood on his hind legs, a forepaw against the wall. He pushed down on the door handle with the other and the door swung open.

The long hall was dimly illuminated by two lamps, both turned very low. Sahib, half into the Renwicks' room and half out, stared toward the far end where a ghostly figure drifted nearer, opening first one door and then the next, slowly approaching Lieutenant Princeton's room. Sahib sniffed . . .

. . . and went utterly still.

At the far end of the hall, a very nervous Lady Anne proceeded stealthily toward the next door on the right. She wished very much she knew which room was the lieutenant's. Then all she need do was open the door, see that he was not suffering for his foolishness in remaining at the party longer than he was accustomed to, and then she could return to her room and manage, finally, to go to sleep.

But the rooms were so terribly dark. This one worse than the preceding which had uncovered windows. Here she could make out nothing at all from the doorway. *Was* it Lieutenant Princeton's room? Should she enter?

Or perhaps not?

Why did she feel so odd, as if she were doing something she should not? It was because she was so worried that she had chosen to come down to check on him. That was all—

Lady Anne felt her cheeks heat.

—was it not?

What else could she possibly have had on her mind? Her inner vision filled with a picture of herself in the lieutenant's arms. Lady Anne's heart beat faster as she wondered if it could possibly be true that she had meant to take the dastardly action of compromising the lieutenant. For his own good, of course.

*Dare I,* she wondered, her eyes widening painfully. Lady Anne took a hesitant step into the room. Another.

Suddenly the door slammed shut and what she had thought Stygian darkness became instantly worse. The *worst* was that she felt as if, suddenly, she were as blind as Lord Renwick.

Then the absolute worst worsened. From behind the closed door Lady Anne heard the soft growl of a wild beast.

"Sahib," she breathed. "It is he!"

And then, of course, she fainted.

# Nine

The following morning Lady Renwick rose early. She wished to check that the servants had completed their work before retiring, and that they'd restored the Tiger's Lair to proper form. It was not that she did not trust her staff, but they worked best when they knew she took an interest. She slipped into a chemise dress which she could easily manage by herself and did no more than brush her hair back, tying it with a ribbon which matched her gown. She rose, turning to the door . . .

. . . which stood open for the whole world to see.

Lady Renwick felt heat in her throat and raised a hand to cover it. Who had opened the door? She glanced toward the bed where Jason slept. For a moment, she was distracted. Lying on his side, he had pulled her pillow near, clutched it . . .

Her ladyship smiled softly.

The smile faded as her gaze shifted back to the door. The standing cheval-glass revealed her mouth had firmed into a stern line. Lady Renwick did not relax it. She must get to the bottom of this. It would not do to have someone, a servant perhaps, opening doors, observing what went forward, and then, very nearly worst of all, *leaving the door gaping open for the whole world to see!*

Lady Renwick stepped into the hall. Farther down the hall lay Sahib. He raised his great head, stared at her, then lowered it back to his paws. His gaze was fixed on the door before him.

"That blessed beast," muttered her ladyship, achieving an understanding of the open door. "He is up to his old tricks, I see. But why did he open the door this time?"

Lady Renwick took a moment to remember that wonderful, fearsome night when Sahib had come to her room, urged her in his beastly way to go to Lord Renwick's room, an action which had led to their marriage. That wonderful night, although fearing something was very wrong, she had hesitated to enter his lordship's bedroom even when encouraged by the tiger. Then, when she discovered his lordship suffering from a terrible nightmare, she'd not known what to do. Sahib had.

"But why, in this particular case, is our Sahib opening doors and wandering the house in the night?" she asked herself.

About half-way down the hall, Jack Princeton's door opened and the lieutenant hopped into the hall. "You are up early," he called softly.

"As are you." She spoke more loudly. "Did you hear anything in the night? An intruder, perhaps?"

Suddenly, from beyond the door Sahib guarded, there was a shriek. "My lady. Is that you I hear? Oh please, my lady, do not allow the monster to harm me! If you are there, please, *do* answer me!"

Recognizing the voice, a combination of horror and humor could be seen in Jack's expressive features. Lady Renwick bit her lip and fought back a giggle.

"Oh, please, rescue me! At once!" called the voice. "I have suffered all the fear and alarms I can bear. The night has been so long, so fearsome, so . . ."

"Full of imagination, perhaps?" said Lady Renwick, but not so loudly she would be heard. She searched for sympathy but found none. Lady Anne had brought this horror on herself. Pointing to his room, she waved Jack back into it. Very softly, she said, "I suspect she came to find you, Lieutenant. It would be best, perhaps, if she does not. Even now."

"I doubt she will try again," said Jack equally softly, nodding toward Sahib who, his great head turned toward them, stared benignly. "Remind me I owe that beast a leg of lamb or something equally tempting."

The string of complaints issuing from Lady Anne had not ceased during their brief conversation, and Lady Renwick continued down the hall. "My lady," she said through the door, "I will return Sahib to our room where I will see he stays and, after a moment, you may make your way back to your room." The comment was followed by silence. But, as Lady Renwick tugged Sahib to his feet, she heard, very softly, a sob.

"I cannot," said Lady Anne. "I dare not be seen."

Curious, Lady Renwick cracked the door open. It was instantly pulled shut, but not before she noted that Lady Anne was dressed in her night robe. Crossly, Lady Renwick considered leaving her guest to her own devices. She sighed as she realized that, as a good Christian woman, she could not allow Lady Anne to suffer still more humiliation for what was mere foolishness and no harm done.

"I will bring you a long cape which will cover you completely. If you are seen, it will be assumed you return from a morning stroll."

The sob was repeated. "You are very thoughtful. Thank you."

Lady Renwick returned with the cape in short order. She did not immediately hand it over, but said, "I do not think I would attempt . . . whatever it was you meant to do. Never again. Sahib was not pleased to have spent his night in a drafty hall, but he is very protective of my lord and does not tolerate intruders."

"I only wished to check that Lieutenant Princeton did not suffer for his rash behavior. Staying up so terribly late, all those inconsiderate people importuning him. It was outside of enough. I felt I must see to him. Surely you understand that I am his nurse and must have a care for him?" She cast a quick look toward Lady Renwick who bore an expression of disbelief. "You will not tell . . . ?" she asked in a small voice.

"No, of course not. But Jack Princeton is not a fool. He left the party when he had had enough. He is neither an invalid nor a child. He does not need a nurse. Nor a nanny. To the contrary. He needs to be pushed into trying what he can do."

"Oh no!" Lady Anne's mood changed instantly to the overly protective mode in which she was most comfortable. "You are so very wrong. He must *not* be encouraged to do anything which would possibly hurt him all over again! He almost died, you know."

"Nonsense. Oh, not that he almost died, but that he is still unwell!"

Lady Anne cast an irritated look at her hostess and opened her mouth, obviously ready to argue the point.

Lady Renwick gently turned Lady Anne toward the door. "Off with you," she said. "I have work to do and I suspect you should seek your bed. This room—" It was a small store room. "—cannot have been very comfortable. You cannot have slept well," she finished.

Lady Anne's mouth snapped shut on any further attempt to convince her hostess of the rightness of her views. Why nobody appeared to understand the necessity of cosseting the lieutenant was beyond her understanding when, to her mind, it was so very obvious. Hoping she would never again find herself so utterly humiliated, and knowing there was nothing else she could do, she went to her room, meeting no one but Lord Bladney on the way.

Wondering why she felt quite so ashamed and embarrassed that it was he who caught her, Lady Anne hurried on her way after only the most incoherent of explanations. Later she decided it was merely that Lord Bladney knew her so well he would be aware she was not one for early morning strolls. Besides, she feared, from the look of disapproval he had given her, he had somehow caught a glimpse of her feet and noticed they were shod in nothing more solid than embroidered bedroom slippers!

In any case, Lady Anne could not bring herself to face any company and sent down a message that she was very tired. She must, she insisted, have a day in which to recover.

Lord Hayworth strolled through the rooms looking for Lady Blackburne and then ruefully decided he was behaving even more foolishly than usual. He reversed directions and went straight to the conservatory where, of course, he found her.

For a long moment he stood quietly watching her deftly, gently, separate exceedingly young sprouts and place them, individually, in another flat of earth. Her work roused an almost forgotten memory from early childhood, and he recalled watching his father's curmudgeonly Scottish gardener doing something similar. He wondered that her ladyship appeared to enjoy getting her hands filthy, to say nothing of her gown, where it was not covered by a large apron.

*Her face as well,* he added silently as, hearing him, she turned. He could see where his lady love had brushed back a wandering strand of hair, leaving an interesting streak of mud behind. He smiled.

" 'Tis you, is it?" asked her ladyship a trifle crossly. "Well, don't stand there. Come here where I can see you." She pointed imperiously at a spot on the other side of her worktable.

Obligingly, Lord Hayworth moved in his loose-limbed manner to where he could lean against a pillar and face her. He shoved his hands into pockets in his trousers, a pretty conceit he'd talked his tailor into incorporating in his most recent pattern. That his stance, his shoulders against the pillar and his hips thrust ever so slightly forward, was a trifle suggestive, was something else.

Lady Blackburne glanced at him, then back at her work and then, motionless, back at him. Her eyes widened and a spot of color appeared high on each cheek. After a moment she collected herself and the eyes narrowed. "That," she scolded, "is no way for a gentleman to present himself to a lady."

"Ah. But ever so comfortable." He grinned. "You know I am addicted to comfort."

Silence fell, but her ladyship flicked several glances his way before finishing her work and putting aside her pick. She wiped her hands free of soil, eying her *enamorado*. "Those pockets. Useful things, are they?"

"Quite."

A smile flickered about her mouth and eyes. She nodded. "I thought so. I suppose your valet would be utterly scandalized if he were asked to show my maid how such were constructed."

Lord Hayworth's mouth twitched. "Do we care if he is scandalized? Perhaps it would actually be good for the old stick to show, er, trousers to a woman!"

Lady Blackburne felt heat rise in her throat. She was irritated that Lord Hayworth had managed to embarrass her, again, when it had been her thought to embarrass him.

He relented and, more softly, said, "If you've a reason why she should see my trousers, then certainly she must see my trousers."

"I have skirts which I save to wear when working in the garden. I believe such pockets might come in very handy indeed," she explained.

Lord Hayworth nodded. Judiciously. "An excellent notion." He eyed her. "And have we now finished with our discussion of my pockets?"

Lady Blackburne scowled. "If you do not wish such a

discussion, you have no business standing there in that exceedingly, er, hmm, well . . ."

"*Lustful* fashion?"

He gazed at her with such utter innocence that she burst out laughing. He grinned.

"You, my lord, are a complete hand—as I believe I have heard the young people say?"

He pulled himself up straight and stepped toward the table. For an instant he shoved his hands still farther into his pockets and then, with effort, relaxed. "I don't suppose," he said in his most insouciant manner, "that you have given my proposal another thought?"

"To the contrary. You must know I've been able to think of nothing else."

"Ah!" When she added nothing more, he asked, "May I know in what directions your thoughts have wandered?"

She lifted her hands in a movement expressing her exasperation. "In *all* directions! Hayworth, I simply do not see how I can—"

"—say anything but yes?" he interrupted. He drew out one hand and raised it. "Say no more, my lady, my love. When your thoughts have traveled all possible paths they will recognize that, as all roads are said to lead to Rome, all thoughts will come together at the point for which I yearn— and I will be the happiest of men. For now, however—" He waggled his eyebrows in a suggestive fashion. "—shall we endeavor a bit more in our experiments to see if we are too old to enjoy those simple pleasures of which the poets speak?"

Lady Blackburne would admit to no one, including Lord Hayworth, that one path her thoughts had taken had led her to wonder if perhaps the solution to her problem was to indulge in a discreet affair with the man. Their last interlude had not led to such an irrevocable decision, but perhaps . . .

"My dear?" he interrupted her thoughts. "Have I shocked you?"

"Oh no. I am more than seven, my lord, and cut my eye-teeth long ago. I have wondered, however, if such endeavors might not be better pursued in less public surrounds?"

Lord Hayworth adopted a shocked look. "You surely do not suggest that one of us attends the other in the privacy of that other's bedroom!"

"Do I not?" She was more than a trifle chagrined by the wistful note she heard in her own voice.

"My dear. You cannot have thought." His voice dropped. "We are not yet wed."

Embarrassment fled. It was Lady Blackburne's turn for raised brows. "Now I wonder why that thought had not occurred to me."

"All I suggested," he said in a wheedling tone, "was that we might indulge in *simple* pleasures, but now—" His hands disappeared back in his pockets. "—you have unnerved me and I have scolded you and I fear that we are, neither of us, in the proper mood." He sighed dramatically. "Ah well." After a moment, he added, "Will you, instead, bundle up and take a walk with me?"

Not too long after that particular tete-a-tete, Patricia Haydon could be seen slipping out a back door. She made her way across the cobbles to the carpentry shop. "Mr. Sawyer?" she called. "Are you there?" She sniffed. She loved the smell of a woodworker's shop, the clean, pungent scent of newly sawn wood, the enticing odor of hot glue, the scented oils and waxes used to finish pieces of furniture made for the house . . .

Mr. Sawyer approached from the depths of the large room. "Mrs. Haydon. Welcome. Come for your crutches, have you?"

"You made more than one?"

"It is easier with two. I know. I broke m'leg once, you see."

"Easier? Should we have another made for the lieutenant?"

"If he wants it, I'll do it."

Gingerly, Patricia accepted the crutches. "Ah! You've already padded them for me!"

"That makes it easier, too," said the man, a chuckle rising from deep in his barrel chest.

Still more gingerly, Patricia set them under her arms.

"Now—" A frown creased her brow. "—all I must do is learn to use them!"

For the next few minutes Renwick's carpenter gave Patricia advice in the proper use of her new crutches and off she went to practice. It took her longer than it had Jack to become proficient, but when she had mastered them, she was pleased to discover she could swing along quite speedily. Her practice had gone on for some time and she had begun to tire when Lady Blackburne and Lord Hayworth turned around the end of a hedge and caught her at it.

"Oh, dear," she said and grimaced.

Lord Hayworth chuckled while Lady Blackburne's brows climbed up her forehead. "What have we here?" asked her ladyship sharply.

"It is *supposed* to be a surprise," said Patricia, removing the crutches from under her arms and holding both together.

"A surprise for whom?" asked her ladyship a trifle frostily. She drew herself up. "Mrs. Haydon, I cannot believe you would mock our dear Lieutenant Princeton in this manner."

Patricia's smile faded and she paled that anyone would think such a thing. "No, never." Her chin rose. "Actually, it was he who suggested I learn the art."

*"He* suggested . . . ?"

Patricia relaxed. "I have difficulty keeping up with him and he said I would just have to get my own crutch! So I have. Except that Mr. Sawyer made me two."

"And do you think you can keep up with the lieutenant now?" asked Lord Hayworth.

Patricia's features twisted into the faintest of grimaces. "I doubt it," she admitted, "but I shall have fun trying," she added and then grinned a bit more broadly than a high stickler might consider proper.

Lord Hayworth nodded. "Yes, my dear, I believe you will and I promise we shall not give away your secret—" He smiled a quick mischievous smile. "—on one condition!"

Patricia tipped her head and gave him a slightly suspicious look. "And that is?" she asked.

His smile widened. "That you give us advance warning when you mean to spring your little surprise on the good gentleman, of course. I would not miss this confrontation for the world."

Patricia was not forced to promise as Lady Blackburne shook her head just then. "Hayworth," said her ladyship, "is a tease. *Such* a tease. I do not know why we poor women put up with *any* of them."

"Any of them, my lady?" asked Patricia.

"Men, my dear child." Her ladyship cast Lord Hayworth a darkling look. *"Men,"* she repeated in a tone implying utter disgust.

# Ten

After the ball the Renwicks' front door knocker was never still. If a young lady did not coax her mother into making a morning visit, one or even several of the young gentlemen was asking the butler if Lieutenant Princeton was at home.

Jack flirted lightly with the girls and did his best to give the young men a realistic notion of war, but, after a day or so, the whole business palled. He asked Patricia if she still wished to drive into Lewes.

"I had almost forgotten, but yes. Most definitely I do. Soon it will be too late to do the embroidery."

"Then," he said, "let us escape before anyone deems it late enough in the day for a visit!"

Patricia's eyes widened. "What? You would disappoint love's young dream?"

He chuckled. "Not only the cooing doves but also those young hawks with their dreams of glory. How quickly can you be ready?"

Patricia told him half an hour and, picking up her skirts, took the stairs in a decidedly unladylike manner—not that Jack objected to the glimpse he got of her trim ankles. He was not so pleased, however, when, turning to tell the footman to take a message to the stables, he discovered the man had been rewarded with the same view.

Jack frowned. When the footman, mouth agape, continued

to stare up the now vacant stairs, the lieutenant cleared his throat.

The footman blinked, turned. He noted Jack's glower and swallowed, his Adam's apple bobbing. "Yes sir?" he asked, his voice rising in a squeak.

"Take a message to the coach house. I wish the gig brought around." His eyes narrowed. "And in future . . ."

"Yes, sir," interrupted the footman, his neck red. "I will, sir."

"You will?"

"I will keep my eyes where they belong, sir," said the footman, standing at attention and looking at nothing at all.

"See you do. *Not*—" The one-sided grin that had the enlisted men under his command idolizing him suddenly appeared. "—that I blame you. A decidedly tempting sight!"

Patricia and Jack were soon on the road. The horse was full of frisk and, as usual, they had much to say to each other, so that it seemed no time at all before they sighted the ruins of Lewes Castle. Very soon after that Jack turned their horse into the inn yard.

"I meant for us to separate to do our shopping and then meet again when finished, but it occurs to me that we forgot your maid and that you need my escort." Jack frowned down at Patricia. The frown faded. "Aha!" He pointed, first at himself and then at her. "I will come with you now, while you shop, and later, while you put up your feet in a private parlor, I will take some few minutes to purchase my bits and pieces."

Patricia wondered at herself for having dispensed with her maid. To be alone in an open carriage with Jack when riding along country lanes was one thing. Coming into town together, well, that was quite different. And how was she to accomplish that one special bit of shopping while in Jack's company?

Patricia resigned herself to another trip into Lewes at some later date and cheerfully accepted Jack's arm for a foray into the haberdashery where she meant to purchase handkerchiefs on which she would embroider the appropriate initials for each gentleman.

The room, lit by an oversized chandelier, was crowded. The patrons milled about, some looking at the merchandise, some being helped by a clerk. A harried young gentleman glanced up from the ledger in which he recorded his latest sale, noted the style of the new customers, and sidled behind another clerk who served a young woman fingering some material. He approached Patricia and Jack.

"Yes sir? Madam?" He glanced from one to the other. "What may I do for you today?"

The stocks were low and the selection of handkerchiefs limited. Patricia looked the young man in the eye. "Are you very certain there is nothing of better quality than this?" She flicked the thin, white cotton, her nose wrinkled in a disparaging way. "In back? Forgotten, perhaps?"

"Well—"

Jack, standing a trifle behind Patricia, tossed his purse in the air, caught it, and tossed it again.

The clerk caught sight of the movement. He eyed first the purse and then Jack who allowed one brow to lift.

The clerk drew in a deep breath. "I shouldn't, but seeing as how the lady never came back for them, well—"

Jack chose a half crown, returned the purse to his pocket and began tossing the coin.

"—they aren't doing anyone any good on the shelf, are they?" The clerk disappeared behind a curtain, and returned with a small package. "A dozen of the best linen, madam! The very best."

The package was unwrapped, the linen inspected, and, agreeably surprised at the quality, Patricia paid. When she turned toward the door, Jack tossed the coin once more, turning away as he did so. The clerk deftly caught it and pocketed it, hoping with all his might that Mrs. Foggerty really had forgotten to return for her handkerchiefs!

Clutching the parcel's sturdy string in the same hand with

which he clutched his crutch, Jack led Patricia to a nearby wine merchant where he made a careful selection from the wines available. He ordered that the case chosen for Renwick be carried to the inn and stored in the Renwick gig.

Then, since it was right next door, they went to the saddlery. Jack was astonished at the quality of the stock. "I could find nothing better in London," he said, choosing several crops from those available.

"Thankee, sir. We do all our own work. Been working in leather for generations, we have, sir. My granddad learned the trade from *his* grandfather and can still build the best saddle you ever sat!"

Jack swallowed. "I'm sure," he said shortly and, paying for his purchases, left the shop in something of a rush.

In fact, Patricia was forced to pick up her parcel which Jack, in his haste, forgot. She followed him out and, after they'd stalked a short distance up the street, she asked, "What is next, Jack?"

He glanced down at her, obviously upset.

"Jack?"

He grimaced, drew in a deep breath and blew it out. "I apologize." He made an effort to put aside his anger and grief that he could never sit on one of the saddler's well-made saddles. "Where, my dear, do *you* wish to go next?"

Patricia hesitated, hiding it by looking around, and brightened. "Jack! There is Lady Blackburne. *And* her maid. I was unaware she had the intention of coming into Lewes today."

Jack looked beyond her ladyship. "And I spy Lord Hayworth. Do you, too, suspect they came on the same errand as ours? Lady Blackburne!" he called and, when her ladyship paused, he and Patricia caught up with her. "We decided, on the spur of the moment, to do a trifling bit of shopping. It didn't occur to either of us, until we reached town, that Mrs. Haydon should have her maid along on such an occasion."

"Will you act as my chaperon?" asked Patricia.

"And perhaps we might all indulge ourselves in a luncheon when we have finished?" Jack gestured to the inn where he'd left the gig.

"Lord Hayworth has already ordered something for our refreshment. Have you much shopping, Mrs. Haydon?"

"Not a great deal. And you?"

"Only one item to which I *must* attend, but I admit that I love the shops and mean to poke into every single one. Lord Hayworth suggested we meet at two. Will that be satisfactory, Lieutenant?"

He nodded.

They made new arrangements with the inn's host, left the package Lady Blackburne's maid carried along with Patricia's and Jack's, and returned to the street. As Patricia and Lady Blackburne strolled away from Jack, Patricia explained that she had already bought handkerchiefs for the gentlemen of the party, a perfectly acceptable gift from a young woman to gentlemen unrelated to her, but that she had yet to find tokens to give the lady guests.

As they entered first one and then another shop, her ladyship was not surprised by the trifles Patricia selected. Only the herbal book Patricia purchased for Lady Anne caused a trifling astonishment—but only because it seemed to her ladyship that since the two women were not on the best of terms, the book was overly expensive.

And then, with a glance to see the way was clear, Mrs. Haydon turned into the saddlery where she bought an elegant but obviously a man's crop.

Lady Blackburne's brows rose. Then her brow cleared. "For your cousin, of course?"

"Not at all. I've had Alex's present put aside for ages." Her eyes dancing, Patricia added, "This is for Jack."

The brows clashed and Lady Blackburne drew herself up. "Mrs. Haydon, I accepted that you did not mean to mock the lieutenant when we caught you practicing with those crutches, but *this!* It is outside of enough—" Her ladyship looked down her nose. "—when you know very well the man cannot ride and that it is obvious to all he resents his disability. How can you be so cruel? Or perhaps it is mere thoughtlessness that you buy him such a gift?"

Patricia's gaze cooled. "I thought you knew me better than that, my lady," she said, her tone frosty. "Since you do not, I will let you think whatever you will and allow you to find out what is in the wind when it is revealed to everyone. Including Jack."

The women, a trifle out of charity with each other, arrived back at the inn not so very much later than was agreed. They would very likely have been on time had they not discovered a millinery shop in which the hats were surprisingly chic and not so very far from current London styles that they would be despised as provincial. Lady Blackburne purchased two, and Patricia, falling in love with a cottage bonnet, bought that.

Although there was still a faint chill between the women, the luncheon went off comfortably, the men discussing the latest word of further French catastrophe in the Russian campaign. Newspapers had arrived from London and been set out for them in the parlor. Lord Hayworth and Jack had perused them while awaiting the women.

When they finished dining, the horses were put to and the gig followed the Hayworth coach back to the Renwicks'. Any interest in Patricia's lack of maid was lost in their mutual arrival.

The next morning dawned bright and clear and only briskly cold. Patricia decided today was the day in which, assuming an opportunity was given her, she'd reveal her facility with her crutches. She told Milly to have them handy along with her warmest pelisse—just in case they were required—and then took herself down to breakfast.

Only Lord Renwick was there. And Sahib, of course. Evidence remained that others had eaten and departed, but at the moment the room was very quiet. Lord Renwick fingered a newspaper someone had left near his place. She heard him sigh.

"Is that the latest paper?" she asked. "It would be outside of enough if I were to ignore you and read to myself, so may I read aloud to you while I eat?" she asked.

She didn't wait for an answer, but filled her plate with a slice of ham, scrambled eggs, and a goodly portion of the curried kidneys which the Renwick cook did to perfection. Then, before seating herself, she poured herself a cup full of good, strong tea. Renwick groped for the sugar bowl and pushed it toward her and then, almost ceremoniously, lifted the paper and handed it to her.

"I may?" she asked. "Oh good. You will tell anyone who asks that I merely indulge *you* so they will not discover what a bluestocking I have become. You are too kind to tell the others that I have bribed a maid to bring the paper to my room when everyone is done with it! Today she will not need to do so."

Patricia read out items between bites and sips and her food grew cold toward the end of her meal. "There. I see nothing else which could possibly be of interest. Unless you wish to hear the marriage announcements or the obituaries? No? Then I am finished." She folded the paper and set it aside.

"You have a nice reading voice, Mrs. Haydon. I find it difficult to listen to many voices. I believe my ears became more sensitive after I was blinded."

Lady Renwick entered just then in something of a rush. "Jason, there is a boy from the little farm. A fire! In the kitchen chimney. They fear the thatch will catch."

"Fire!" Renwick rose instantly. "Put Sahib in our rooms. You," he said to a footman he'd heard entering behind her ladyship, "call together the men. Send word to the stables to saddle every horse and to all the grooms and groundsmen that they must help put it out." He was out the door before he'd finished speaking. Sahib stared after him with longing but, obedient to Lady Renwick's hand on his nape, remained behind.

"Is it far?" asked Patricia.

"Far? Not at all. Through the home wood and across the long meadow."

"Are you worried about him?"

"I always worry, but it does no good to coddle him." She sighed, then added, "He wouldn't stand for it."

A rumble of voices and tramping feet were heard and, suddenly, a rush of masculine figures passed the open door on their way to the stables. Jack was among them and it was Patricia's turn to feel concern. "No," she said. "None of them ever will allow themselves to be babied. At least, not a man who is worth his salt. Is there anything we women can do? House fires can be disastrous for a family."

Her ladyship bit the side of her lip, thinking. "Come along and we will sort through the bedding for what may be given to the family if it becomes necessary. Clothes are another thing. Just in case. Oh! Before we go up, I will tell my housekeeper to collect supplies of food from the pantry and vegetable cave. A good-sized cheese would be in order and perhaps a ham?"

"Bacon, perhaps?"

"Yes. Far better. Mr. Gates will feel less beholden."

Half an hour later Mrs. Gates and three young, big-eyed and frightened children trudged through the woods and in through the kitchen door. Lady Renwick was called down and Patricia followed.

"Mrs. Gates," said Lady Renwick. *"Did* the roof catch?"

"We thought not and then, just when we were certain all was well, there it went!"

"You've lost the house then?" asked Lady Renwick sympathetically.

"Nay. Didn't mean that. That man on crutches, he saw it. He had men on the roof and buckets passed up like they was all in the army. Never seen anything like it. They put it out.

Now they are checking the thatch to make certain there are no other smoldering spots which might catch."

"How lucky that Lieutenant Princeton noticed!" exclaimed Lady Renwick, "But, even so, the house must be uninhabitable."

"You will have your work cut out for you, Mrs. Gates," said the cook, who hovered, surreptitiously, passing the children one newly baked lemon biscuit after another.

"We will send you help for the cleaning and whitewashing and all the laundry you must do," said Lady Renwick, soothing the white-faced woman. "When his lordship returns, we will know better what is needed. For now, take the children to the housekeeper's rooms and rest. I will send a maid up to the nursery for some children's games and a few toys to keep them occupied. Don't worry, Mrs. Gates. His lordship will see you right. You know that."

Mrs. Gates smiled weakly. "Oh yes. It is just . . ." Tears welled.

"Just?" asked Lady Renwick.

"My grandmother's comforter! The smoke and water. I fear it is ruined!" she wailed.

"Ah. Terrible indeed . . . *if true,*" said Lady Renwick with rough sympathy. "There is no use repining until you know for certain." Her ladyship turned the family over to her housekeeper who clucked and soothed and, with more biscuits, took them to her rooms.

The men returned over an hour later, tired, dirty, and subdued. "My lady," asked Lord Renwick of his wife, "you do have our chimneys swept at decent intervals, do you not?" He only half jested.

"I most certainly do. Are you telling me Farmer Gates did not?"

"Jack made what he called a reconnaissance and tells me the other chimney in the house does not look to have been swept for years."

"Was there much damage?" asked Patricia.

"They must live in the kitchen until repairs are made," said Jack, joining them. "We were forced to tear out a goodly portion of the roof to be assured there was no more chance of fire."

"Actually," said McMurrey, "a part of what was torn out *did* catch. It made a nice bonfire there in the yard. I saw several men warming their hands at it!"

"At least that particular blaze makes it unnecessary to haul away the old thatch," jested Lord Hayworth.

"Very true," said Jack with a grin. "Too bad thatch burns so quickly. By the time I got there, it was ashes. *My* hands are still cold!"

He put them against Patricia's cheeks for a moment before turning away. Patricia was shocked by the surge of warmth his cold touch produced in her, and was very quiet during the continuing discussion of the situation.

Eventually the men took their smoky selves off to their rooms to change. Lord Renwick was the last to leave. "Ian told me," he said to his wife, "that without Jack, we very well might have lost the house. Not only did he see the first signs of fire in the thatch, but he instantly organized the men to take care of the problem. As you know, if a thatch fire has the least little bit of time to get ahold, there is no saving a place."

"Don't tell us," said Patricia sternly, startling his lordship. "Tell Jack. It is he who needs to hear it."

"Ah! Mrs. Haydon! I was unaware anyone was here but Eustacia! But you are correct." Lord Renwick nodded. "I *will* tell him." He oriented himself, and, his cane tap-tapping, went off to his rooms to change.

"I have not seen him use a cane," said Patricia when he was gone.

"When Sahib is near, as he usually is, that is all Jason needs. He uses the cane when he must go about alone."

The two women, fast friends by this time, talked quietly

for some little time. And then Lady Anne burst into the room. "Is it true?"

"Is what true?"

"Was there a fire? Was Jack foolish enough to go with the men? How dare he? What could *he* do? He'd only be in the way! He's crippled! Is he hurt? Oh, tell me, *is he hurt?*"

"Calm yourself! At once!" said Lady Renwick. "Jack was the hero of the hour, very necessary to saving the house, and, so far as I know, *no one* was hurt."

Lady Anne's eyes widened. "But . . . but . . ."

"But he is a cripple?" asked Patricia sweetly.

"Yes," said Lady Anne. *"Yes.* I had thought you did not, but you *do* understand. He must have care. He must not . . ."

Patricia's patience, worn thin by Lady Anne's foolishness, now dissolved. "Nonsense," she said. "Will you please get it into your fluff-filled head that Jack Princeton is no longer your patient and has no need of you coddling him and wrapping him in cotton wool!"

"But . . . but . . ."

"But nothing. The man is perfectly healthy. He limps. And there are some things he'll never do with ease, but he is neither sick nor has he lost the use of his mental faculties." More sternly, she added, "He neither wants nor needs a woman's pity!"

"Ohhh . . ." Lady Anne's face contorted. "You are so hard. You could never understand how it is between us!"

"I hope I do not insult you, Lady Anne—" Clean, in fresh clothing, Jack had returned to find Patricia and had overheard their argument. "—but there is *nothing* between us. I will be forever grateful for the careful nursing you gave me when I was ill, *but that is all."*

This time when Lady Anne said, "Ohhhhhh . . ." it had an entirely different sound, a wailing note. She ran from the room crying.

Jack caught Patricia's eyes. "I should not have said that?"

"To the contrary, Jack, you *should.* We all know she has

built castles in the air concerning you, but I had not thought she'd gone so far as to impute emotions to *you* which you do not feel. That must not be allowed."

"I agree," said Lady Renwick. "You could not permit her comment to pass without a denial."

"Thank you." He moved on into the room, coming close to Patricia. "And thank you," he said more softly, "for your support of me!"

Patricia sighed. "I'd have been more tactful, but she angered me."

"I will remember," said Jack, "that it is unwise to make you angry!"

That wonderful lopsided grin appeared and Patricia's heart did a flip-flop, startling her. Then, finally accepting the truth, Patricia Haydon resigned herself to loving Jack Princeton forever. A love she was certain would never be returned.

Then, although her heart felt as if it were breaking, she forced herself to smile in return.

# *Eleven*

The next morning Patricia once again told her maid to have crutches and pelisse handy. She was determined to surprise Jack at some time during the day. There was no opportunity after breakfast: the men returned to Farmer Gates's house, meaning to confirm the damage report submitted the evening before by Renwick's land agent and to determine what help the farmer needed, if any.

The men returned half-way through the luncheon with which the women indulged themselves and, accepting ale from the butler, stood around the room teasing and jesting with those dining. Patricia wondered if it would not be possible to spring her surprise upon Jack when they rose from the table, but again she was thwarted.

Not only did two young gentlemen arrive, but a neighbor's daughter, Miss Browne, drove over, escorted by her brother. The young lady, using a great many words, insisted the lieutenant would be greatly entertained by driving with her brother and herself to a nearby village where there was a winter fete to raise money for the church roof.

Jack cast a helpless look toward Patricia, which was intercepted by Lady Renwick. Coming to his rescue, her ladyship brightly suggested that others might wish to attend as well. "In fact, it is an excellent notion," she added. "Why do you young people not wait until I discover who wishes to go? Then we may all bundle up and travel together as a party."

The young people were well-trained, but Patricia noted the girl could not totally hide her chagrin that she'd not have the lieutenant all to herself for the afternoon. A quick look of loathing cast in her direction alerted Patricia to the problem. A minx if Patricia ever saw one. And very likely up to all the tricks. Jack must not be left to such a fate! She joined her voice to those agreeing with Lady Renwick's proposal that the drive would be the perfect outing.

Only Lord Bladney and Lady Anne, who still smarted from Jack's reprimand of the day before, remained at home. The rest piled into carriages, sorting themselves out as well as they could, and, in the end, only the young lady and her brother were dissatisfied. The young lady because she was not in the same carriage as Jack, and the young man because he had to listen to his sister's complaints for the whole of the journey into Bascombe Cross.

The fete was combined with the usual weekly market day activities, so the square was crowded. Around two sides were those who had come to sell goods, such as winter produce, chickens, ducks, and other meat. On the green were the booths and games common to such a fundraising event.

Lord Hayworth steered Lady Blackburne to Jack's side where the lieutenant pulled on soft leather gloves while Patricia held his crutch. "Let us see what is offered in the way of amusement?" suggested his lordship, taking Lady Blackburne's elbow.

As they moved onto the frozen grass, they were joined by Miss Browne who pulled her reluctant brother along behind her. His obvious embarrassment pricked both Patricia's sense of humor and her caring nature. She was torn between putting the young man at ease and protecting Jack from the sister!

Protecting Jack won and, when the other ladies strolled up, Patricia linked her arm with Miss Browne's and, although unhappy, the girl did not object when asked if she did not wish to join the other women seeking out the jumble sale.

Each found some small item to buy and then moved on to

where a table was loaded with baked goods and jams. A friend of Lady Renwick's was finishing the judging and everyone stilled as she made her announcement. Muted cheers and a few losers' tears followed, soothed when Lady Renwick bought these items for a good price. They were tucked into a basket, and a lad sent to put them into the Renwick carriage.

The group of women strolled on, occasionally stopping at a table, or to watch a game of chance, and, finally, at the tea tent to purchase a cup of hot tea. After that they moved toward the far end of the green where they meant to watch the organization of still another of the contests planned for both young and old.

This particular race was a three-legged race for men. Unfortunately, it appeared there would be no race. A pair of twins, a farmer's sons, stood there grinning broadly. Patricia overheard one man say to another, "What's the use? They always win."

Quiet was demanded. "It has been decided," said the vicar into the silence, "that two prizes will be offered. First and second place."

"Well, in that case! Care to join in, Freddy?" the man asked his friend. Several others came forward to have one leg firmly tied to a friend's and, finally, laughing, the men of the Renwick party pushed forward.

"Oh no!" muttered Lady Renwick, her complexion paling slightly. "He wouldn't!"

Patricia looked to where her ladyship pointed, only to see Jack standing next to his lordship, their arms around each other's waists. "But it is so apt, is it not?" said Patricia. "The halt leading the blind, I mean?"

Miss Browne gave Patricia a look which should have sent her reeling, and then, nose in the air, she moved away, joining Lady Blackburne, who also frowned ferociously.

"How will they manage?" a resigned Lady Renwick asked.

"Manage? Quite well, I'd guess. Your husband is a strong man. There is nothing wrong with Jack's *eyes*. Have faith!"

The men, Jack's weak leg tied to Lord Renwick's, took a few practice paces. They stopped, discussed something, then tried again. It seemed to go more smoothly.

*In fact, if they will only stop laughing,* thought Patricia, *they are likely to do very nicely indeed.*

The pairs were lined up with the twins in the middle. The starter called out, "Ready? Set! . . . *Go!*"

Almost instantly one pair tumbled to the ground. Several others took too long to get themselves coordinated and were left too far behind to have hope of winning. The twins were well ahead, but not so far behind them, were, of all people, Jack Princeton and Lord Renwick. Patricia could see Jack talking, but could not hear what he said. Directions, she assumed.

A murmur ran through the crowd. Everyone knew Lord Renwick was blind. Someone passed about the word that Jack limped. Badly. The crowd grew.

Then, only a yard or so from the finish line, one of the twins stumbled. He pulled his brother off stride. One loudly swearing at the other, they tumbled into a heap right in Jack's path. Then Patricia did hear what was said: "Jase! They are in my way. I must jump!"

Patricia saw Lord Renwick's arm tighten around Jack's waist. His lordship half lifted Jack over the extended legs of the twins and the two went on. A roar went up when they crossed the finish line only a foot or so ahead of a pair of farmers from up Spithurst way. Lord Merwin and Lord Wendover came in a close third.

Patricia looked back to where the twins lay on the ground. Still tied together, they pummeled each other, each disclaiming fault, each accusing the other. They were rapidly surrounded by men urging the combatants on.

Patricia kept up with Lady Renwick who moved gracefully, if with unladylike speed, to her husband's side. Patricia thought there was a bit of an edge to her ladyship's voice when she congratulated Lord Renwick, or perhaps it was relief, but whichever, it was certainly true that his lordship looked a trifle sheepish!

Jack, on the other hand, appeared to be elated.

"You did it!" she said, extending her hand to him.

"So we did!" He pulled her close and dropped a kiss onto her forehead. *"So we did."* He hugged her—and very nearly fell, taking her with him, when Lord Renwick tried to turn away in order to accept congratulations from one of his tenants. His lordship had forgotten they were still bound together!

A lad brought Jack his crutch, but the lieutenant did not release Patricia. Instead, he tucked her under his arm, obviously determined to see everything offered by the fete. Jack led her back toward the games and booths which offered fairings to lucky winners, or handiwork and jumble, and food, of course. He tried his hand at the dart board, bought Patricia a chance at the Lucky Dip, and purchased, to the obvious delight of the child who had baked it, the sorriest looking tart Patricia ever saw. He proceeded to eat it, smacking his lips and telling the girl she would grow up to be the finest cook in the region if she only practiced the art diligently.

"I cannot believe you ate the whole thing. Will you not be sick?" asked Patricia, half laughing and half worried.

"I hope not," he responded, grinning. "Not that the filling was bad. It had a very nice flavor, but she needs someone to show her how to make decent pastry! Hers was greasy. Far too much lard!"

They found the others at the refreshment tent. Lord Wendover was sent off to locate the laggards and very soon they all climbed into the carriages for the journey home. The young people followed them and could not be gotten rid of. Lady Renwick was, thought Patricia, forced to ask them to remain for dinner, and it was not until late in the evening, when the moon finally rose, that the guests took their reluctant departure.

Patricia went up to her bed berating herself for thinking as she did. It was *not* true that Lady Renwick was *forced* to ask them to stay. The young people were an entertaining bunch, the girl more than usually proficient on the pianoforte and the boyish voices blending into a delightful trio as they sang one old song after another.

"I am cross," she told the bedpost, "because, having decided to spring my crutches on Jack, I have been unable to find a time when I could do so!"

"Talking to yourself again?" asked Milly, coming in at the end.

"Yes I suppose I am. Tomorrow. *Tomorrow* I *will* manage to show off to Jack, even if I have to drag him off by the ear! You will be ready?"

"Never fear. Your crutches are in Mr. Reeves's room just beyond the baize door. He was kind enough to allow me to put them in a corner so they'd be handy."

"I'll have to thank Reeves for putting up with them. My pelisse?"

"Draped over them. You see your chance and you'll not have to wait for a moment!"

"Milly, you haven't been gossiping about this, have you?"

"I wouldn't! Of course, Mr. Reeves demanded to know why he should keep the things and I had to tell him, but he's not a gabster. Not Mr. Reeves."

*Not,* thought Patricia, *to you, but what about the senior staff?*

Patricia did not exactly gnash her teeth, but she was not particularly happy, either. She could all too easily see Reeves telling Mrs. Climpson, the housekeeper. Mrs. Climpson would tell Lady Renwick's abigail who would tell Lord Renwick's valet and all too soon all the valets would know . . . including Black who would tell Jack. Patricia let slip a few swear words gleaned from her late husband's choice collection. And then wondered why men bothered to swear. The oaths didn't ease *her* feelings at all.

* * *

Warmer weather set in over night. Melting snow dripped from shed roofs, ran in rivulets between the cobblestones paving the stable area, and generally made the out of doors a place to avoid. But by afternoon, the worst was over. No one had the least intention of attempting the roads which would be a mire of mud and virtually impassable, but those who wished exercise were not adverse to walking on the wet grass or along the well-gravelled drive. The men went out first. It was only when she happened to look out a window that Patricia saw Jack strolling, in his own particular style, up the drive. She saw her chance.

Patricia excused herself from the others in a rather absent fashion as she hurried from the room. She knocked on Reeves's door, collected her possessions, and, the pelisse only half-fastened, rushed out the front door. She drew to a halt at the top of the stairs. Jack was no longer in sight. She looked both directions.

"Ah!"

Hurrying down the steps, she reached the bottom where she settled herself on her crutches and took a shaky step or two. Then, more sure of herself, she hurried after Jack who was wending in his overly quick way to the end of the house and, very likely, the side door to the Renwick's wing in which his ground floor room was situated.

Which reminded Patricia: She still had to determine how the man had climbed stairs! "Jack, wait up!" she called.

He swung around. His eyes widened and then he grinned that funny half grin. "I see you took my advice!"

"Yes. I'm pretty good, too. You won't be able to leave me behind now."

"I won't?"

"No you won't."

"Hmm." He got that mischief look any of his friends could have warned Patricia meant devilment. "I'll bet I could."

"Not anymore," she crowed. "I've mastered these things."

"Want to put your money where your mouth is?" he asked, his eyes flashing.

She eyed him. "You would suggest a race?"

"Exactly."

She pursed her lips. "Hmm . . ."

"Think maybe you would lose?"

"Of course not," she said scornfully, knowing she would.

"Then we'll have a race."

Patricia nodded. "Very well."

The details were decided and they returned to the front of the house where the gravelled drive would provide a flat surface for both. There they met Lords Wendover and Merwin returning from a ride. Lady Blackburne and Lord Hayworth appeared in the doorway, obviously prepared to go out. A groom came up behind her leading their mounts.

"I don't wish to make a spectacle of myself," Patricia muttered just loud enough for Jack to hear.

He grinned down at her. "You *do* think you'll lose."

"It isn't that. Lady Blackburne already thinks badly of me. This will simply cap her determination to see me in the blackest way possible." She sighed. "Ah well. A bet is a bet and it cannot be helped. Lord Hayworth will wish to watch, and if that groom is allowed to return to the stables, he is likely to have them all hiding in the bushes, more bets laid and the whole thing becoming a farce."

"If Lord Hayworth will not ride off, then the groom will be needed to see to their horses." Jack stopped, pulling her to a halt. "Patricia, we can postpone our race, if you wish."

"And it will snow and then what? I will not race over ice and snow!"

"Nor I. The one encounter I had with ice was one too many! Wendover, will you be our race official?"

"Race official?"

"Patricia and I have decided to race. From here to that first chestnut."

"You'll need a starter as well as someone at the end," said

Lord Hayworth. He descended the steps, abandoning Lady Blackburne, who glowered. "I will be your starter if one of you others will go down the drive and observe the finish."

Their voices reached the footman on duty in the hall. He abandoned his post to inform Reeves, who ordered him back to his place . . . and instantly went, himself, to find Mrs. Climpson. He returned to the hall where he took up a stance at the window opposite the one the footman occupied. "I will," he said in stately manner, "put a crown on Lieutenant Princeton."

The footman sighed, but knew he'd avoid a reprimand by taking up the bet. "A crown, then. On Mrs. Haydon."

Lady Anne, in the blue salon, wandered to the window just then. Her gasp of dismay drew the other women. "He wouldn't!"

*"He! What of her?"* The neighbor's girl's eyes flashed with a touch of anger. "And at her age, too! What a hoydenish thing to do," said the young lady guest who, braving the mud and riding to the Tiger's Lair, had hoped to have a few words with the romantic lieutenant.

Out on the drive, Jack and Patricia were lined up and ready. A handkerchief waved from between Lord Hayworth's fingers. "When I drop the handkerchief, you will begin. No crowding. No tripping. Just a good clean race," he intoned in a pompous manner which drew smiles. Even from Lady Blackburne.

An instant later the square of linen dropped and Jack and Patricia were off. "You are good," said Jack, studying her style. "I think having two crutches gives you better balance. I will have to see to getting another."

Patricia cast him a smile, but hadn't the breath to speak. She soldiered on, swinging ahead, placing the crutches, swinging ahead, doing her best to actually outpace Jack. He drew ahead, then fell back a trifle, then ahead again . . . Until finally they were within a few feet of the chestnut. Jack slowed and Patricia pulled into the lead.

Lord Wendover awarded the win to Patricia. She glared at Jack. "You let me win."

"Me? Let you win?" Jack pretended innocence. "Ask Tony. I would never do such a thing."

Wendover grinned. "I will merely say that Jack is the most competitive of us and I have never ever seen him allow an opponent an advantage."

"Never *before* seen him do so?" asked Patricia.

The men chuckled. "No flies on this one, Jack," said Wendover, admiringly. He slapped Patricia on the back in a masculine fashion and then apologized.

"No flies indeed." Jack's gaze rested on Patricia, a light in his eyes she could not interpret. "*I* knew that long ago," he added softly.

"Well, we'd better get back up to the door, Jack," said Lord Wendover, "where it looks to me as if you've a welcoming committee."

Jack turned and stared at the house. Patricia looked over her shoulder. "Oh, dear," she said.

"Oh dear indeed. I think half the household is there."

"At the least."

"You look worried."

"I should never have allowed myself to succumb to your cajoling, Jack!"

"Did you enjoy it?"

Patricia grinned. "Yes. And you?"

"Oh, very much indeed. I don't believe I've ever met a woman who would indulge me as you have done."

"Indulge you! I thought I'd nagged you and scolded until you would be tired of hearing me."

"Oh, I am! Have you not seen how much I've mended my ways? I do so merely that I need not listen to your nagging. Shrew!"

"Ha. I see you still need a bit of nagging about your attitude. It is not for *that* ridiculous reason you should improve yourself, but for your own sake!"

"That happens as a consequence, of course," said Jack.

"And now if that is settled, shall we return to the house?" asked Wendover. "My feet are getting wet."

"My dear?" asked Jack, sobering. "I suppose we will have to face the music?"

"I suppose we do. Alex would, I suspect, refuse to order the carriage and allow me to disappear!"

"If you were to disappear, then I would, too. Searching for you. And that would really put the fox into the henhouse, would it not?"

"It most certainly would. Well, then, if there is no escape, let us go." Patricia set her crutches and began the long trek up the house. *Why,* she wondered, *had it not seemed so long coming down.* She was aware that, later, her shoulders would ache abominably. *How,* she wondered, *does Jack bear it?*

They were nearly to the house when a mud covered carriage, the wheels shedding clods with every turn, pulled into the drive and rolled toward them. Patricia, Jack, and Tony moved to the side and the carriage and horses passed them by.

"That wasn't . . ." said Jack startled. "No. It cannot possibly be . . . ?"

"You thought so, too?" asked Wendover.

The two men ignored Patricia and hurried after the coach, Jack arriving some yards ahead of Wendover, Patricia behind his lordship. Since she had been hopping along as fast as she could manage, she knew for certain that Jack had allowed her to win their race. Thinking of Wendover's carefully phrased comment, she wondered just *why* he'd allowed it. Could he possibly have . . . ?

But they arrived just then, and the men entered the hullabaloo around the carriage.

Patricia, realizing there was no longer any reason for her to use the crutches, took them from under her arms and, moving around the coach, went in a brisk manner up the steps to the house. It was only when inside and climbing the stairs to her room, that it occurred to her to wonder *who* had arrived so expeditiously, saving her from the embarrassment which was certain to have been hers without that distraction. Ah well, it made no difference *who*. Whoever it was deserved her thanks! She would learn their identity when the party met in the salon before dinner and the new arrival was introduced.

In actual fact, much to the distress of several of the women, none of the Six came in to dinner. Instead, they sent excuses for abandoning everyone and promised to come for the tea tray.

"Who is it?" asked Patricia of Lady Renwick.

"A rapscallion and rogue!" she said, laughing.

"Which particular roguish rapscallion?"

"His name is Miles Seward."

"I should have guessed," said Patricia.

"How could you guess?"

"I met the six of them many years ago when I spent the summer before my marriage at the Merwin estate where they had gathered for a month or so before going up to University. As I recall, Seward was a very strange boy, a wild-eyed youth who could never be still."

"He has grown into a wild-eyed man—" Lady Renwick's tone was dry as dust. "—who can never be still! As you will see."

Patricia contained her curiosity, but not easily. *At least,* she thought, *I do not complain aloud as does Miss Browne who has once again managed to overstay her welcome!*

Not, of course, because she did not wish to complain. She was uneasy about how Jack really felt about her using crutches, and she desperately wished to know! Especially since she had been forced to endure still another scold from Lady Blackburne, who was convinced no man could possibly appreciate such a subtle jest.

Her ladyship ended her rebuke by saying, "If it *was* a jest, of course."

Surely Jack had seen the humor in it . . . had he not?

# Twelve

Patricia was the first to leave the table and go to the blue salon, still fretting about Jack's feelings about their race. Perhaps his look, the one she'd thought was approval—or maybe *more*—did not mean what she'd thought it meant? Or, perhaps the teasing he'd undergo from his friends would change approval, if it was that, to something different?

Patricia nodded to the footman who opened the salon doors for her. A frown creased her brow. Just inside the doors, she was pounced upon and warmly kissed. Alarm turned to amusement when Miles Seward, his deeply tanned face as red as such skin could get, swore softly.

"Really, Miles," scolded Patricia, "if that is the way you mean to greet all the female guests, I think I shall exit and come in again!" She heard a deep laugh. Chagrinned that not only had they been seen, but that someone had heard her jesting words, Patricia, in turn, blushed a lovely rosy color. She glanced beyond Miles Seward to where McMurrey and Jack sat near the fire.

Seward put an arm around her waist and bussed her cheek. "Never say you will leave," he said, gesturing theatrically. "I could not bear it. I will oblige you with kisses as often as you wish—" He gave her another. "—but do not remove the sun from my eyes, the moon and the stars and the . . ."

"Miles," said Ian sternly, "you are embarrassing Mrs. Haydon."

He leapt back. "Mrs.? Mrs. *Haydon?*" He cast a bewildered look around the room. "But who is Mrs. Haydon?"

"Me," said Patricia. She caught a clearer look of Jack and wondered why he glowered into the fire. Had the teasing been so unmerciful, so unbearable that he was truly angry? Her cheeks turned very nearly as red as her shawl. "Just me," she repeated but more absently.

"No, no, no," said Seward, drawing her attention by prowling around her. "My memory cannot be so poor. It is only a few years since last we met and you, my lovely, can be no one but Patricia Conners."

"Of course it is Patricia. But it has been more than a few years and it is no longer Conners," said McMurrey sharply after another glance at Jack. "Nor is she Lady Blackburne, so you may just put yourself back beside the door. Or—" He grinned a grin which was very nearly a smirk. "—will you pay up like a gentleman and cease harassing the women?"

Seward swung around to face McMurrey. "I will kiss Lady Blackburne—" He pointed a finger at the Scotsman. "—and you will hand over the ring I was forced by Alex's trick to relinquish just before I left London." He moved into position beside the door where he lounged against the wall, awaiting his true victim. "How, by the way, *did* you win the ring from Alex?"

"I didn't," said McMurrey. "I won it from Tony. He bet me I would not wear the most outrageously over-sized boutonniere ever seen into Almack's. Since I'd not had the ring for far too long, I did it. Princess Esterhazy has not spoken to me since and Lady Jersey still teases me by making me stand still while she inspects me for any new nonsense before allowing me in."

Seward grinned. "That sounds like our Tony, all right. Patri—" Again he turned that odd bronzy red. "—Mrs. Haytown, Hayturn, Haywhatever . . ." And then he paused, looking bewildered. Then he scowled. "I cannot remember to call you by that ridiculous name and, at the same time, remember what I meant to ask. I will call you Patricia."

Before Patricia could respond to what, in any other man, would be unforgivable impertinence, the door opened. Lady Renwick, entering, was caught in a close embrace and kissed.

Her ladyship disengaged herself, gave Seward a speaking look, and passed on to where Patricia sat. "Is it a wager?" she asked softly.

"Of course," said Patricia, rolling her eyes. "What else could it be?"

"With Miles Seward, one can never tell," was the dry response.

"You appear to know him well."

"Not at all well, yet one feels one has known him forever. He made a brief visit during which he learned of a problem concerning the health of an elderly servant. He immediately took our ward, a prince from India, and his entourage, to Portugal where they'll spend the winter. His was a brief visit, but quite long enough to take his measure! Ah, Lady Blackbu . . ."

Lady Renwick broke off, giggling, when Seward roared, "Aha!" He grasped Lord Renwick's aunt in a firm embrace. "Prepare to be kissed," he hissed in a stage villain voice. Lady Blackburne was not a small woman, but he swung her around, tipped her, and kissed her soundly. "There," he said, beaming. "I am so glad you were next into the room, Lady Blackburne. Thank you very much." He swung on his heel and prowled toward the other two women. "Now," he said in a gloating tone, "I may return to teasing Patricia."

When she was finally able to stop laughing at his nonsense and get in a word of her own, Patricia asked about the ring.

"Ah! The ring! Ian, I want my ring!"

"Varlet! I had some small hope you would forget." The Scotsman rose and strolled to where Seward had crowded Patricia into a corner. "Will you please cease and desist?" said McMurrey softly, when near enough. "You are behaving badly, Miles." He cast a look to where Jack still stared into the fire, silent and morose.

Seward frowned. "Behaving badly? Because I have cornered the most interesting woman in the room and work myself to a frazzle in the hopes of entertaining her?"

"Yes."

"You would say I should share my entertaining ways with others?" he asked. Plaintively, he added, "But I have so few opportunities to enjoy such delightful companionship." He pretended to pout. "*Surely* you realize it is unfair that I be forced to give it up when all too soon I must return to my lonely ship?"

The Scotsman bit his lip. He glanced at Patricia and then back to Seward. Finally he shrugged. "Well. I tried." He returned to the fireplace where, an elbow on the mantel, he did his best to jolly Jack from his megrims.

Patricia, noticing for the first time just how quiet Jack had grown, wondered if she should go talk to him. "Mr. McMurrey has a point," she said. "You, Mr. Seward, must sing for your supper." She glanced around the room. "I believe you should begin with Miss Bladney."

Miles followed her gaze. "Not that bland creature on the settee."

"Yes, although *I* would not call her bland."

"Compared to you she is. Have you tired of me already?"

"You are an entertaining rascal, Mr. Seward, but one does tire of nonsense." When he refused to move, she sighed. "If you will not go away, then tell me of your adventures."

He sobered instantly, his features blank. "I think not," he said crisply.

She looked at him askance. "You would say *none* were of a nature you can repeat for a lady's ears? Nonsense. I heard you went up the Nile disguised as an Egyptian laborer." She frowned. "Can it be true?"

"One of the biggest mistakes in an ill-spent life," he said promptly. But his voice still carried a bit of that sharpness and none of the languorous teasing of earlier. "The Egyptian worker is little better than a slave, Mrs. Haydon. I managed to jump ship, braving the crocodiles, and by then, I knew enough to adopt a persona which allowed me to travel far more freely the rest of the way to Luxor."

"Luxor! I have read of unbelievable ruins," she said.

"Quite unbelievable. And now," he said sardonically, "I suppose you wish me to describe them?"

"I would like that very much."

He shook his head, his lips forming a pout. "A dead bore to talk of what is done and over. You have ceased to be entertaining, Patricia Conners Haydon. I will, as suggested, go tease someone else."

He bowed and moved away, glancing back to see, she guessed, if he had discomposed her. Smiling slightly, she waved him on. She joined Lady Renwick. "The man is outrageous to the point of being unforgivable," she said, but smiled.

"Most outrageous," agreed her hostess. She too smiled. "But *never*," she added, "is he boring!"

Patricia laughed. "Yes. He left me because I asked him to tell me of his adventures. First he pokered up and said he thought not, and, when I suggested that not all of them could do me harm, he said that it was a bore to discuss what was past." One of Patricia's brows arched. "I think, when we are next at a meal where he cannot escape us, we should do our best to insist he tell tales! He will hate it."

"You mean, get a little back for the teasing he puts us through?"

"Yes. Shall we enlist Lady Blackburne? I am certain, after that kiss, she too will wish to pluck a feather or two!"

They joined Lady Blackburne and made their suggestion. Her ladyship looked down her nose. "It is outside enough that you suggest annoying a guest under your husband's roof in such an ill-bred manner, Eustacia. Surely it was not *you* who came up with the notion. No, it is obvious that it was

Mrs. Haydon who suggested so uncouth an idea!" Then her lips twitched. "Now, having scolded you royally, how—" Her voice lowered to a level suitable to conspiracy. "—do we implement your plan for discombobulating Miles Seward? The boy deserves everything he gets!"

The next evening, somewhere in the middle of the fish course, Miles, perceiving he'd been outwitted by the three women, gave in gracefully. He told one tale after another. The sardonic looks passed among the other men and a twitch of the lips now and again suggested to Patricia that the tales were scrubbed of that which would make them dangerously titillating or frightening. She was especially convinced that his story about his capture and escape from a pirate, complete with the villain's ship, should have been far more hair-raising than the humorous escapade he made it.

Dinner ended and the men stood while the women exited the room. Seward sat back and, taking out a handkerchief, mopped his brow. "Ian, I have earned that ring. Now hand it over as you did *not* last evening in the drawing room!"

"Someone had better take up the challenge," rumbled McMurrey, removing from his smallest finger a triple band of old silver which had been braided into an intricate knot. "If he goes off with it on his hand, we may never see it again. His luck cannot go on forever. One day he will come a cropper. Miles—" The Scotsman frowned, his deep voice rumbling to a still deeper note. "—I wish you would come to the end of your adventuring and settle down! We worry about you."

"Worry?" Seward's lips twisted into cynicism. "Perhaps," he said. *"When* you think of me. Which is not often."

"Far more frequently than you obviously suspect," said Lord Merwin with a casualness which fooled no one except, perhaps, Miles. "I heard an odd rumor just before I left town." He looked at his nails. "Is it possible you *will* be around and about England more than in the past?"

"Round and about?" Seward chuckled, his mood toppling from cynical to comical. *"Round and about?* Why, yes, you might say that."

Merwin pursed his lips. "Then it *is* true you have become a free agent for the Horse Guards in their fight to suppress smuggling?"

Seward glanced quickly around the dining room, found the servants had departed, and nodded. "It is not generally known. So, Alex, where did *you* hear it?"

"From a very green lieutenant who is secretary to the colonel to whom you report. When you remember to report, that is. The lieutenant thinks it a great joke. His colonel has a most colorful vocabulary, you see, which he exercises whenever he is reminded of you. He has invented, we are assured, a great deal of picturesque description of your humble self, Miles. The lieutenant wasn't completely lost to discretion. He names you the Privateer."

"Blast the cub's well-oiled tongue! News of his folly goes into my next report. Which means I must write one." He met Ian's startled look. "You are not startled that I hate writing them, so it must be that I'd rat on the young'n, but Ian, *think*. If he talks about me, which he knows he is not to do, there is no telling when he might reveal something truly important!"

Merwin agreed. "That thought occurred to me as well, so I had a word with his colonel. I doubt our young friend will ever again learn anything of a sensitive nature. That assumes, of course, that he is allowed to remain in London. I suspect he will be packed off to the Peninsula before he knows where he is!"

"Probably not," said Seward, acidly. "He is likely one of those sprigs of the nobility whose fond mama has forced an indulgent papa to insist the boy be allowed nowhere near any nasty French guns which might hurt the poor lad."

"That is possible. There *are* a few of those cluttering up the Horse Guards, but perhaps not so many as you think."

The conversation turned to the war. Seward listened to Jack's comments and nodded now and again. McMurrey sat back and watched the two. Jack seemed to have come out from the black mood into which he'd fallen the evening before, but even so, he was not at ease. And he never once looked directly at Seward. McMurrey's brows drew into a heavy frown and he rubbed his chin in a thoughtful manner not lost on Merwin who, wishing to discuss the situation, went to knock on the Scotsman's door once the household was quiet.

And then, his hand raised to do so, he refrained.

Merwin turned on his heel, his ears burning. He had forgotten, until the very last instant, that McMurrey and his wife shared a room!

The next morning Seward joined Patricia and a few others at the breakfast table. He suggested he and Patricia go riding. She demurred.

"Do you mean to tell me you do not ride?" He pointed a finger at her. "Ha! I know better. You ride like a centaur. Or should one say a centaurix?" When she didn't even smile, he asked, "You would suggest you no longer ride? That too must be nonsense. No one who rode as you did could later come to dislike it."

"Oh, do go, Patricia," said Jack from his place farther down the table. "Enjoy yourself."

There was only a hint of crossness in his voice, but Patricia heard it. Her lips pressed into a firm line. "I think not."

"I cannot recall when you last rode," said Jack, startled that it had not previously occurred to him. "By now you must miss it very much."

"If I did, I would have had a horse brought round for me.

I can go any time I wish," she said, trying for a lightness she didn't entirely feel.

"Indulge me," urged Seward. "I wish to ride with you."

"Your wishes should be paramount with me?"

Seward's eyes widened. "But of course! How could it be otherwise?"

"Very easily," retorted Patricia.

"Go," ordered Jack, staring into his plate. He looked up at her, glaring. "I'll not have you thinking you must not because of some misguided notion . . ."

"You egotistical grump!" Patricia spoke sharply. "How dare you think I refrain simply because of you!" Although it appeared otherwise, she was angry with *herself* that Jack had guessed her motive for staying away from the stables. "Very well," she added, "since it is what everyone wants, I will ride."

"What I want is irrelevant, Patricia," said Jack, sounding exceedingly weary. "What I know is right is another thing entirely."

"Ooohh!" Patricia glared at him, wondering what bee he'd gotten in his bonnet this time. She stormed out of the breakfast room, leaving behind a deep stillness.

Realizing there was some strong emotion between Jack and Patricia, Seward frowned. "Have I put my foot into it?" he asked.

Jack grimaced. "She has taken it on herself to jolly me out of my sour humors. That means she spends far more time with me than she aught. I just realized she hasn't ridden in weeks and, as you said, Miles, she loves it." Jack struggled to his feet and accepted the crutch handed him by one of the footmen. "You will see she is royally entertained. As she deserves."

Jack didn't exactly storm from the room, but he too left behind a half-eaten breakfast—and several worried friends.

"Has he a tendré for her?" asked Seward bluntly.

McMurrey nodded. "Perhaps more. In my humble opinion

he has fallen deeply in love with her." He studied his nails, looking up, meeting his friend's gaze. "I have not, however, determined Mrs. Haydon's feelings for him. It is not impossible, as Jack suggested, that she merely wishes to help him, to see him returned to the man we all remember."

Seward's eyes narrowed and he stared into space, considering that last bit. "We shall see," was all he said before choosing himself a large and varied breakfast.

He finished eating as Patricia returned to the room, dressed in her well-worn riding habit. He held up one finger as he finished his coffee, then rose from the table. "Shall we go?" he asked, his smile blazing as he offered her his arm.

"We shall." Her smile was brittle. She nodded to the others standing around the table. "Come along, Mr. Seward, so these gentlemen will feel free to finish their breakfasts before they become inedible. And I will prove to you I still ride."

There was a recklessness to Patricia that her cousin had never before seen. He frowned after her as she turned on her heel and departed.

"What is it, Alex?" asked Ian.

"I almost wish Miles had *not* appeared just now."

"For whom do you have the most concern?" Ian asked after a moment.

"The most? An impossible question. Jack is falling back into his old feelings of self-pity and inadequacy. And I fear Patricia's heart is involved, that he will hurt her badly. We cannot have *Patricia* falling into despair. It is she who jollies others out of the megrims!"

"Jack appears to be doing quite well for a man who, I am told, was shaking hands with death," said Seward. He and Patricia had run the fidgets out of their mounts and now jogged along a quiet lane.

"I *thought* he was. Suddenly he is acting as badly as he ever did."

"What do you mean?"

"Have the others not told you how he ran away from London? He hid himself up in Yorkshire and would be there still, very likely freezing to death or starving himself, and those with him, if Alex and Lord Wendover had not hunted him down and brought him away."

"He is not hiding now. Is that not an improvement?"

Patricia sighed. "He yearns to ride as he once did."

"Alex told me of a special saddle 'we' are buying for him." Seward's teeth flashed white. "You will, I hope, note that 'we?' "

"I noted it. I hope it helps, but who can tell? Perhaps he thinks half a loaf worse than nothing."

"Jack?" He rode in silence for some paces. "I don't recall him as that kind. But, in those days, our wants were simple, were they not? A good horse, time and space in which to ride him? When Jack received his inheritance from his godfather and bought himself a commission, you would have thought he'd entered a state of bliss!"

"If his man is to be believed, he was an excellent officer."

"From what I heard in Portugal, I'd say it was more than merely good. He was an outstanding officer and a friend of the highest order. When word went around that he wasn't expected to live, there were a lot of sad hearts."

"Yes. I can believe he was a heartbreaker."

"Women?" He cast her a sardonic look. "I wouldn't know about that."

"But you said . . ."

"What I meant," he interrupted, "was that there were many *men* greatly distressed by the news. His peers, enlisted men, and even some native Portuguese. He was very well-liked."

"Then why have they not written? Or," added Patricia, "is it possible they *have* but that the letters have yet to find him!

They may be sitting with his disreputable brother, for instance, who would not think to order his brother's mail sent on. Assuming he knew where to send it, of course."

"Disreputable brother?"

"Lord George Princeton has lost the family fortune, mortgaged the entailed estates, and run up debts he has no hope of paying. Very likely he will end his days in debtors' prison or in exile. Since running away was Jack's method of dealing with a problem, perhaps it will be his brother's as well."

"Hmm. Do I hear something of a bite to that?"

She didn't answer.

"Are you angry with him?"

"Angry? Why should I be angry?"

"Either you are or you are not."

He cast her a sideways look when she didn't respond. Her features were cast in ice. Was it disdain or the sort of grimness that comes with deep and unpleasant thoughts?

"Do you care to talk about it?" Seward's softly spoken words brought Patricia's gaze to him. For half an instant he thought she might, but she shook her head.

"No thank you. Time will solve my problem. One way or another." Without a pause she asked, "Shall we indulge ourselves with one more run before we return to the house?"

They did. He proposed a race which he won handily, gloating over her in his teasing manner as they returned to the stables. "I should have demanded a forfeit," he said. "Another kiss, perhaps."

"I think," contradicted Patricia sternly, "the first was more than enough." But her eyes twinkled.

"One," he said, just as sternly, "is *never* enough."

Jack, watching from shadows deep in the stable, saw Patricia laugh. When she and Miles Seward were out of sight, he too headed for the house, but he entered by the side door, going to his room where he found Bill Black placing newly washed linens in a drawer.

"Pack," he ordered. "We are leaving."

*"Leaving!"* Black clutched the shirts he'd just ironed, wrinkling them all over again. "But I thought we were set for the holidays!"

"I'm leaving. If you go too, then see to our packing." Jack threw himself into the comfortable chair set before the fire. "And don't make a to-do about it or I'll have your head for washing. No one needs to see us off. I'll leave a note thanking Lady Renwick, and another for Alex. Blast! You must hire a carriage. Or might I borrow one? That would be best, perhaps. Well?" He scowled. "Don't dawdle. I leave tomorrow at first light." He lifted his chin. "And quietly. Understand?"

"No I do not. Nor do I approve. But when did you ever listen to the likes of me. Can I ask," added Black a trifle sarcastically, "where we're going?"

Jack hadn't gotten so far in his thinking as to decide *where* he'd go. He just needed to *go*. Quickly. "When you need to know, I will tell you."

# Thirteen

Lord Hayworth prowled the conservatory, but Lady Black-burne was not there. He waited. She did not come.

*Why does she not come?*

It wasn't as though she didn't know he'd be there. Nothing had been said, but they had met here every day since he'd first proposed. She would be innocently occupied among her plants. He would be not so innocently *pre*occupied with her. And, usually, they would indulge in a trifle of dalliance before her ladyship would remind herself it was improper to behave in such a way and take herself off.

*Did she, today, manage to think of the impropriety first?* he asked himself. *Did she tell herself she could not, with proper decorum, come?*

"And if she will *not* come, then where may I go to find her?" he asked a particularly flamboyant red flower for which he had no name.

It was no surprise that the flower gave him no answer, but it was with a touch of depression that Lord Hayworth set off on his search, for this was not a good sign. The unthinkable might happen and she might yet say him nay!

The footman stationed in the front hall had no notion where she could be found. The maid Lord Hayworth encountered polishing a mirror in the blue salon was equally uninformative. Nor had the butler so much as an inkling of her ladyship's present whereabouts.

A sudden inspiration sent Lord Hayworth out to the stables to see if she had left Tiger's Lair. He discovered from a lad polishing tack that, indeed, she had, that Ian McMurrey, Lady Serena, and Lady Blackburne had gone off very early that morning for a visit to Lady Serena's home.

Lord Hayworth strolled off, frowning. Hadn't Lord Renwick once mentioned that Lady Serena's father was an ogre of the worst sort? How *could* Lady Blackburne have agreed to visit such a man's home? Lord Hayworth sighed softly, knowing that, of course she would—especially if Ian had the wits to suggest that Lady Serena was less likely to suffer if a stranger accompanied her!

Lady Dixon's eyes lit up at the sight of Lady Serena. "How wonderful, my dear child, that you come to visit!"

Serena eyed her mother who was thinner than formerly. Her hair showed more gray threads as well.

"And how pleased I am to meet you, Lady Blackburne," added Lady Dixon politely, her eyes feasting on her daughter.

"We stopped briefly to see Vicar Morton," said Serena, impatient with social niceties. "I feared you were ill when he told me you had not been to church for some months."

Lady Dixon's hand went to her throat and her pale skin seemed to lose still more color. "Your father feels it is unnecessary," she said in a choked voice.

"The older the man grows, the more insane he becomes!"

"Serena! Child! You must not say such things!"

Serena glanced at Lady Blackburne. "I apologize, Mother, but it is outside of enough that you are no longer allowed the solace of weekly church services."

"Your father reads the Bible and says prayers each morning, dear. That, he says, is more than sufficient for nonsinners such as ourselves."

"You, perhaps," said her daughter, "but does he have the nerve to consider himself sinless?"

"Serena, you will not say such things! I will not have it!"

Serena sighed. She wished Ian had not gone off to the village with her brothers. Still, it was a blessing that her father was away from home and not expected to return until tomorrow. She wondered if, somehow, Ian had known Lord Dixon was gone. Then she told herself not to be so silly. There was no way he could have known!

To the contrary. Ian had known. The man he had set to discover proof of Dixon's infamy, which would give Ian ammunition for blackmail to help remove Lady Dixon from her husband's power, had sent a laconic message to the effect their man was off on a journey and that he meant to follow. Word was Lord Dixon would be gone some days.

Ian had decided it was an excellent time to bring Serena to see her mother. They had also brought gifts for Boxing Day giving. Ian hoped Lord Dixon would not take it upon himself to forbid his wife the wearing of the lovely warm cloak Serena had chosen for her. As Ian and Lady Serena knew, Lord Dixon was capable of doing just that.

Lady Serena's youngest brother, Jonathan, sat beside Ian in the village inn and fiddled with his mug. He sported a split lip and one of the most colorful black eyes Ian had ever seen.

"What happened?" asked Ian bluntly.

Jonathan glanced around. His brothers were vying for the attention of the barmaid and too far away to hear. "Punishment."

"For what?"

"I was fool enough to object to his treatment of our mother."

"Your father?"

"Yes." He touched his eye. "He watched."

"Then it was your brothers . . . ?"

"One held me and the other beat me," said Jonathan sulkily.

Ian considered his brother-in-law thoughtfully. "You don't have to remain here, you know."

Jonathan's shoulders moved inside his jacket. "Where would I go? M'father refuses to buy me a commission. I'm afraid of the water so can't run off to sea the way my one brother did. There ain't nothin' else," he said.

"If you wish it, I will buy you a commission."

Jonathan straightened, staring at Ian. "You would?" After a long moment he asked, suspiciously, "Why?"

Ian shrugged. "Perhaps because I think it would please Serena to see you away from here."

Jonathan drained his mug. He set the pewter pot down carefully and eyed Ian. "You mean it?"

"Yes. If I give you some blunt, can you hide it until after the holidays and then, sometime in January, make your way to London where Serena and I must live for the next month or two?"

"You try me," said Jonathan.

Unfortunately, just then, his brothers' tempers erupted and a brawl broke out. Jonathan, at the urging of the inn's host, along with Ian, pulled the two apart and marched them from the inn and into the stable yard.

"Have you—" Ian's icy voice chilled everyone within hearing. "—had no training in proper behavior? None at all? Surely you have been told that, if you must indulge yourselves in fisticuffs, then you should take yourself out here where it will do no harm to anyone or anything but yourselves."

Serena's middle brother looked a trifle sheepish, but the elder looked merely defiant.

"Now, gentlemen," said Ian, his tone sarcastic, "you may proceed to do your best to kill each other." He stepped back, bowed, and turning on his heel, marched back into the inn.

Jonathan followed. "That money," he said under his breath. "Quick. While they are outside?"

Ian went up to the bar and Jonathan followed. "Host!" The man appeared. "I hear you are trustworthy."

"Yes sir," he said. He was only half listening, his ears cocked to the rumpus outside where the brothers had resumed their quarrel.

"I've a purse I want you to hold in safety. When Jonathan, here, comes for it, turn it over to him."

When Ian's words registered, the host's attention turned entirely on him. Ian explained as he sorted out the coins and a few flimsys, returning the rest to his pocket for their trip back to Tiger's Lair. He pushed a crown across the counter before putting the rest into the purse which he also passed over.

"I'll keep it safe, my lord," said the man, wiping his hands in his apron before picking up first the crown, which disappeared, and then the purse which he tucked out of sight in the back of a drawer. "When you want it, you come for it, Jonny."

"Don't tell anyone." Jonathan cast a look toward the stable yard.

The landlord grinned. "I'm no blabbermouth!"

"Now that is settled," said Ian, "how about another mug of your excellent home-brew?" Once they were seated with another mug of ale, Ian reminded Jonathan that he must, in secret, inform his mother he was leaving. "You don't want her worried about you," he said.

Ian picked the ladies up an hour later. When they were out the drive and onto the main road home, he told Serena what he had done. "I wonder that it has never occurred to your brothers that, if they cooperated, they could put the fear of God into their father."

"It will never happen," said Serena, shaking her head. "They can never agree on anything, you see."

Ian nodded. "And your mother, Serena?"

"She is in a constant fret she will do something to bring his wrath down on her head." Serena stared unhappily out her window. "I had a word with the housekeeper and she told me it isn't too bad. Only very occasionally does he lose his temper with her. It is enough, of course, to keep her on tenterhooks, which is not good for her, but I do not think she is in danger of . . . of his . . ."

"Of his doing her, er, permanent damage?"

"Yes."

"Would any husband truly harm his wife?" asked Lady Blackburne.

Her ladyship had been shocked by how old Lady Dixon looked when she knew very well the woman was several years younger than she was herself! She remembered Mary Hallowell-that-was from when the chit had had her first Season. Lady Blackburne had been married only a short time but had not had such stars in her eyes she'd been unaware of new arrivals on the London scene. Of course Mary Hallowell Dixon never again graced a Season. Perhaps that was why the woman had slipped from memory?

Her ladyship was informed that yes, Lord Dixon might very well lose his temper to the point where he'd badly hurt his wife.

"Perhaps she would find it comforting if I were to write her? A correspondence between us?"

"Do not bother," said Lady Serena, her voice caustic. "My father would never give her your letters."

Again Lady Blackburne had difficulty understanding such conduct. To her way of thinking, it simply wasn't done to behave in such a manner! And yet Ian McMurrey was not one to exaggerate.

Lady Blackburne wished very much she'd not gotten up so early that morning. If she had not, then she would not have been asked to join them on this journey. And if she had not, she would have had the guilty pleasure of another tete-a-tete with Lord Hayworth in the privacy of the conservatory and, as a further benefit of late sleeping, would not have been forced to become aware such evil existed in this world!

* * *

While the McMurreys and Lady Blackburne enjoyed a late luncheon along the way home, Lord Bladney sat with Lady Anne in her favorite parlor. Lady Anne set delicate stitches in the slippers she embroidered for Jack for Christmas while Lord Bladney read aloud the newspaper which had arrived that morning.

"You will be pleased to hear that the Marquess of Wellington is visiting both Cádiz and Lisbon this month. He is to add still another style to those titles he has already earned, that of Duque da Victoria." Hoping to nudge Lady Anne into one of the arguments she enjoyed so much but would not initiate, he added, "I suppose there will be those who think he has been honored in such a way far too often. Why, was it not just this past August when he was named Generalissimo of the Spanish armies?"

"Which was a long delayed decision," said Lady Anne, biting off another length of thread. "The war would have gone far more smoothly had he had control of the Spanish troops long ago."

"Would you have agreed to allow a foreign general to lead our troops?" asked Lord Bladney provocatively.

It was enough. Lady Anne set aside her sewing and leaned toward him. His lips tipped just a trifle as he listened to her harangue. Occasionally he nodded. Once or twice he shook his head, setting her off into still more vehement argument.

Finally Lady Anne ran down, out of breath and panting in a delightfully tantalizing way, her breasts heaving and her lips slightly open. Lord Bladney considered kissing her, but, reluctantly, gave over the notion. "Well," he said, "I see you have considered the question from all sides. I have felt Wellington overly praised for less than he *should* have accomplished, but I see there are extenuating circumstances over which he has had little or no control."

When Anne looked a trifle too complacent, he added,

"You are wrong, however, when you say it is all the fault of Parliament. You must know that Parliament is forced to consider far more than mere support of the war. There is the whole of the country, our people here, and how Parliament's decisions will affect the decisions of other countries. Napoleon has set all against us, Lady Anne. We cannot beggar ourselves or he will find us easy prey."

"Nonsense. A solid push and it would be done. Napoleon would be finished and the world could get on, in peace, making life better for all."

"We will have to agree to disagree, my dear."

"Agree to disagree? But, Horry," she said earnestly, "you are so *wrong-headed*. How can I convince you?"

"I fear it might take a great deal of time and effort. It is true you convinced me the enclosure movement has gone far enough, but . . ."

"Far enough! Too far. Way too far . . ." She was off and running and Lord Bladney, sitting back in his chair, enjoyed her easy flow of words, her cogent arguments, and rediscovered what he had long ago suspected: It was too bad Lady Anne had not been born a man. She would have been a great orator and would have done the party proud if elected to Commons. Which gave him a notion.

"My dear," he said, when a break occurred in her lecture, "have you thought of writing letters to the papers? You could use a pseudonym, you know."

"Oh!" She put her hand to her cheek, her eyes widening. "Oh, Horry, would I *dare?*"

"You've more sense than many whose letters are full of sound and fury, as they say, but little content! Why should you not exercise your wit?"

"You know very well why not," she said in a dry tone, her eyes catching and holding his. "I would, as you know, be vilified if it was ever discovered I did such a thing!"

"Why do you not write a letter which I may copy over and see is mailed." When she merely bit her lip, still holding his steady gaze, he added, "I will read it and we can argue your points if I feel you have gone too far or are, as you call me, wrong-headed."

Lady Anne's gaze wavered. Then, in a very soft voice, she said, "I'll do it!" And then she turned glowing eyes to meet Lord Bladney's and held out her hand. "Horry. You have made me so very happy. Thank you."

"You are surprised. Why? You know I would do anything in my power to make you happy."

Lady Anne instantly pulled away, her expression closed and impenetrable. She picked up her sewing and caressed the part she'd finished.

Lord Bladney silently cursed his tongue, watched her set her needle for another stitch, and picked up the paper. He found another item of interest which he read. He was still reading when Lord Merwin put his head in the door and asked if either of them had seen Jack.

# Fourteen

"What the bloody hell is going on here?" yelled Jack in his best parade ground voice. When he'd tried, more politely, to discover what was happening, he'd failed to get anyone's attention. Now he stepped into the way of a man exiting his brother's town house.

The man carried a very bad portrait of a Princeton ancestor. "Out'a my way. If'n that bastard owed you somethin', you move your stumps in there and get what you can get. 'Twon't be much, I kin tell you that."

The burly man shouldered past Jack, pushing him off balance and, if Black had not been at his side, Jack would have fallen. The incident added coals to the fire burning inside him. Struggling with the steps, he managed to get inside where he found a second scowling man, this one far better dressed. As the gentleman moved toward the door, Jack caught him by his lapel and held on. "Tell me what is going on."

The man removed Jack's hand from his coat. "Who asks?"

"If it is any business of yours, I am Jack Princeton. Now what . . ."

Before Jack could finish the sentence, his arm was grasped firmly and he was pulled into a salon bare of anything but the ashes in the grate. "You, my lord, are a very difficult man to locate," said the stranger. "I held the wolves off as long as I could, but one cannot perform miracles."

"I have no title. Just plain Mr. will do. Who are you?"

"Your solicitor, my lord, Mr. Tremble."

Jack's eyes widened painfully. "George?"

Mr. Tremble cleared his throat. "Dead, my lord. Your brother appears to have fallen asleep in, er, a, well he, hmm—"

"Spit it out," roared Jack.

"In a doorway, my lord," said the solicitor, hastily complying. "A side door. To, er, a gambling house, my lord." At Jack's glare, the solicitor mopped his brow with his handkerchief.

"Drunk, I suppose," said Jack, bitterly. "Was the weather so bad he froze to death?"

"Oh, no, my lord. Stabbed and robbed, my lord."

"My father predicted he'd come to a bad end," muttered Jack. He continued to glare, but now it was at nothing at all. After a moment he swore. Fluently. "I suppose I inherit his debts?"

"Only those which are official, my lord, unless you mean to pay any debts of honor which can be proven valid. The mortgages alone will be a heavy burden and there may be loans of which I am ignorant."

Jack's mind worked furiously. "This house," he said, glancing round. "The location is excellent, is it not?"

"It is, my lord."

"It is mortgaged?"

"Oh, yes, my lord. Everything that could not be sold is heavily mortgaged."

Jack sighed, thinking of the bit of property he'd managed to save from the wreck. The least valuable bit.

"Do you think to rent this house, my lord?" asked the solicitor, sounding hopeful.

"I don't know what to think." But the notion had crossed his mind. "George. Dead."

"I do not wish to press you, my lord, but decisions must be made."

Jack ignored him. *"When* did it happen?"

"A little over a month ago, my lord."

"A *month!"* Jack's mouth fell open. He closed it into a firm, hard line. "Where did you bury him?"

"In the family vault at the Court. A private service, my lord."

"I have been with friends. Why did none of them know of this?"

The man's ears reddened. He cleared his throat and mopped his brow again. "I, er, kept it from the papers. I thought if I could find you before the rats stripped you bare, we might hold them off. I failed, my lord, in my every attempt to locate you."

"Someday you must explain how you thought to find me if you did not advertise. There is nothing left here?"

"A few pieces too large to carry off, my lord. Anything which could be moved has been removed. Not, my lord, that there was much left. Your brother sold everything he could."

"There was entailed silver and a small collection of paintings. Those are gone?"

"Everything, my lord."

"Everything but a couple of heavily mortgaged estates which have been run into the ground—and this house."

"Exactly, my lord."

For the second time, Jack's vocabulary, learned from the most picturesque of His Majesty's enlisted men, came into play. When he fell silent, only the clatter of ironbound carriage wheels traversing the cobbles beyond the windows, the ring of shod hooves and the drivers' voices, muted by thick walls, gave form to the stillness.

The solicitor tentatively cleared his throat.

"Give me your card," ordered Jack, his attention caught. "I will come to your office tomorrow and you may detail the horrors of my position down to the last jot and tittle. Tonight I wish to—" Jack discovered he would not mourn the brother who had never been like a brother to him. "—think."

"Yes my lord. And where will you put up?"

"Why, *here,* of course."

The man stared, appalled. "Here! My lord, you cannot stay *here.*"

"There is a law against it of which I know nothing?"

"No, of course not," the solicitor hastened to say. "But there is nothing here. And no servants to see to your needs. I doubt there is so much as a mattress, my lord."

"I was a soldier for most of a decade, sir. Here I have a roof over my head which does not leak—" Jack's eyes narrowed. "—or at least I assume it does not leak?"

The man nodded. "You need not concern yourself about that. The house was well-built, my lord. It is sound."

"Then I will do very well. Until tomorrow." Jack bowed slightly and the solicitor bowed deeply. He left, an obviously unhappy man. "Black," said Jack once the door closed, "see the house is locked up tight. I wouldn't put it past George's creditors to have unlocked a window here and there, meaning to return and pull down the chandeliers and the marble off the fireplace."

When Black had gone off on his errand, Jack stared up at a lighter spot over the mantel where his mother's portrait had hung. "I wonder where you are now," he whispered, and then, turning, he toured the main floor of the house.

The place was in decent condition. It needed the painters in and the paneling and chandeliers polished. That sort of thing. But the windows were intact and there were no gaping holes in walls or floors.

When he moved upstairs in his idiosyncratic manner, there was, Jack discovered, even a bed. A huge bed, the mattress ancient and in need of replacement, but nevertheless a bed. Covered by their great coats, he and Black would be snug as bugs in a rug!

Black found Jack in what had once been his mother's room. "Orders, my lord sir?"

Jack grimaced. "Give over the 'my lording,' Black, since I am obviously in no position to be lording it over anyone!"

Black grinned. "Orders, sir?"

"Check the kitchen. See if there is a pot to cook in and if any coal remains. Which I doubt. Then—" He tossed Black his purse. "—buy supplies. We need to eat, so that means food and a fire. And don't forget the pot if there is none!"

When Black departed, Jack returned to somewhat maudlin memories of what his life had been like as a boy before his mother died and he was sent to school a year earlier than intended. There he'd met the others of the Six, none of whom had had a totally satisfactory family life, except Wendover. Wendover had been blessed in that regard. Merwin, as next best, had had a conventionally normal childhood. His family had been absent more than home, but that was not out of the way. Many children never saw their parents from one month to the next.

Renwick had been reared by a dissolute father who ignored his son's existence. The Renwick house and grounds, the estate, everything, had gone to rack and ruin. And when Ian McMurrey's mother died, his father had become a sot—although that was not until they were all within a year of going up to University.

And Seward? Who knew if Miles had ever had a family! Jack had some vague recollection that Miles's childhood was overseen by a pair of dusty old solicitors who had had charge of the lad from infancy. So only Wendover had had a truly loving family life, the care and support Jack had once sworn he would give his own children.

Back when he'd thought it possible he might have children.

Enough. Jack forced memories of his mother and his friends back into the corner of his mind where the past lived on. His brother was dead and he was in for years of work and worry and little else. A quick review of his resources

told him they were worth nothing when put beside his in-
herited debts. As he wandered through the empty rooms, he
finally concluded it was no use trying to make decisions
until he knew more, since the only positive thought he'd had
during the whole of his cogitations was to get this house
leased as quickly as possible for as much as possible.

Black returned from his shopping by way of the tradesman
entrance into the kitchen. The clattering and banging drew
Jack down there.

"The place is a cave," he muttered, looking around.

"Better'n some quarters you had in Portugal!"

"Much better," agreed Jack. "Can you manage?"

"There isn't much to work with. Some chipped plates and
a bent fork or two. A pan so dented no one wanted it. But
I'll manage just fine. Won't compare to what you got used
to at Lord Renwick's, though." There was a wooden bench
built against one wall of the huge fireplace and Black pointed
to it. "You had a shock. Sit yourself down and let me worry
about the edibles."

"Shock?" Jack laughed, a wry humorless laugh. "I suppose one might call it that." His eyes went hard. "Damn
George! Have you a notion of what I'm left with?"

"Debt up to your neck," said Black promptly.

"My *neck?* Oh no. You are wrong, Black. From what little
I gleaned, it is more likely I am so far over my head I'll
drown in it!"


Ian McMurrey, returning to Tiger's Lair after the visit to
Lady Serena's mother, was ready to discuss his plans with
the rest of the Six. He called a Forum as they'd named such
meetings when still in school, where ancient history and
Latin were of major concern.

Everyone gathered in Renwick's study but Jack. "What,"
asked Lord Renwick of his butler, "do you mean he isn't to
be found? Jack cannot have gone anywhere."

"But he has, sir. He left two messages."

"Why was I not told?"

"No one of importance knew, my lord," said Reeves, looking down his nose. "The maid who cleaned his room this morning discovered it had been cleared of the lieutenant's gear, but she didn't think it her place to inform anyone because she assumed everyone knew."

"That is only reasonable," rumbled McMurrey. "She is a maid, after all. She did her work in Jack's room and went to her next duty as would any well-trained maid."

Seward's brows arched. "Ran away, did he? He makes a habit of it."

"And if he did? Could you perhaps tell me why?" asked Merwin, his voice faintly coated with ice.

Sahib pushed up onto his hind quarters.

"Me? What have I to do with it? Jack has grown decidedly antisocial. I couldn't get him to warm up at all."

"*You* couldn't, perhaps," said Merwin.

The tiger stood. His tail lashed once.

"That sounds very near an insult, Alex. You'd better explain."

"You have enjoyed a delightful flirtation with Mrs. Haydon, have you not?"

Seward was silent for a moment. "Oh, oh."

Sahib subsided.

"You hadn't a clue, had you?"

"Well, I don't know that I'd go that far, but *she* made no objection," responded Seward, frowning.

McMurrey spoke before Merwin could say something he'd regret. "You are a very difficult man for a lady to put off, Miles. You never were known as overly sensitive to others. I do not say that to insult you, but because it explains why you never take a hint. The usual sort of social snub a woman uses when wishing to avoid a man's attentions does not work with you."

Seward's spine straightened. "You would say I am unbearably pushy?"

"Not at all. You are delightfully insouciant, with a sense of humor which draws one in. Anyone. That means that only by firmly stating her feelings in just so many words may a woman tell you to go to hell, for fear that your attentions might blight her hopes with another man."

Miles features fell into a grim expression. "I've been a fool, you would say."

"Assuming you were only flirting and were not pursuing Mrs. Haydon seriously, then, yes," said McMurrey in a judicious tone, "I would have to agree you've acted the fool. Or at least, you have chased away Jack, whom I'd guess, *is* seriously interested in her. Given enough time, he might actually have come to believe his limp made no difference to her."

"Then," said Seward, "I must apologize to Mrs. Haydon and when I've done that, I must find Jack. I'll bounce his head against the wall a few times so he'll get it through his thick skull he's as good a man as he ever was."

"That might work if you allow *him* to bounce *you* off a wall or two in turn," said Merwin. He grimaced. "And that says it all, does it not? You will note I said that you must *allow* him to do so. Which implies I do *not* think him the man he was. Which makes me at least as bad as anyone else."

While this discussion was progressing, Lord Renwick gave orders to his butler who went off to set in motion the inquiries which were the first step toward discovering where Jack had gone.

"I just hope he isn't fool enough to attempt to reach that tumble down wreck of a house up north!" said Merwin.

"He wouldn't," said Wendover, his eyes popping. "No one would be so foolish as to try to live there over the winter. The place is a hovel!"

"He might manage in the rooms he fixed for his house-keeper."

"Come, Alex! You cannot say you think him such a num-skull!"

"He is not happy, Tony. There is no telling what he will do."

"At least he has Black," said McMurrey in his deep sooth-ing tones. "Black is competent and has Jack's well-being at heart. We must be glad of the man."

"Yes, a good man. Wouldn't mind adding him to my crew if he were a seaman," said Seward, which was, from him, high praise. "There is nothing we can do until we discover what direction Jack headed and, if I am not wrong, Ian called us together for a reason. Ian? Why do you not discuss your problem?"

"Jase and Alex know about it." Ian proceeded to fill the others in on the situation at Lady Serena's home, including the shocking information that her father was a bigamist.

"Surely you don't mean to confront him with this?"

"With that or something else. I'd not make the information public since bigamy makes Serena and her brothers bastards. It would also put a mentally defective man, his son by his real wife, in line for the title. His real wife is not in dire straits. She owns the house they live in and has an annuity which continues to the son. She thinks herself a widow and I see no reason to change that. She is, after all, better off without the man. Believe me!"

"So, what is the problem?"

"So far my ferret has been unable to come up with the proof to tie that wedding to Dixon rather than another by the same name. He has nearly given up finding it and has taken to following Dixon in the hopes of discovering something else which will do the trick."

"And this Forum?"

"To put all of you in the picture and, at Jason's insistence, ask for volunteers who will go with me when I finally confront the man with whatever information I choose to use. He is vicious and not to be trusted. On the other hand, he likes his place in the world and will not wish to jeopardize it."

"Write up your information before you face him," suggested Merwin. "Add whatever proof you have and leave it all with your solicitor. Tell Dixon it exists but not so much as a hint as to where it may be found. Just in case he thinks to solve his problem by having you killed."

"Excellent advice, Alex, and something which would not have occurred to me. You see why I need one of our Forums? Anyone else have anything to add?"

"Only that I will join you if I am around," said Miles.

"And I." It was a chorus of voices, including Lord Renwick who, conscious of his blindness, felt he was useless, but that Sahib would be a valuable resource.

"So," said Miles, standing, "if that is all, I must find Mrs. Haydon and apologize. Jason, when your men return with news, you will pass it on?"

"Of course. We'll have a second Forum and plan what we must do to get Jack back where he belongs. With us."

"I doubt apologizing to me will do any good," said Patricia. She eyed Miles Seward, who had dropped to his knees before her, his arms spread wide in supplication. "Especially since the histrionics with which you indulge yourself tend to make one less ready to believe your sincerity."

He sighed theatrically, drooped so that his shoulders sagged. He cast her a hangdog look. "But what can a man do? Born a clown, he must stay true to his nature." His tone became confiding. "Clowns are not, you know, particularly happy people."

Patricia grimaced. "So you say. But one judges by what one sees and you, Mr. Seward, appear light-hearted to the point of inanity."

He stared beyond her shoulder and, for just a moment,

she saw the depths hidden behind the facade he presented to the world. Patricia's eyes narrowed and she wondered what she might say to . . .

"Inanity," Seward said, interrupting her thoughts. "I see," he added. "Yes, of course. But—" He forced a touch of his usual insouciance. "—that is life, is it not? One huge jest the good Lord perpetrated on humanity to make us humble? Best that one accept that and make the best of it, do you not agree?"

"I doubt I do. Agree, I mean," said Patricia, her expression wry. "I will think about it. Oh, the devil," she added. "Do get up. If someone comes in and thinks you proposing, the fat will truly fall into the fire!"

Seward looked down, adopted an expression of surprise, as if he'd forgotten he was on his knees, and hopped up in an agile fashion. He bowed. "May I assume you have forgiven me?"

"There is nothing to forgive. Or, if there is, then I must forgive myself as well, must I not? I cannot accept Alex's assessment that Jack left because of our bantering, but if he did, then I am equally at fault for indulging you."

"I remember you as a wide-eyed girl-child, unhappy and afraid," he said, staring thoughtfully. "But life appears to have treated you tolerably well after all. You are anything but a child, no longer unhappy, unafraid of life and living, or what the future brings. Is that not so?"

"I was very much that fearful girl-child when we first met, Mr. Seward. But you forget that while you were off adventuring, I was growing and changing as one does when one lives for more than the moment." She eyed him. "You know, somehow I have conceived this odd notion there is far more to you than you allow the world to see. Why?"

"Why is there more?"

"Why," she said gently, "do you not allow the world to see it?"

A rush of red flooded up into Seward's ears. "Oh well,"

he said and looked at nothing in particular. Several nothings-in-particular. "Well, you see, it is this way . . ." At which point he stopped and gave her a look which pleaded with her to change the subject. When she did not, he drew in a deep breath and said, "I suppose because I do not wish the world to know?"

"I could again ask why, but I will not. The world will not, you know," she added in a gentle voice, "condemn you for feeling things deeply."

"Will it not?"

The response was so dry that Patricia wondered just how—and *how badly*—Miles Seward had been hurt. What led to his sinking all seriousness beneath a facade of carefree behavior and lighthearted jests?

"Perhaps," he said, "I have been away from England so long that our world has changed, but I doubt it. Very much. I prefer to go on as I've begun."

"Rather than take a chance that someone—" Her brows arched. "—will hurt you again?"

He swallowed. "You witch."

"No." Patricia considered the man. "It is simply that I like people. I like to know what makes them the way they are. You are an intriguing man, Miles Seward. A complex man. Yet you act as if you are a court jester. I doubt you managed to laugh your way out of the various pits you dug for yourself, or into which you were thrown, so there is far more to you than a laugh or a grimace or the off-hand manner you show even your friends. Do not hide from them to the point they find you less than they'd thought."

He grimaced and made a joke to the effect one could not conjure up something from nothing.

Patricia chuckled. "You have done it again, have you not? It is a habit with you, to turn off anything which might probe into your inner self."

"I suppose Jack allows you to touch all the tender places inside him?"

Patricia sobered. "To a degree, yes. But only to a degree. It is human nature to protect oneself from hurt, but you carry that to such extremes no one can know you at all."

"Ah! But, as I said, it is safer that way." He bowed, excused himself, and went off to ponder Patricia's words and wonder if there might not be something in them.

But—how did one go about changing? He was still worrying away at the problem, when a footman found him and asked that he join the others in Lord Renwick's study.

The grooms had returned with what little information they had managed to discover.

# Fifteen

The men were deep in plans when Patricia stormed into their study. "Reeves tells me Jack took the gig, leaving the message he'd have it returned in a week or two."

"Yes," said Lord Renwick. "It suggests he has gone on a rather long journey, does it not? Why," he asked plaintively, "did the fool not take a closed carriage if he meant to travel? At this time of year a gig is foolish beyond permission!"

Patricia frowned. "You think he has returned to where Alex and Lord Wendover found him?"

"Where else?" asked Wendover, surprised.

Patricia cast him a look. "There is the whole of England and Scotland, is there not? Why not London? Or The Wells or Bath or any number of other places?"

"Was there not an estate in Sussex?" asked McMurrey. "The one he liked best?"

"Hampshire, but it belongs to his brother, does it not?" objected Wendover. "Jack and his brother were never close. Would he go to a place owned by George?"

"Not if it is in the same condition as the lodge you described!" Lord Renwick grimaced.

"Jack was in the army," said Seward thoughtfully. "You have no notion how miserable winter quarters in the Peninsula can be. That house, even if stripped of all amenities, would be cozier than what many of our officers endure in Portugal."

The group fell silent. Finally Lord Renwick tapped his desktop. "Do we conclude we will split our forces? Someone goes north to Yorkshire and someone checks the Hampshire estate?"

"My father has requested my presence in Scotland. I said I would come in the New Year, but can do so now after checking that Jack has not gone to Yorkshire," said McMurrey. "That is, I will if you, Jason, allow my wife to remain here in comfort."

Lord Renwick nodded. "Of course Lady Serena must not attempt such a journey in her condition. Eustacia will be glad of her company. You will, of course, return for Christmas?"

"I should return by then if I take only my groom and ride."

Wendover cast McMurrey an appalled look. "Ride? All that distance?"

McMurrey chuckled. "It is possible, you know," he said.

"You Corinthians frighten me," drawled Wendover. "I never know when you will suggest I join one of you active souls in some mad flight of fancy!" He raised his quizzing glass and looked around. "I suppose you think I should ride west. Well, I will not." When his friends blinked at this sudden and adamant refusal, he smiled. "I will take my carriage, my groom *and* my valet."

Patricia smiled. "Very well done, my lord. I do believe you had them going!"

Wendover cast her a shy smile. "Occasionally I manage to send them up," he said.

"I will ride with Ian," said Seward. "I can return and report after we check Jack's hunting box while Ian continues north to Scotland."

Lord Renwick nodded. "I wish I could help, but I fear I'd be no more than a hindrance. *Damn my eyes!*" He instantly recalled Patricia's presence and apologized for swearing.

"Never mind, my lord," she murmured, only slightly

shocked. It was the first time Patricia had heard Lord Renwick complain in any way of his blindness. She wondered if she had been insensitive to his true feelings or if, these days, his lordship was only occasionally overset by his condition.

"You and Alex will see to the women," rumbled McMurrey. "They will need you."

The Forum broke up, those who were travelling taking themselves off to order their packing. Lord Renwick and Merwin sat silently and Patricia wondered if she should leave, when her cousin spoke. "You said he could be anywhere, cousin. *Why* did you suggest such a thing?"

Patricia frowned. "I do not believe Jack went north. He *might* have gone to the Hampshire estate if it was a place he liked as a child."

"What do you think he did? Very likely you know him better than we do. He is so changed I have wondered if he is the same man who went off to war."

"I doubt any man is the same after experiencing war!" she said, her voice sharp. "I have been trying to think what I would do if I were bitter and unhappy. If I had tried isolation and it did not help, and if I were beginning to accept my condition, I think I might want to lose myself among as many people as possible."

"London?"

She nodded. "Alex, will you accompany me there?"

Alex ignored her question. "I could take a day or two and check the hotels, I suppose. Or it is not totally unthinkable he has left word at his brother's, even if he would not stay with the man . . ."

"Alex, will-you-escort-me-to-London?" Patricia spoke slowly, making each word distinct.

Rudely blunt, Alex said, "No," and continued thinking aloud. "Would he perhaps do something so odd as go to one of our town houses, Jason? Not yours, since it is leased, but mine or Ian's? Or might he talk his way into Tony's rooms?"

"What about Wendover's family?" asked Renwick. "Do you remember how Jack adored Tony's mother? As did we all, for that matter."

"That suggests a journey into the Cotswolds, does it not?" Merwin drew in a deep breath and let it out. "Jason, when we find Jack, I think I'll land him a facer. It is outside of enough, making us travel all over the countryside at this time of year!"

"Alex," said Patricia a trifle loudly, "you will escort me to London or I will go on my own."

"Patricia, you act the fool when you are not one." More gently, he added, "There is nothing you can do, so why not remain here in comfort?"

"I will go to London!"

Merwin cast a look toward Lord Renwick begging help, forgetting his friend could not see him. "Why?" he asked.

"I do not know how I know," she said, suddenly stubborn. "But I *must* go to London."

"Mrs. Haydon, truly, it would be better if you do not."

"Lord Renwick, I know you men mean well and wish to cosset and care for me, but you do not understand. I suddenly feel very strongly that I must get to London and that I need to do so quickly. It is *imperative.*"

Alex eyed her. "I remember a tale. That time, too, you insisted you must do something. Instantly. As I recall you averted some disaster, something quite horrid, by getting your own way. I do not recall the details . . . ?" he finished on an interrogatory note.

Patricia felt her ears grow hot. "It has happened more than once. I've no notion what particular occasion you might mean."

"And how often does it happen and *nothing* occurs?" asked her cousin shrewdly.

"When I feel this strongly, I am forced to give into my forebodings. Always."

He sighed. "Very well. Be ready to travel in the morning. You may stay with Grandmother."

Patricia grimaced. "She will forbid this and demand that, and will comb my hair when I will not do her bidding. Alex, you know she is so independent herself, she cannot bear anyone around her who knows her own mind!"

"Still, if you wish to go to London, I see no alternative."

Patricia's lips tightened. "Neither—" She spoke so forlornly the men were forced to chuckle. "—can I."


"So," summarized the solicitor, the tips of his fingers touching, "you begin to understand, my lord, why I contend the only solution is to marry a woman who will bring you as large a dowry as possible. I have made a study of the situation and know of several cits who seek a noble bridegroom for their daughters. Should I approach one? Or all of them, perhaps?"

Jack's eyes narrowed. "Was George looking into that as a solution to his problems?"

The solicitor looked at the corner of the room. "It had not gone so far as an approach, but I had gathered the information."

"I wondered how you had the names of buyers at your fingertips. I doubt, however, any father would pay to get *me* as a son-in-law." He rubbed his leg which ached abominably. He had done far more walking than he was used to doing and suffered accordingly.

"You will not, I hope, feel insulted when I tell you it is the title they buy. As long as the man is not a drooling idiot or evil, they care little what comes with it."

"I pity their daughters!"

"Pity yourself, my lord," said the solicitor bluntly. In fact, he verged on rudeness. "One chit has a squint which is quite off-putting. Another is a poor little dab of a thing. And the third is overly tall, far too thin, and has a particularly shrill laugh. Now. Which should I approach?"

"You go too fast, Tremble. You tell me the estates earn enough to cover the mortgages. Barely. If we rent the town house for the sort of rent you suggest is possible, then that I may use to begin making improvements to the estates which will increase the income they bring me."

"My lord, how can you possibly keep up appearances if you use your only source of income to improve your property? On what will you live?"

"On one of the estates. Probably the one in Hampshire where I may help forward the necessary improvements."

The solicitor goggled. "My lord! You cannot mean you would go into the fields and grub in the dirt!"

Jack laughed heartily for the first time since he'd learned of his new status. "And why not? Is not our king known as Farmer George? Surely there can be nothing out of the way if one emulates his Royal Highness!"

"Of course it is wrong. All wrong. You must take your place in society and your seat in the Lords and . . ."

"Spend my evenings losing money I do not have? As did my brother? I think not." Jack struggled to his feet, more angry than he'd been in some time. "And think of the figure I would cut if I had a look-in at Almack's, perhaps. Or wooed some sheltered miss who has never been allowed to know there is anything ugly or bad in the world? You are a fool, Tremble."

"My lord, I have not suggested you wed a young miss from your own class. I suggested you marry a cit's daughter. It is not the same."

Jack's eyes narrowed. "Just how high a value does such a father put on his daughter?"

"Ten thousand, easy. Perhaps as high as twenty, depending on how desperate he is to get himself a toehold into society!"

"And he believes wedding his daughter to a noble will buy him that toehold?"

"Yes. Along with continuing funds on which you would live, of course."

"They are all fools."

"But exceedingly rich fools, my lord," said Tremble slyly. "Do not put the notion out of court, giving it no thought whatsoever."

"I will think about it. For now, find me a renter for the town house." Jack settled his crutch under his arm and exited before he said or did something unforgivable!

As he swung along Fleet Street toward the Strand, he scowled so harshly that an old friend, thinking he recognized Jack, decided not to approach him after all. Jack hadn't noticed. His thoughts were as bleak as his future looked to be. Even though he had refused to allow his solicitor to approach any of the wealthy city men seeking a noble bridegroom, it seemed likely that that was the only solution.

Perhaps if Miles had not arrived at the Tiger's Lair and shown him how hopeless was any thought of a future with Patricia, he might feel differently. He'd been a fool. The biggest fool alive to fall in love with a woman of Patricia's caliber! She deserved the best.

Not Miles, of course. Miles would never be a good husband for any woman. There wasn't one alive who could hold his interest for any length of time, nor one who could keep up with him if she managed the first trick. No, Miles was not for Patricia, but watching them laugh and joke and enjoy each other's company had underlined how impossible it was that she might ever look at Jack himself with a lover's eyes. And Jack wanted no less of her.

Since he could not have what he desired above all things, then would it not make sense to accept Tremble's offer to find him a bride who could save the estate, so there would be something for his children to inherit?

"But would it be fair to the woman?" he muttered, his scowl deepening.

A beggar veered off.

There wasn't a woman born who could replace Patricia in his affections. He wondered if he could even look at another female without feeling revulsion at the thought of bedding her. Would any woman be fool enough to take him under such conditions? Want a coronet so badly she would overlook his limp and his lack of any proper feeling?

"And if she is such a fool, would I have *her?*"

"Have her what, guv?" asked a cheeky lad of ten or twelve, falling into stride with Jack.

"Have her . . ." Jack focused on the lad and growled deep in his throat. In his huskiest voice, he said, "Keep your hands off my purse, boy. I haven't enough for myself and my man as it is."

"Why not?"

"Why not? Because I'd a brother who was a fool and now I've only his debts and no hope of an acceptable solution to my problems."

"Ah. A wrong'un, was he? Known some like that m'self," said the boy, skipping jauntily along beside Jack.

It occurred to Jack the boy actually kept up with him. He wondered if he had slowed down or if the lad was particularly quick on his feet.

"Might help ye, guv."

"How could a brat from the Isle of Dogs be of help?"

The boy grinned. "Recognize m'yap do you? How come a swell like you knows that?"

"I was in the army, boy. I had lots like you under me."

"Then maybe my dad was one of them. He went into the army. Took the King's Shilling, he did, right after m'mam told him he had to wed her, having got her a bun in the oven. Me, that is."

"I doubt it," contradicted Jack. "I was in the cavalry, and the enlisted men under me had to know the care and feeding of horses."

"That's m'dad. Worked in the stables, dinna he? Cared for a brewer's beasts, he did."

"Truth?" asked Jack.

The boy grinned a perky confiding smile. "I like to think it, anyway."

Jack chuckled.

"Know where you can get vittles cheap. Know where to pick up coal for free. Know how to snabble a purse when needed. Know all sorts of useful things."

"Know how to get yourself into Newgate or on one of the boats to Botany Bay, is what *you* know!" Jack found himself amused by the lad. "Tell you what. You come home with me. Black will find a use for you and you'll no longer need to run from the watch."

The boy stopped. Jack, perforce, halted as well. "You mean it?"

"I said it, didn't I? What I say I mean. And I mean it when I say you aren't to get on the wrong side of the law! *And* that you'll have to sit to your books and learn to read and write." He watched the lad's eyes grow huge. "And what is more, you'll do it for a hard bed on the floor by the kitchen fire and your food. I told you I haven't an extra coin in my pocket."

"You'll learn me to read and write?"

"I'll *teach* you to read and write." *And why not? It will give me something to do. The boy is sharp enough.* "It won't be easy."

"No sir. But to read and write!"

It occurred to Jack there might be someone who would worry about the boy. "Do you need to inform your mother?"

"Nah. She died. I take care of m'self."

"Very well. Follow along and don't get lost. I'd not know how to find you again."

He heard the boy mutter that he'd find the guv if anything so stupid as that happened. So, not long after, he led the boy in through the kitchen door to the town house.

"Where you been?" asked Black. "I been worrin' my head to sawdust about you."

"I've been finding us help."

"Help?" Black's eyes flicked to the boy and settled. "What's your name, lad?"

"Dickens. When I was born they said I was the Dickens boy." He grinned, his eyes dancing. "Or maybe it was, 'The dickens. It's a boy.' Anyway, Dickens stuck. Been Dickens all my life."

"Very well, Dickens. I haven't a notion what you'll do to help and if I know boys, which I do, you will eat us out of house and home. But if the lieutenant says you are ours, then ours you are. First off," said Black, wrinkling his nose, "out of those duds. I'll heat water and you, m'lad, will have a new experience in your young life. A *bath*."

Dickens looked horror-struck. "Take off m'trousers?"

"You can't very well bathe with them on. While the water heats I'll duck out and see if I can find you something to wear that isn't full of holes or too small which that jacket surely is. Now, you help haul the water, boy. And you, sir, you take yourself up to bed. I need to see to that leg, don't I? Aching more than a bit, isn't it? Damn and blast, I suppose you ran all over London on it and didn't take a hack. Not once is my guess. Saving a few pence and suffering for it so I'll have to spend the pence on liniment! Boy—" Black turned to glare at the lad. "—this man is the most foolish creature you ever met!"

Dickens, full of hero worship, disagreed, but was far too canny to say so.

As it turned out, Dickens was shy. Black agreed to let him bathe in privacy if he'd promise to do so thoroughly. All over. Including his hair. Dickens swore to do so on the grave of his father—which didn't convince Jack since the boy hadn't a notion where, if at all, that grave existed, but Black was complaisant.

"He'll do it," said Black later as he worked to reduce the knots in Jack's leg. "Boy like that, he wants a father, you see. He'll have pretended all his life he had one somewhere, but now he has you and he can let the man go peaceful into his grave. Assuming, as you say, the fellow's dead. Dickens will be clean when you see him again."

Which he was. And proud as a peacock of his new clothes.

Even better, once Black had a moment to follow him about, the boy came through on his promise of knowing where the best and cheapest food was to be found and, whenever he was given the time to do so, he scrounged up coals.

Black was afraid to ask where he found it.


Patricia sat in a straight-backed chair and listened to Lady Merwin expound on why she, Patricia, could not possibly help in the search for Jack Princeton. "It isn't the thing and you know it," finished her ladyship, her tongue as tart as the lemon she was carefully squeezing into the punch she was concocting for the two of them.

Patricia wondered exactly why it was not the proper thing for her to search for Jack when it was acceptable for Lady Merwin to drink rum punch mixed to her own recipe. She forbore to express the thought because it was likely, if she were stupid enough to do so, her ladyship would construe her words to mean Patricia did not approve. Lady Merwin would, as a result, deny her a glass of the heady drink which, Patricia mendaciously told herself, she needed for medicinal reasons!

Instead, she asked, "Can we not attend at homes and see if anyone mentions his name? Perhaps someone has seen him."

"Alex is far more likely to discover news of him in the clubs or find him at some small out of the way hotel. Assuming he is in London. Why—" The elderly termagant eyed her uninvited but welcome visitor. "—do you believe he is?"

"You wouldn't understand," said Patricia and, before Lady Merwin could take umbrage, added, "*I* do not understand it.

only know I must seek him, must prevent some disastrous
vent. I do not know what it is, but it will ruin the rest of
is life if it is not prevented."

Patricia might have been startled to discover that the in-
nsity of her expression convinced her ladyship where
ords would not have done so. "You have the sight?" asked
ady Merwin, stirring the warming brew.

"The *sight?*" Patricia looked blank. "Oh. That sense of
e future it is said some Scots possess?" She looked
oughtful. "I never thought of it that way, but perhaps that
 what it is. Which—" She adopted a brisk manner. "—is
onsense. Such things must be nonsense."

Lady Merwin ladled out a portion of punch and handed
atricia a glass nearly too hot to hold. She gave another stir
 the punch simmering in the coals of the fire and ladled
ut her own. Ever since Patricia had stumbled on her lady-
hip mixing this particular concoction one cold winter eve-
ing when her ladyship had been visiting in the country, the
wo had occasionally shared a bowl, a secret they divulged
 no one. As had crossed Patricia's mind earlier, it was *not*
uitable behavior for two ladies presumed to have the char-
cter of women of quality!

"In actual fact," said Lady Merwin, referring to Patricia's
enial, "I disagree. I once had a Scottish maid who had the
*ight*. There is nothing the least nonsensical about it! So—"
er ladyship reversed her earlier stand. "—let us put our
eads together and see what we may do."

They sipped and talked, drank and planned and, as the
vening progressed, discussed possible ways and means in
ore and more outrageous terms. Finally Patricia yawned.
I hope," she said, patting her mouth, "that we do not recall
is discussion in detail come the morning. I fear we have
ecome more than a trifle ridiculous!"

Lady Merwin nodded, an injudicious tipping of her head
llowing her turban to slide even farther down her forehead
nd half-covering one eye. "You may be correct. So, to as-

sure that we do *not* remember, perhaps we should have one more teeny weeny sip apiece?"

With great care, Lady Merwin removed from her chair to where the almost empty bowl beckoned. Almost as carefully, Patricia joined her. With the utmost care to be fair in her sharing out, Lady Merwin ladled the last of the punch into their glasses, squinting at each portion to see which should get the very last drops.

The two women clicked glasses.

"To saving Lieutenant Princeton!" said Lady Merwin.

"To finding him so we *can* save him!" responded Patricia.

They turned bottoms up and then, simultaneously, cast their crystal glasses into the fireplace, where they shattered in a more than satisfactory manner. Arm in arm, the women wended their way up the stairs to their respective beds.

Luckily, Lady Merwin's servants were unusually fond of their mistress and, with great self-restraint, did *not* spread the tale of the broken glasses among their acquaintances!

Jack's sleep was troubled. He pictured the tenants on his father's farms, pictured the neat houses and productive lands of his youth . . . and wondered what he'd find now. Would anyone he remembered still live there? He imagined the suffering. Imagined cold and hungry children. *Were* there children? Or had all the young people fled his brother's cruelty, moving into the manufacturing cities where life was also cruel, if more impersonally so.

Lying rigidly still so he'd not disturb Black who snored softly on the far side of the wide mattress, Jack's mind returned again and again to Tremble's proposal, shied from it, thought again of his tenants' probable living conditions, and, finally, forced himself to think about a squint-eyed female, an overly tall female, a little dab of a female . . . and, giving his mental memory of Patricia Haydon a wistful farewell . . .

decided it was the little dab of a woman who would most likely suit him best.

Thus, reluctantly, Jack made the decision to order his lawyer to approach the cit, direct him to suggest he and the chit meet so that they could each know what bargain they'd make, assuming a bargain *was* made.

And Jack, with one last inner vision of suffering tenants over-laid and confused by a vision of a glowering Patricia, finally slept.

# Sixteen

It was full daylight, such as it was, when Lord Wendover arose from the worst night's sleep he had ever endured. Even his nights on the floor in Yorkshire had not been so bad. Not only had these sheets been unchanged since the last patron slept in them—or perhaps the last several patrons—but the noise from the taproom had risen through the floor long into the night. Then, when finally he fell into a restless sleep, some horrid fowl sang its morning hymn to the moon, awakening him. He had nearly roused the inn, called for his valet, who was likely dead to the world in a quiet little cubby in the attics, and demand they leave at once. Instead he'd returned to the arms of Morpheus, only now rousing for the second time.

A different sort of noise was very nearly as undesirable as that disturbing him only a few inadequate hours earlier. Tony Wendover peered through the low window into the street. He sighed. Just his luck, was it not, that today was market day in Petersfield? That it would be hours before his coach could squeeze through the narrow streets now crowded with pedestrians, carts, animals, and what-not, for its final leg to Underhill, Lord George Princeton's Hampshire estate?

Resigned to the inevitable, he allowed Abley to shave and dress him and then took himself down to his private parlor where he ate an excellent breakfast, the first good thing he experienced in this particular inn. Then, picking his way, he minced up the street. Reaching the square, he raised his glass to peer curiously at chickens and ducks, warily eyed a brace of rambunctious calves, sauntered by a display of cheese and jam and a scanty showing of winter vegetables. He sighed at the paucity of good food and wondered how long before spring peas would be available. About this time of year Tony always yearned for a goodly portion of luscious sweet green peas doused in rich country butter!

A stall selling handiwork did a brisk business. He moved close and, surprised by the quality of the work, bought several items for his mother. The woman behind the makeshift counter laid out an overly ornate nightgown and slyly suggested there must be a lady in his life who would enjoy it immensely.

The notion of buying a nightgown, even for a mistress, made Tony blush. More quickly than was good for his dignity, he moved to the next stall which exhibited woven objects, reminding him he had yet to buy presents for his friends. After long cogitation, he chose from among the gaudily striped scarves.

Returning to the handiwork stall, he ignored the buxom proprietor's slightly bawdy advice that he buy half a dozen shifts for his nonexistent wife, and chose, instead, a dozen daintily embroidered handkerchiefs to give to the women at the Renwicks' house party. And finally, on impulse, because it reminded him of her, he bought a well-made apron for his old nanny who, long retired, lived in a cottage near the gatehouse on his family's estate.

Then, the streets clearing of the major part of the crowd, he returned to the inn where he handed his packages, neatly tied up with string, to his valet. Good smells from the kitchen recalled his excellent breakfast, so he asked the innkeeper to supply him and his men with a basket for the road, and finally entered his carriage.

Wondering crossly why he had offered to make what was very likely a wild goose-chase of a journey, he prepared to suffer the jolts and jiggles of still another day's travel. Usually a gentle and happy man, Lord Wendover was never quite himself after a short night's sleep!

"Do you think he'll be there?" asked Seward of McMurrey. They had left Ilton behind, following the byways leading to the derelict hunting lodge.

"No. I agree with Mrs. Haydon. Still, it must be checked. Jack must know we'll search for him, and it is possible he might think that simply *because* we know he's too smart to come here, that that is what he must do."

"I don't understand why he is so bitter."

"My guess is that Jack always assumed he'd either survive the war or not. Life lacking the ability to ride was not a future he envisioned. He finds his condition not only unexpected but a burden beyond what can be borne. Death might, actually, have been preferable."

The Scotsman sighed softly, recalling how his interference had aided Jack's survival. Jack had refused amputation when his leg became badly infected. Everyone, including Jack, had expected him to die when Lady Serena told Ian of a possible cure. A cure almost more terrible to contemplate than death. But there was that *almost*. Ian had introduced maggots into Jack's wound and sat with him all through that night, wondering if he had done the right thing.

The cure, ugly as it was, had worked. But, now and again, Ian wondered if he should have left well enough alone.

"This is beautiful countryside," said Seward, interrupting his thoughts. "Bleak and lonely, but striking the soul to its core. I had forgotten."

"You've been gone a long time, Miles," rumbled McMurrey. They had become more deeply reacquainted while traveling north. "I suspect the exotic places you've been to and the exciting things you've done drove such peaceful scenery from your mind."

"I suppose it was exotic. Usually I was too on edge to care. I wonder what drove me to explore places never before seen by an Englishman. Ian, I dined on fat-roasted grubs. I ate luscious fruits you cannot even imagine. I escaped death more often than I like to remember and do you know what I longed for more than anything else in the world?" His laugh was a touch bitter.

McMurrey glanced his way. "It must be something unexpected."

"I am embarrassed to admit it. What I wanted—!" He glanced sideways. "But no! You cannot possibly guess." Seward cast Ian a roguish look. "Try!"

"A glass of good home brew."

"Beer was never a problem. I don't care where you go in the world, Ian, there is always something similar to an ale."

"Good English roast beef done to a rare turn by a master chef and served in its own juices?"

"I occasionally thought I could eat a whole side of beef if only it were available, but that isn't what I ached to sink my teeth in."

"A crisp apple you yourself picked from the tree," suggested McMurrey.

"You will never guess," said his friend, satisfied he was correct. "What I wanted above all was a nursery fire and a toasting fork. A good firm loaf of bread and a wedge of cheddar cheese! It was as simple as that old nursery treat, cheese melted on toast! Now you may laugh."

"I cannot laugh, Miles, because what you *truly* longed for was the time before your parents died, a time when you were still wrapped in their love and care. You lost that when that accident took them and have, I think, been seeking it ever since."

"Why should I want what I cannot recall?"

"Because deep inside, it is what we all want. If we are lucky we find it again. Oh, not exactly the same sort of thing, of course, for we are no longer children. Still, a good mar-

riage gives one that same sense of comfort. Of companionship. Of—" Ian frowned. "—of something I cannot name,
but, whatever it is, it gives life meaning."

"Bah." Seward stared between his horse's ears. "You
spout fairy tales, Ian. Fairy dust daydreams!"

"If it is a fairy dream, Miles, then I hope I never wake,"
said Ian gently. "Jason has it with Lady Renwick. I with
Lady Serena. I pray the rest of you find it."

Seward cast McMurrey an uncomfortable glance.

Realizing he had discomfited his friend, McMurrey obligingly changed the subject. "Things look different in the winter, but, assuming I've not forgotten the way, we should sight
the lodge from the top of this hill."

"Have we come so far?" Seward touched spurs to flanks
and, obligingly, his mount lengthened his stride up the gentle
slope. He pulled up at the top and waved his hat at his friend
whose horse continued its ambling gait. Given his size, he
never pushed his horses unless he had very good reason.
Even a strengthy beast, such as the one he rode, would soon
tire if he did.


Alex Merwin stepped down from the hack he'd hired to
bring him to his grandmother's house. He'd been delayed by
a friend and Lady Merwin would not be pleased. The door
opened and her haughty butler stared down his nose at him.

"Yes, Bates," said Alex with a sigh. "I am very late and
have put Grandmother's temper on edge. If she has thrown
something at your head I apologize."

Bates permitted himself the barest hint of a smile. "It has
not come to that, my lord. Merely she is a mite twitty." His
voice lowered. "I believe it is Mrs. Haydon's influence, my
lord, which kept her sweet. Mrs. Haydon knows how to manage her ladyship a fine treat!"

"I had better get myself in there and draw her fire or my
cousin may disown me that I have put her to the trouble."

He handed over his hat and gloves, allowed a footman to relieve him of his great coat, and twitched his cuffs into place.

Bates opened the salon doors himself. "Lord Merwin, my lady."

"Complete with apologies and excuses," he said as he moved gracefully to take his grandmother's hand, and, just as gracefully, kiss it in the old-fashioned manner the elderly woman liked.

"Wendover would approve," said Patricia, eying his movements judiciously.

"Wendover," said Alex with a laugh, "taught me the trick of it!"

Lady Merwin tapped her grandson's hand with her fan. "Rapscallion. Well, I will forgive you on this occasion, even without excuses. But only if you open your budget and tell us, at once, what you have discovered. We are all impatience, Alexander."

Alex sobered, his mouth drawing in and lines appearing. "It is easily told. *Nothing*. Nothing at all. About Jack, I mean. I discovered something else, however. George is dead. Jack's brother? If rumor is correct, Jack has come into the very devil of an inheritance. George was in debt up to his ears."

"Oh, dear," said Patricia, her expression darkening. Did this have something to do with the disaster she foresaw? "First his leg and now his fortune."

Alex glanced at his cousin, and noted her concern. His grandmother was less sensitive. "Debts? If he has the sense with which I credit him, he will instantly marry himself a rich bride and use her dowry to make a recover."

Alex, his gaze on Patricia, noticed how hard the notion hit her. He drew his grandmother's attention, giving his cousin time to recover. "Before Jack can do anything," he said, "he must be found. The knocker is off the door of the town house and no one, not even a caretaker, is there. I asked a neighbor, who left his home just as I left George's, what he knew about it all. The man put his nose in the air and said *he'd* be surprised if so much as a marble fireplace or a chandelier remained. He added that, only a few days ago, George's creditors carried off everything they could bear away. He'd never seen such a thing before."

"They simply walked out with what they could carry?" asked his shocked grandmother. "Why, what is the world coming to? And why was the house left unprotected?"

"That I do not know. Or perhaps his solicitor, too, was owed more than he liked and was among the first to raid the house?"

"Such a cynical thought," said Patricia. "Alex, do you know the solicitor? Might that be a place to start?"

"I haven't the least notion who George used, but that will be my next endeavor. Perhaps my man can discover his identity. But, Patricia, with his brother dead, finding Jack has become far more important than we dreamed. I hope he went into Hampshire. That would be the best thing for him to have done. You shake your head, Patricia. Why?"

"I feel it strongly. He is here, Alex. In London. We must find him. And quickly."

"You've another premonition?"

She answered obliquely. *"If we do not find him in the next few days, it will be too late. I feel it in my bones!"*

# *Seventeen*

Several days passed and Patricia grew more and more agitated. She could settle to nothing and, often, a footman in attendance, she stalked the streets.

And was rewarded.

Finally.

Piccadilly was crowded with pedestrians, men on horseback, carriages and carts. Traffic was slow. Even walking was difficult. Especially when one refused to watch where one was going but scanned faces, seeking the one countenance in all the world one yearned to see.

Then, coming toward her on the far side of the busy street, she saw him. *Jack.* Driving the Renwick gig.

Patricia very nearly stepped into the street, her eyes never leaving his face. She was stopped only when the footman, quite literally, put his hands on her and held her back. She glanced up at the man, discovered how worried he looked, and then glanced at the carriage suddenly blocking her view of Jack. A painful blush reddened her face and she ducked her head for a moment.

"Thank you," she said softly. "I left my good sense at home, did I not? But I saw him."

The footman knew Mrs. Haydon sought a friend who had not left a forwarding address, that it was important the man be found quickly. But he blinked at her comment since he had never believed she'd discover him in this odd fashion. "Where?" he asked. "Perhaps I can reach him for you?"

The traffic cleared for a moment. The gig was nearly across the street from her. "There," she said, indicating it.

And then, just as it moved ahead so that the hood hid the occupants, Patricia noticed there was a young woman seated beside Jack. Her blush, which had not totally withdrawn, faded abruptly. And, as the footman looked both ways, seeking to cross over to catch him up, Jack turned the gig into a narrow side street, disappearing.

"Never mind," said Patricia, her voiced choked. "It is too late. But at least we know he is in London."

She felt a trifle faint. The implication of the woman, testimony to what Jack's terrible mistake might involve, hit her even harder than when Lady Merwin suggested Jack wed a rich woman as quickly as possible. Jack, it appeared, had reached the same conclusion.

"Find me a hack," she ordered. "I must return to Lady Merwin's."

Jack leaned near the soft-voiced woman seated beside him. He was bored to tears by her prattle which was strained in the extreme. He had previously wondered if it was merely that she had been taught she must provide conversation, or if it was that she talked of trifles to avoid a conversation on a topic she did not wish raised. Still, if he heard the details of one more bonnet or where she had found the silk made up into one more gown, he feared he might say something completely unforgivable.

Somehow he must get beyond a discussion of fripperies and discover how she felt. "My dear Miss Cunningham," he said when she paused to draw breath, "I believe you told me of that particular purchase while we passed the Serpentine. Instead of discussing your wardrobe, tell me this. Are you completely happy with the notion of a possible union between us?"

Shocked silence followed his question. "It is," she said faintly, her voice fading nearly to nothing, "my papa's fondest wish."

"But I asked about *your* wishes," said Jack. A muscle worked in his jaw. This not-so-*very*-young lady, her dumpy little body encased in a gown with too many flounces and too much lace, was the best of the three maidens of whom Tremble had spoken and to whom he had provided introductions. This was the second time he had taken Miss Cunningham for a drive and he still wondered if he could go through with the negotiations his solicitor pressed him to begin.

But if he did not? That was the rub, was it not? "I'm sorry. That was exceedingly rude of me. I asked you a question and then my mind wandered. Tell me again, what is *your* wish in this?"

"I would like above all things to have a lovely town house . . . and attend all the balls and salons during the Season . . . and have a great house in the country where I would host parties during the hunting season . . . and to have all the fine clothes and furbelows I ever wanted. . . ."

Jack's mouth dropped open. He grimaced and then asked, "Surely you were told it will be years before I can manage a Season in London and that my country estates need a great deal of work before any may be considered even comfortable? My brother was not—" His voice took on the tone of understatement. "—the best of landlords. In fact," said Jack, thinking it best to be blunt in order to get through to her less than sterling intelligence, "he stripped his houses of everything of value long ago."

"Papa explained all that," she said in that complaisant voice he was coming to dread. "He says it was not your fault and that he thinks you a right one. So he will see everything put into proper order. And he will frank our Seasons here in

London until you've managed to bring your land up to snuff and have the income you should have from your properties."

Jack felt chilled. Was he to become a cit's pensioner? Was that the depths to which he was fallen?

"I see you wish the trappings of the *ton,* Miss Cunningham, but I doubt *I* will ever spend a great deal of the year in London. Perhaps no more than a week or so each Season. I prefer the country and country pursuits, you see. Besides, I would raise my family there. I would be there while my children grow up. The happiest family I know is my good friend Anthony Wendover's. I would model my own behavior on his parents'."

"I don't know his lordship's family, of course, but surely it is not proper for a peer to hide himself away in that manner? Or to have so big a hand in the rearing of his family?" She looked wide-eyed and a trifle out of countenance. "Is it not the proper thing to have nannies and governesses who bear that responsibility?"

"It is a common pattern but not one I wish to follow."

Miss Cunningham sighed and wrinkled her nose. She gave him a quick glance and then looked straight ahead. "Does Papa know of this?"

"I have not discussed my philosophy of child rearing with him, if that is what you ask."

"No, no." She waved serious thoughts away. "I mean that you would not wish to spend the Season in London. That you would not hold balls and salons and fancy water parties and jaunts to the opera and see all the new plays and . . . and I do not know, do I?"

"Nor have I discussed that aspect of my life with Mr. Cunningham."

"He won't be pleased," said the young woman, scowling. Suddenly she brightened, leaned forward. "Stop! Oh do, please, stop."

Jack pulled up, hoping there was no one behind him who would be discombobulated by his sudden halt.

"Maurice! Oh Maurice, I am here!"

Jack glanced down at the chit and discovered she was, for the first time in their acquaintance, animated, her eyes shining, and her mouth turned up in a smile. In fact, one might even call her pretty. He looked toward the young man who approached the gig. The stranger frowned.

"Mary," he said sternly. "You are aware this is forbidden."

"But I must speak to you." She held out her hand and, seemingly unable to deny her, the man clasped it. "Oh! Maurice, this is Lord Princeton. Papa introduced us a day or two ago." The man cast a quick scornful glance Jack's way. "My lord, this is Maurice Johnston. He is Papa's partner's heir."

Extending his hand, Jack eyed the stocky young man, a rueful look in his own eye. So this was the reason he'd found Miss Cunningham less than willing to show him her best side?

"Miss Cunningham has honored me with her company in the park," said Jack noncommittally.

"Maurice, please," whispered Miss Cunningham in a voice she perhaps thought Jack could not hear. "Come to the garden? Tonight?"

"No," said Maurice, making no pretense of hiding his words. "We have been forbidden to hold converse, Mary. It would be totally improper as you know. *This* is improper."

"Mugwort!"

"Not at all," Jack said. His scolding tone was just a trifle stern and brought a glare his way before she adjusted her features into a pout. "Mr. Johnston is merely an honorable man. May I ask if there is an understanding between the two of you?"

As Johnston said *no* Miss Cunningham said *yes,* and continued, "We have said since we were children that we would grow up to wed." Miss Cunningham's voice had a breathless note. "I understand it cannot be, but—" Her voice changed to a wail and her features took on a look of bewilderment. "—why can we not at least be friends?"

Jack caught the look of pain in Johnston's eyes. "Mary, it is not possible. I have told you that."

"But I do not see why!" whimpered Miss Cunningham. "Maurice, you have always been my friend. Don't you see? You *must* be my friend. Maurice, *I need you.*"

"Mary, I will always be your friend, but we can no longer see each other as we once did. *Your father has forbidden it, Mary.* Why will you not understand?" Johnston glanced at Jack, read something in his expression which brought the blood up to his ears. "My lord, try if you can explain to her. If not now, then once you are married and she has the, hmm, experience to understand?"

Jack felt his own neck redden. "It has not yet come to a betrothal, Mr. Johnston. We still consider whether we are two people who can make a marriage together." He glanced down when he felt Miss Cunningham's gaze on him and found her staring at him, open-mouthed. "I have not asked for your hand, Miss Cunningham, have I?"

"But Papa said . . ."

"Miss Cunningham," interrupted Jack, "it is not a question of what your father says. It is a question of what *you* say. This is England in the year 1812. There are laws. You cannot be forced to wed where you do not wish to wed."

Maurice Johnston blinked and then shook his head. Repressively, he said, "Surely a good daughter is subservient to her father's wishes."

"My papa says he knows what is best." Miss Cunningham spoke at the same moment. She went on to add, "He tells me I am a flibbertigibbet and haven't a notion of what will make me happy."

"But you are not happy, are you?" asked Jack softly. He glanced at Johnston and saw his heavy brows drawn together.

"Oh yes. Papa says I must be deliriously happy."

Jack met Johnston's eyes. They communicated their muual lack of understanding of a woman's mind. "It is getting late, Miss Cunningham. I had best see you home."

"Maurice," she said hurriedly. "Please? Come?"

He shook his head. "I am glad to have met you, my lord. You are not the man I thought you would be. Have care for her."

*"Nothing—* " Jack was beginning to feel just a trifle desperate. "—is settled."

His mouth set in a grim line, he gave the reins a gentle shake, and they set off for the last of their drive to Miss Cunningham's home which was situated inside the walls of the City itself. There he closeted himself with Mr. Cunningham and came away from the interview grim of feature.

Lord Merwin, upon receiving the rather incoherent note which a harried footman handed him late that evening, excused himself to his friends and immediately took himself off to Lady Merwin's town house, a much relieved footman trailing in his wake. The footman was certain he had been all over London, searching for her ladyship's grandson.

Lord Merwin entered his grandmother's salon to find Patricia pacing from one end to the other, his grandmother staring at her and frowning in a ferocious fashion.

*"At last!"* Lady Merwin twisted in her seat. "Alexander, I know I am sadly addicted to the theater, but will you tell this woman that dramatics of the sort in which she indulges belong on the stage and *not* in a drawing room?"

"Patricia, what is it?" he asked, concerned to find his cousin in such a state that she had ruined her coiffure, untied the ribbons decorating her gown and, somehow, torn the lace trimming the hem.

Patricia turned on her heel and rushed to him, holding out her hands. "He is *here,* Alex. In London. *You must find him.*" Squeezing his hand too tightly, Patricia moaned. "Or perhaps it is already too late? No, no, there has been no announcement! But it *will* appear. Oh, at any time now! It must *not,* Alex. *Not.* He will be so unhappy. Oh, Alex, what am I to do?"

"You have seen Jack," he said, drawing from her spilled words the only important point. "Now calm down. This is not at all like you." He led her to a chair and insisted she seat herself. "Now," he said soothingly. "Tell me a round tale with none of the histrionics with which you have upset my grandmother."

Patricia glanced at Lady Merwin, noted her frown, and flushed slightly. She drew in a deep breath, folded her hands in her lap, and instantly picked them up again. She began wringing them. "I was walking on Piccadilly. I was searching for him. It is the only thing I could do, Alex."

"Obviously it was not a totally futile endeavor," he said.

"Not at all futile! *I saw him!* But he was driving on the other side of the road, and you would not believe the traffic. I could not reach him, Alex, and—"

Her skin paled to the point that Lady Merwin began to search her reticule for vinaigrette.

"—he had a young woman up beside him. Alex, I know what he would do. He would marry for the fortune he needs."

"A very sensible solution to his problem," said Lady Merwin.

She was ignored. "He would sacrifice himself," continued Patricia, "and for what? A few acres which might, the sooner, be returned to productivity? A house here or there which, if he were not so impatient, might be restored without giving up the whole of his happiness?"

"And that of the woman he would wed," said Alex, nodding.

"Alex, *you must find him.*"

Alex stared into space. "Miles has arrived back from Yorkshire. He suggested he drive on down to Tiger's Lair, but I will send instead a note, and engage him in our search here.

Patricia, if Jack has already asked for the woman's hand, it is too late. You know that, do you not?"

"I know. But I think it has not gone quite that far. Not yet. That is why I feel it is imperative we find him. Quickly. He is on the verge of a decision. I know it. And, Alex, he will choose wrongly. I am sure of it! And then you did not come for hours and hours and—" Patricia's voice rose toward hysteria totally out of character. "—what could I do? He must be stopped!" She jumped to her feet and, again, began her pacing.

"Make her stop that, Alex. This carpet was woven to order by a French firm. If she persists in wearing it to the backing, it will be a disaster. There can be no replacing it until this blessed war has ended!"

Alex rose to his feet and went to his cousin. "Patricia, you must not tire yourself so. You will be of no use to Jack if you destroy your health."

She cast him a scornful look.

He chuckled. "Very well, that was maladroit. I know you are far too healthy for such trifling activity to wear you down. But your worrying *will* and it does no one any good." Slyly he added, "I do not feel I dare go off on a new search until I know you will not make yourself ill while I am gone."

Patricia stopped in her tracks. She stared straight ahead and her shoulders slumped. "Very well, Alex," she said. "But find him. Quickly."

"I have attempted to discover the name of his solicitor, but George appears to have gone through a dozen or so in the last few years and I have yet to track down the man who currently holds that position." He stared at the carpet and then sighed. "Since you believe haste is important, I will try another way."

"Alex, please return to his town house. *Please?* You say there was no one there, not even a caretaker, but that seems unlikely, does it not? Perhaps Jack and his valet are camping out there and both had gone out? Perhaps if you were to return at an hour when they would *not* be out? Very late perhaps? Or early? Very early?"

"I will do that," he said soothingly, but with little hope of finding Jack in the deserted mansion. The neighbor's tale had been specific in his story, saying that the house had been stripped to the bare bones. Surely no one could live in a house under such conditions.

Jack sat in his kitchen watching the boy, Dickens, play mumblety peg on an old three-legged table whose surface was already marred by nicks and scratches. It was in such poor shape that George's creditors had not bothered to remove it. He could see nothing wrong with the boy adding more gouges with his play. On the other hand, he thought, the lad must learn he cannot do such things to better quality furniture. Should he give the lad a lecture now? Or should he ignore the whole thing until the time came when he had a table of some quality?

Jack grimaced. Why did he think of such things when what he must do was make a decision concerning Miss Cunningham.

He recalled his careful talk with her father. The man was not unintelligent and not totally without compassion, but the cit had a blind spot which convinced him the best thing for his chit was to marry her into the peerage and *not* to Maurice Johnston. His last words were that if Jack did not come up to snuff, he would merely wait until his agent came up with another needy man and a new offer was forthcoming.

*Which would happen,* thought Jack.

There was always someone on the *ton* at point-non-plus who would take the route of marrying for money and care nothing for the woman except that her father towed him out of the river tick—and very likely with the expectation that Mr. Cunningham would continue franking equally wild behavior.

Unfortunately, Cunningham, with his unrealistic notion of what was expected of a *tonish* man, very likely *would* pay the piper if only his daughter—and incidentally, of course, his grandchildren—joined the nobility.

The man seemed to have a decidedly skewed notion of the average life of the average peer! Or perhaps *not?* Not of the sort of peer who would find himself forced to wed a young lady such as Miss Cunningham? A Miss Cunningham very much in love with Maurice Johnston?

Jack's thoughts veered away from his memory of Miss Cunningham's glowing features as she stared down at Johnston, at her unhappiness when her beau denied her plea. Instead he thought of the people who were his tenants, and the state of the land which was also his responsibility. He, by all moral and ethical reasoning, must do what he could to ease them in their plight. It was his duty to take whatever route necessary to see all returned to prosperity.

Even if that meant sacrificing his future happiness.

But that of Miss Cunningham, as well? Jack could bear to surrender his own hopes of the future, since they were of the nature they were and hopeless anyway, but could he be responsible for ruining those of the young lady? Why would her father not see that her happiness was paramount? Could he possibly manage to convince the cit he was wrong to tear his daughter from the arms of the man she loved? A man who, Jack suspected, returned that love?

Perhaps Mr. Cunningham had not considered the fact that, if the two wed, his grandchildren would inherit the whole of the business which, in their few discussions, Jack had come to believe was Mr. Cunningham's sole interest in life. Other than his dreams of joining the *ton,* at least vicariously, through his daughter.

But perhaps the argument would bear weight. If he cared to use it.

So. Did he ask for Miss Cunningham's hand, marry her for what her father could do? Or did he play Cupid and attempt to bring about a happy ending for the young lady? A wry chuckle escaped him.

"So what's so funny, guv?" asked Dickens. He frowned ferociously, having just missed his throw.

"Hmm?" asked Jack. "Funny? Ah! Just a thought, Dickens. The thought of me in the role of Eros."

"Eros? And who," asked the boy, suspicious, "would that be?"

"A Greek god with a bow and arrow who was believed to be responsible for aiming the darts of love at people's hearts."

Dickens cast Jack a disbelieving look. "What nonsense is that? Why would he hurt people that way?"

"From the mouths of babes! How correct you are, Dickens. Love does hurt," Jack murmured and fell back into reverie. This time it was not Miss Cunningham on his mind but Patricia Haydon. Thoughts of her red hair and fiery temperament brought a smile to his lips. What would Mrs. Haydon have him do in his current dilemma?

Jack sobered instantly.

Mrs. Haydon, he thought, would push him to *do*. Do something and stop his havering. Had he not known, ever since Tremble first broached the topic, that his only solution was to marry for money? Well, no. There was one alternative. He could, he supposed, leave the country and live somewhere cheaply on the little Tremble could send him. That was an alternative.

But, an alternative which left his tenants in sorry straits. And the land as well.

It was, he told himself, the coward's way out. Jack drew in a deep breath and let it out slowly. Whatever else he became, he would not be known as a coward. The decision was made. Tomorrow he would ask for Miss Cunningham's hand and he would force himself to treat the girl fairly and well. She might never know the love she'd have with Johnston, but she would not be used as another might use her. She would not be wed for her money and then abandoned to her own devices. He would do his best to see she suffered no more than was necessary for this very sorry arrangement.

Jack firmly banished Patricia Haydon's laughing features from his mind's eye and told Dickens to find the piece of slate and the chalk so that they could practice his letters. Jack found teaching the lad rewarding. Dickens was quick and, like a sponge, sopped up whatever bits of learning Jack sent his way. Very soon now Dickens would begin reading. And then, thought Jack, a fond eye on the boy, there would be no stopping him!

# Eighteen

The next morning, early, Alex Merwin and Miles Seward turned into the mews behind the row of houses which included Jack's. Merwin was certain they would find no one.

Seward told him he'd no imagination. "You have led a pampered life, Alex. Visit our troops in Portugal. Travel in the east. Or just go north to Scotland where the enclosures have beggared so many, leaving them landless and, too often, with the roof burned over their heads. If Jack lives here, he is dry, has a fireplace to provide warmth and in which cooking may be accomplished without eating the smoke of a campfire. All in all, he is not badly off. Have you remembered to count?"

Merwin pointed to the next gate. "That one."

It required no counting. The gate, unpainted for years, was the only one along the row in such shoddy condition. Seward, instead of opening it, turned the other way and entered the ramshackle stable. The stamping of a horse's hoof caught his attention and he moved along the row of empty stalls until he reached the one occupied.

"Is that Renwick's?" he asked Merwin.

"I don't know his stock well enough to tell you, but it is a horse and it is in the Princeton stables. And there," he pointed into a shadowy corner, "is a gig. I was wrong. Jack must be here after all."

"So—let us go beard the fool in his uncomfortable den."

A sudden, belligerent, and uneducated voice stopped them. "Don't you coves move an inch. I've my sticker, I have, and I'll skewer you where you stand. Won't no thieving scum steal the guv's 'orse. Not while I'm here to see they don't."

Seward slowly turned his hands out to his sides. "We are neither thieves nor scum, rascal," he said in a pleasant voice. "We are Jack Princeton's friends and must speak to him."

"Then you jist tell me why you're prowling around his stable, hmmm? Not the way of friends, sneaking around behind their backs, now is it?"

"Boy, you are an able defender of a good man," said Seward without a hint of condescension, "but is not the best solution to your problem to take us to Jack and let him decide?"

The lad scowled, looking undecided. "Yes, but I let you out this door and you take to your heels and then what?"

"Except that we will not take to our heels. We want, above all things, to speak with Jack."

The boy sighed. "And that's another thing, isn't it? You can't."

*"Cannot?"* asked Merwin, sharply.

"Ain't here, that's why. Gone off to that silly trugmoldy's place—"

Merwin was shocked by the low word for a woman.

"—isn't he? And when he'll be back, *I* don't know. So what to do with you, tha's the question," he finished.

"Is his man here?" asked Merwin, feeling some of Patricia's concern, sharing her foreboding that time was running out. "Black, his name is."

"Black's off choosing the guv's dinner, isn't he?"

"Black," said a new voice, "has returned. How may I serve you, my lords?"

Alex stepped forward, stopped when the boy raised his throwing arm, knife at the ready.

"Here, brat! You put that away," ordered Black. "The lieutenant would have the hide off your back if you harmed one of his friends!"

"Well, how was I to know? Come in here and find them poking around. Nice way for friends to behave, I *don't* think." But he slid the knife into his boot and stood back, his arms crossed and his scowl well in place.

"Where has Lieutenant Princeton gone?" asked Merwin. "We must, if at all possible, catch up with him."

Black glanced at Dickens. "How long ago did Crazy Jack depart?"

"About so long as it takes to toss down a couple of noggins of gin," said the boy. "When he went off, he sent me out to feed and water the nag."

"Not so very long, then. He is on foot? Or did he mean to take a hack?" asked Black.

"Said he'd catch him a hack, dinna he? Said we had to see to that wheel—" He nodded one sharp nod in the direction of the gig. "—afore he could go back to using that, dinna he?"

"And *where* did he go?"

"Tol' you," said the boy, exasperated. "To that trull's place."

"The lieutenant," said Black, cuffing the boy for his language, "visits a young lady. He dressed extra carefully this morning." Black drew in a deep breath, his eyes narrowing. "I will not be surprised," he ended in a doleful tone, "if he returns to us with good news."

"*Not* so good if it is what I think it might be. Boy," said Seward, "can you take us to where this chit lives?"

" 'Course I can. You think I'm one with attics to let?"

"What *I* think is that you were born to be hung," retorted Merwin, "but, gallow's bait that you are, it is up to you to guide us. Come quickly. We must catch up with Jack." He exited the stable and headed toward his curricle and horses.

\* \* \*

Jack didn't know whether to bless or curse the accident which had held him up far too long. The delay was a blessing in one sense because it postponed that which he didn't truly wish to do. In another, he wanted the whole thing settled. *Done.* Finished with, and no way to turn back. If his leg were not aching to beat the devil, he would get down and walk.

"How much longer?" he asked the driver who sat higher and could see the road ahead.

"They getting to the end of clearing up the mess. Be easier if'n it 'tweren't beer. The mob been catching it up in any sort of container, and the men clearing away the tuns are sympathetic. They don't try too hard to make 'em stop it. Even saw one wench with a thundermug!"

Jack chuckled for the first time that day. "I hope she washed it first," he said when he could speak, "although I can't say *I'd* want to drink from my chamber pot, no matter how well washed!"

"Nor I, guv. Nor I. Ah! I do believe they're movin' now."

In the next few minutes they managed all of five yards before they were once again forced to halt. Jack sighed. "Now what?"

"Two men and a boy, guv. They are in the street going from carriage to cart and whatnot. Appears to me they're searching for someone."

Jack pulled himself up and stuck his head out of the hack's window. "Hell and damnation," he muttered. He paid off his driver and quickly made his way to the entrance of a narrow alley. Where it led he'd no notion and he didn't much care. He'd made a difficult decision and, having made it, wanted no interference!

His driver, looking after his departing fare, frowned. And then, however nice the man had seemed, wondered if Jack was a wanted criminal. The driver stood up and waved. "Hoy, there. A great limping sod of a man?"

Miles heard and loped through the crowded vehicles to the hack. "A limp? Tall with a rather shaggy mop of hair?"

"That's him. He loped off down that alley there."

The man pointed and Miles halooed. Alex and Dickens caught him up and the three headed down the alley. The byway was narrow, curved, and filthy. Dickens raced off ahead and, farther on, they heard him yell.

"Hol' up now," shouted the boy. *"Do."*

The two men came around a curve and there, ahead, Dickens and Jack stood in converse. Jack looked up. He grimaced. "What the devil are you doing in London?"

"Hunting you, of course," retorted Seward. "When I thought to have a restful holiday in comfortable surroundings, what did I find? I'm riding hell for leather nearly as far as York and then still more quickly back again—and why? Because of you, old friend, that's why. Why don't you leave a forwarding address when you take yourself off?"

Jack looked at Merwin. "This adventurer who goes off for years to no one knows where asks another why he has left no forwarding address?" he asked wryly.

Merwin chuckled. "He's got you there, Miles. The only difference is that we never tried to track *you* down, whereas we *had* to find Jack."

Jack stiffened. "Oh?"

Merwin's mouth thinned. "You have no notion how insistent my cousin can be when she is convinced disaster is in the wind. Nag? Socrates's wife had nothing on Patricia! She wouldn't let up until we said we'd find you." Alex shrugged. "So here we are. And you, my buck, will return with us to my grandmother's so we may prove to my cousin you have not come to grief. Or, perhaps you have?" Alex's expression revealed his concern. "Did your brother's death leave you in as deep as we fear it did?"

"You've learned of that, have you? Yes, quite as deep. Or perhaps no. My guess is—" There was a touch of strain in it, but Jack's monkey look creased his face. "—that I'm in *twice* as deep as you fear!"

"We can discuss that elsewhere in comfort. We'll see what

may be done," said Merwin. "But for now, come and reassure Patricia."

Jack didn't move. "There is nothing to discuss," he said, his jaw set at a pugnacious angle. "I have everything in hand."

"If'n you mean to buckle ye'self to that trol . . ."

Jack glared at Dickens.

"Um, featherhead?" amended the lad. "Anyway, the one you been courtin', then you better think agin." He made a rude noise. "That one would have you killin' yourself with yawnin' afore the marriage bed had cooled!"

"Shut your trap, young one," ordered Jack. "But Dickens is correct about one thing. My solicitor located a handful of young women who wished to buy themselves a coronet. This young woman's father is more than willing to buy me out of difficulty."

"And leave you, for the rest of your life, hating the woman who made it possible?" asked Alex, putting no particular emphasis on any part of the statement.

Jack's lips compressed and a bleak look appeared about his eyes. "I can see no other solution, Alex. There is the land which has had no money put into it for years, and I've tenants to think of. They cannot be allowed to suffer, can they? Not when such a simple solution is available."

Merwin glanced at Miles. "But does it have to be settled now? Today? This instant? Patricia is exceedingly worried, Jack. She has tramped the streets searching for you and worn herself to a thread. Please, at least postpone whatever you mean to do until you have seen her?"

The bleak look around Jack's eyes deepened. Alex wondered what went on in his friend's head but doubted if he'd be told, even if he asked.

"One more day cannot matter," said Seward gently.

"Come on, guv," urged Dickens. "Do what these here swells say. They have your interests to heart. I know they do."

"Et tu, Dickens?"

"Et who?" Dickens looked bewildered. "What's this two,

then? I ain't et no one, let alone two. Not since breakfast anyway." He was affronted when the men laughed.

"Very well, then," said Jack. "I will come. There is nothing anyone can do, of course, and I only hope I can bring myself to the sticking point again tomorrow, but of course, Alex, we cannot have your cousin wearing herself to the bone, can we?"

"Cut the sarcasm, Jack," said Seward. "You haven't a notion in your head whether any of us could help you. You didn't ask, did you? I would think it behooves you to discover the answer before you do something which requires sacrificing yourself to this degree!"

Jack seemed to slump. "I have thought and thought, Miles. I can see no other solution."

"Well, *I* can. Once you have reassured Mrs. Haydon you are not about to go off half-cocked and, as she puts it, ruin everything, you and I will go somewhere quiet. We'll discuss it."

Jack stilled, ignoring Seward's offer. "Ruin?" he said. "Everything?" He glanced at Merwin. "What, do you suppose, does she mean by everything?"

Merwin debated telling him what he believed was meant. Then he decided his cousin's tender emotions were not something he had a right to reveal. "You'll discover the answer only if you have the opportunity to discuss it with her."

"Everything . . . ?" muttered Jack. *But surely,* he thought, *she cannot mean what I hope—no! That I fear she means?*


Patricia's current round of pacing had reached the far end of the room. She turned as the door opened. Her eyes widened and a happy expression lightened her features for the first time in days. She rushed down the length of the room, stopping at the last moment, and *after* Jack had braced himself to receive her in his arms. He was, he realized, bitterly disappointed that she recalled herself to proper behavior.

"Jack," she said, a trifle breathlessly. "And not . . . not . . . ?"

She obviously had no notion how to finish, so Jack did. *"Not* betrothed to the young lady I am told you saw driving with me down Piccadilly."

Patricia drew in a deep breath and let it out equally slowly. "Thank the good Lord for small favors," she muttered softly, "and," she added, "for the large ones, too."

Seward, hearing, grinned. "You haven't a notion how near a thing it was. He was on his way to do the foul deed and I fear that if there had not been an accident involving beer kegs he would, even now, be asking for our blessing and congratulations."

Merwin shook his head. "Whitbread will not be happy. A whole load of his largest kegs, smashed to smithereens."

"But why should Whitbread *not* be pleased?" asked Patricia, her voice lilting and eyes sparkling. "Was it not he who brought in a new proposal for the poor laws? Back in ought seven? Just think how many of the city's poor were made happy by today's accident?"

She could not believe how light-headed she felt now that Jack was here. It had been some time since she could deny that she loved him. That thought sobered her and she allowed the others to take up her comment, the jests flying until the door opened and Lady Merwin stalked in.

"Aha!" she said and pointed a rather gnarled finger at Jack. "The jackanapes is returned, is he?"

"Or perhaps," suggested Seward, "one should say the *jackass* is returned?"

"Or perhaps that Jack is back in his box and we will not let him out again?" teased Merwin.

"Or that Jack is about to lose his temper?" asked Jack himself. His expression denied it, however, his relief at finding himself still unbetrothed and free made anger impossible.

"Temper! Speaking of distempered freaks, Jack," put in Lady Merwin, although they had *not,* of course, *"where* did you find that lad who is even now exploring my house? He calls himself Dickens and swears he is yours?"

"Dickens? I sent him to the kitchen where he was to await me! Is he, instead, making a nuisance of himself? I'll have his lights and liver if he breaks anything!"

"Softly, Jack!" Lady Merwin exclaimed. "The boy has his hands in his pockets and his eyes starting from his head. One of my footmen is shadowing his every step. And his *language!* I'm sure I didn't understand the half of what he said to the poor footman whose ears were quite red. So perhaps it is as well I did not understand?"

Merwin laughed. "The boy has a salty tongue on him! Where *did* you find him, Jack?"

"He meant to pick my pocket, I think, but when I twigged to him we fell into conversation instead." Jack shrugged and a rather tight version of his one-sided smile appeared. "I found I couldn't let the imp fall back into the gutter so I took him home."

"He said you were teaching him to read and write," said Lady Merwin, her gaze softening.

Jack's expression suggested embarrassment and he shrugged again. "It is something to do of an evening," he said.

Patricia smiled. "Yes, but you would not do it if the boy were a poor student. How did you know he was worth saving?"

"One learns how to judge a man when one is an officer for any length of time," said Jack. He looked around the elegantly comfortable room and thought of the rough quarters in which he had been housed. When he shrugged this time, it was with discomfort. "Well, I guess I should be going. I'll just collect Dickens and . . ."

"And nothing," said Lady Merwin firmly. "Now that we have you, you will not escape so easily. As Alex said, Jack, you are back in the box and we will not let you out again to get up to more mischief, which will send our Patricia back into hysterics."

"Hysterics!" Outraged, Patricia glowered at her hostess. "Never! I didn't! You maligned me!"

"Well, whatever you call it, I'll not have you doing it again. My carpet will not stand for more of it! I've ordered dinner put forward. For all of us. And then we will have a counsel of war."

"I will stay for dinner, my lady," said Jack, his earlier depression returning and, along with it, the bleak look which had become common with him the moment he realized the mess his brother had bequeathed him. "And I thank you, but I fear it is a forlorn hope that any sort of skirmish can make this battle easier."

Seward sighed dramatically and rolled his eyes. "Jack, I *told* you I've a notion. After dinner, you and I will repair to whatever room Lady Merwin promises will be private. We will sit down and discuss this problem. What I do not understand—" He did look a trifle bewildered. "—is why you did not come to your friends at the beginning."

Jack looked from Seward to Patricia and back. "I had my reasons," he said, the bleakness replaced by grim resolve.

"If, at the time, you had given me a hint," said Miles, this time making no tactful pretense of a lack of understanding, "of *that* particular problem, I'd have backed off. Jack, I'm a flirt. If you had only thought, you would have remembered you used to accuse me of knowing no other way of communicating with a female. So I flirted with the only woman at the party who was at all interesting and accomplished at flirting back. But for neither of us was it more than a game. Now stop pretending you are more of a fool than I know you to be!"

Jack's ears were red and Patricia played with a bit of ribbon, her head turned slightly away. And then, slowly, they turned to look at each other. Volumes were spoken in that exchange of gazes.

Unfortunately, neither knew if the other understood what was said.

# Nineteen

Miles Seward forced Jack into a seat, started to sit, but, instead, paced the stretch of rug in front of his friend. Then, his neck bright red, he turned on his heel. Twice he began to speak, then shut his mouth. Finally, throwing up his hands, he began.

"There is no modest way to explain! Jack, I did not waste my time while gone. I've become a very wealthy man. It just sits there in the three percents doing nothing." He held up one hand when Jack looked as if he were about to object. "Rein in your pride! I know better than to suggest I give it to you. What I propose is that I loan you enough to pay off the mortgages and a bit over, perhaps, and charge you that same three percent. Just what it would earn anyway. What do you say?"

Jack's hands clenched the arms of his chair. He leaned forward as if he'd rise. Then he fell back. "As easy as that?"

"You're good for it."

"It will take forever to pay you back. You've no notion how bad things are."

Seward shrugged. "So it takes forever. That's sooner than if you pay the usurious interest the cent-per-cents charge. You've at least a hope of clearing the debt."

Jack looked a trifle dazed. "I cannot believe . . ."

"Why not?" interrupted Seward. "Would you not do the

ame for me? If I thought you would take it—" He flashed
a quick grin. "I would just give it to you!"

"I've never managed an estate," said Jack slowly. "I don't
now a mangel-wurzel from a mandrake root and have no
notion how to go about such things."

"You'll learn. You've both Alex and Jason to advise you,
o say nothing of Ian. Ian is likely to have a brother or a
cousin or a friend in need of a position as land agent. Go to
him and you will have honest help."

Feeling a trifle light-headed, Jack nodded. "Yes. If Ian has
a hand in recommending a man, then you may depend on
his honesty and ability. I'd not thought to ask him, but I will."

"When he returns from Scotland, be certain you do so.
Are we agreed?"

"Miles, I . . ." Jack motioned to the other chair. "Sit
down," he said, "so I need not break my neck looking up at
you."

Seward sprawled, his legs stretched before him, his elbows
on the chair arms, his fingers intertwined under his chin.
"So," he repeated. "Are we agreed?"

"I cannot afford not to. As things are, the interest takes
every bit of income which can be squeezed from the farms.
If I've something to put into improving them, there will be
more income. But—" He frowned. "—not instantly. My first
priority must be to repair the homes of those working the
land. I was told there is not one roof that does not leak." He
shrugged. "Just as an example."

"We will take the next day or two to pay off those mortgages and have my solicitor write up new ones. Tell me your
solicitor's name and I'll have mine contact him—" He
paused, frowning. "You shake your head. You haven't
changed your mind, have you? About a loan?"

"Up to the point you mentioned my current solicitor,
Tremble, definitely not. It may be prejudice because of the
mess to which he introduced me, but I cannot like the man.
I've a notion he played a double game with me. He came

out with a plan for marrying me off to a cit's daughter so smoothly I hadn't time to think, and he pushed hard for it. It is not unlikely he receives a fee for finding men in my position, do you not agree?"

"Very likely. And if he gave you no time to think through your situation, I'd say it is still more likely."

"Does that mean," said a new voice, "that you won't be a'leg-shakling yourself to that light skirts—"

*"Dickens!"*

Dickens, crawling out from under the desk, sighed deeply. "Oh very well, then. That *ninny*. Well?"

"If you are asking, will I marry Miss Cunningham—" Suddenly every bit of tension flooded out of Jack and his half-smile was truly back. "—I will not! By God, it is no longer necessary!" His laughter was utterly contagious.

Patricia, sticking her head in the door just then, smiled. "That is good to hear. Oh! May I come in? Have you finished?"

"Come in, come in. Patricia, I am told it was at your urging that I am saved from a dreadful mistake. I thank you."

"I am happy to have been of service. But have you and Miles finished your business?"

"Ya, they done it." Dickens swaggered into the light. "They jawed and jawed and took forever and a day, they did. Seems the guv's friend, here—" He jerked a thumb toward Seward. "—is rolling in it, and will let the guv have what he needs, so that's that." He rubbed his hands together. "We can go home now."

"Which reminds me," said Jack, forcing himself to his feet. "Just what are you doing here in the library when I told you to await me in the kitchens?"

"That's your fault! Well, it *is*," Dickens insisted when Jack glared. *"You didn't warn me,"* exclaimed the boy. When Jack did not relax, he continued with something approaching a whine. "I et my supper and I thanked the cook just like you said, but then I hadta get away. That woman was a huggin'

ne and a kissin' me 'til I couldn't stomach it, guv. You'd not
had me a tossin' all that good food, would you? Why, I
niver et such food afore. So," he finished, his tone returning
o normal, "can we go now?" He looked around, his hands
stuffed deep into his pockets. " 'Taint so bad here, but all
his folderol! Never knew there was so many *things* anywhere. And, guv, *they'll break* if you so much as sneeze on
em."

Seward and Patricia smiled. Jack grimaced, but it hid a
smile. "I guess you must avoid sneezing, Dickens, since I
am not yet ready to leave. Or perhaps—" Jack thought of
Black and how worried he must be. "—you go on without
me. You can find your way back to the house, can you not?"

Dickens cast Jack a look pregnant with disgust. "Find
m'way?" He threw back his narrow shoulders and swaggered
owards the door. *"I,"* he said, "could find m'way outta hell."
At the door, he turned around, bowed in a surprisingly
smooth fashion to Patricia.

Patricia curtsied and watched the boy leave the room.
"Who," she asked "was that?"

"Everyone has a cross to bear. To keep them humble,"
said Jack, tongue in cheek. *"That* is mine. He goes by the
name of Dickens."

Patricia had a vague recollection of Lady Merwin speaking of a boy and presumed this urchin must be he. She made
no comment, however, because Jack and Seward were firm-
ing up plans to meet in the morning. Then Seward excused
himself to make his adieus to Lady Merwin, reprehensibly,
leaving Jack and Patricia alone. He even shut the door as he
left, which he surely knew he should not do.

Jack knew it, too. "Patricia? Shall we too join the others?"

"In a minute. Tell me what you have done. If it is not too
private?" She strolled nearer and seated herself in the chair
Seward had vacated. "Unless—" She immediately returned
to her feet. "—you feel we *must* return to . . ."

He smiled. "I am certain we *should,* but perhaps no one

will notice if we do not." He described Seward's offer a
his relief at receiving it, and then asked, "Tell me, Patrici
why were you so very insistent I must be found?" Then
flushed. "If it is not too personal a question," he finishe
echoing her thought of a few moments previous.

"Jack, I cannot explain it. It is simply that, occasionall
I get a strange sort of feeling. The experience is always o
of great urgency. So urgent, in fact, that I must give in to
This time your departure roused it."

"You cannot explain it and I do not understand it, but
am very happy you experienced it. Patricia, you cannot kno
how near I was to asking for Miss Cunningham's hand, ar
I would have regretted it forever. I was actually on my w
to speak with her father when the others caught me up.
fact, I *should* have reached her home. If it were not for a
accident ahead of us which closed off the street and made
impossible to move—" He shook his head in bewildermen
"—I would already have proposed and been accepted."

"But the street *was* blocked, you *were* stopped, and the
*did* catch you. Perhaps the accident was the answer to m
prayers, Jack."

"You would say I was blessed by a miracle, is that it?
he asked, speaking far more lightly than he felt.

They fell silent. Neither could mention the one thing
most importance—and neither could think of anything els
to say. Finally, unnerved by the silence, Patricia rose to h
feet. Jack followed suit, his struggle to rise much less n
ticeable than days earlier. All the walking he had done ha
strengthened his bad leg somewhat.

"Perhaps," he suggested, "it would be best if we rejoi
the others."

"Yes. Yes, we must, must we not?"

"Yes. We must." *Or, the thought filled Jack's mind, yo
will find yourself compromised and Lady Merwin insistin
on an immediate wedding.*

The light-headed feeling shifted to a more light-hearte

feeling and Jack wondered if that might not be the answer to his problem: Forced to wed him, he need never know if she would refuse his proposal—assuming he ever had the courage to make it!

*Which,* he thought and a touch of the old bleakness returned, *I never shall.*

His interview the next day with Miss Cunningham's father was stilted in the extreme, the two men parting in mutual dislike. But Jack had managed to plant the notion that, if allowed to wed Maurice, her heart's desire, the partnership would be continued and united in Cunningham's grandchildren. The notion had held the cit quiet for fully half a moment. Perhaps it would take root and come to full blossom and Miss Cunningham and her Mr. Johnston would wed after all. Jack hoped so.

Letters exchanged with those at the Lair informed the Renwicks' guests remaining there of all that happened in London, with the exception of Jack's aborted wooing of Miss Cunningham. *That* was an episode Jack hoped he would manage to forget. Eventually. So, with Jack's problems on the way to a solution, life at Tiger's Lair went on pleasantly.

Since Jack's departure, Lady Anne was much in Lord Bladney's company. He encouraged her to write her letter to the *Edinburgh Review* and they spent a hilarious hour discussing possible pseudonyms. His lordship did not, however, nerve himself to lay his heart before Lady Anne. Each time he'd done so in the past, she had trampled all over it with her little feet. He could not, he knew, bear another rejection.

Still, he began to feel some hope. Lady Anne did, now and again, give him the sort of hint a well-brought-up maiden was allowed to give. So maybe . . . just maybe.

While Lord Bladney's star rose, Lord Hayworth's fell. His wooing was not faring nearly so well. While Lady Blackburne was perfectly happy to indulge him in a little light dalliance, she would say him neither yea nor nay when it came to marriage.

Still, he would not despair; the fact that she did not say nay was enough for now. If she did not agree during this visit, then perhaps she would on his next. Lord Hayworth was determined to ask as often as necessary.

Lady Serena was less content. She spent much of her time fretting. It was a bad time of year for travel, so when she was not worrying about Ian, she worried about her mother. Only Lady Renwick's company eased her. The two women talked about their condition and how much they looked forward to the time when they would hold their babes in their arms. And it was fortunate, they told each other, that there were no mothers attending the party who would tell horrid tales of childbearing. No one to replace the wonder of it all with Dire Warnings and Dreadful Experience!

Still, the house party was happier when the wanderers returned. Only Ian remained away. Lady Renwick held several small dinner parties with carefully chosen guests. And she had the annual party for Renwick's tenants for which all the guests helped. It was, thought Jack, just the sort of afternoon he hoped, someday, to enjoy with his own tenants.

# Twenty

The days until Christmas passed quickly, quietly, contentedly. Jack continued to discover depths in Patricia which made his heart alternately sing that she was the woman she was—and die a little that he dare not ask her to wed him.

Until one day Lord Hayworth invited the two of them to join him on a visit to the conservatory and, of course, Lady Blackburne.

Jack had never before entered the overly warm room with its smell of damp earth and growing plants. He was impressed. "I don't believe I have ever seen that particular flower before," he said, cupping a delicate bloom that scented the area for yards around it.

"It is called an orchid. A friend, far wealthier than I am, collects them. He gave me cuttings from two or three, but that is my favorite. He has men all over the world tracking them down and pays well for the new varieties they bring him."

"Are they difficult to grow?" asked Hayworth.

"Once they have accepted a new home, they thrive, but they require more warmth and greater dampness than some plants."

"I will have to see to having a conservatory built onto my home," said Lord Hayworth, casting a sly glance toward Lady Blackburne. Her ladyship blushed. "You must advise me."

"Of course," she said just a trifle sharply.

Patricia caught Jack's gaze and arched her brows. He shrugged. Both thought that, just perhaps, there was more going on between his lordship and Jason's aunt than they had suspected.

"You, Jack, must come to me when you decide to add a conservatory to one of your houses," said her ladyship, recovering her poise. "I highly recommend the diversion of growing things. There is much joy in seeing a seed become a seedling and, eventually, a lovely flower. A never ending pleasure," said Lady Blackburne.

"I doubt I'll have the funds for anything so out of the way as a conservatory. Not for years. But I will keep your offer in mind when that day comes."

"Then things are as bad as I had heard?" asked Lord Hayworth, a touch of sympathy in his tone.

"Very likely worse," said Jack shortly. "George spent every groat he could wring from his estates. And," he added, unable to avoid just a touch of bitterness, "from any other source he could find."

"I could return one item he should not have sold," said Lord Hayworth. "In fact I will. I shall write my butler and direct him to ship it wherever you tell me you'd like it sent. It is your mother's portrait," he finished when Jack looked confused. "I bought it some years ago. A lovely woman, your mother."

"I wondered where it had gone. It is one of the few things I regret losing," said Jack. "But, frankly, at the moment, it is far safer where it is. When I've a place to hang it which will do it justice, I will not let pride stand in the way of informing you I am ready to receive it."

"You have your work cut out for you, have you not?" said her ladyship. "You should wed, my lord, and have the aid and solace of a good wife."

Spots of color marred Jack's cheeks. "To the contrary," he said, speaking stiffly. "I could never ask a woman to share the difficulties I face. Think, my lady," he continued. "I have no decent place to which I might take her. I have no furnishings, no family jewels to give her, cannot, for years, provide a Season in London for her. I cannot even afford to gown her as she should be gowned! Every cent I can find must be poured back into the estates until they are returned to what they were."

"There are many women who would deem it an honor to share your travail," said Patricia. She spoke so quietly that, for a moment, the meaning behind her words did not register.

Jack studied her for a long moment. "Perhaps," he responded, "but it would cause dishonor in me to ask it of her."

They stared at each other, fighting a silent battle. Then, repressing a small sob, Patricia turned on her heel, stumbled over a loose brick, and then, catching herself, rushed out the door.

"Occasionally—" Lord Hayworth stared off into a high corner of the conservatory as if the wet panes were the most fascinating of things. "—love and happiness turn dishonor into honor."

Jack's eyes narrowed. *"You* would ask the woman you love to suffer deprivation and discomfort for what may be years?"

"Hmm. Perhaps. Depending on the woman, her character, her love for me, and her fortune." He held up a hand in a fencer's gesture. "I do not mean that *I* would use the fortune. I would have it put safely into her own hands so that she would *not* be deprived of any of the elegant trifles to which she is accustomed."

Jack made no pretense that their discussion was hypothetical. *"Has* Patricia a fortune?"

"Her husband left her comfortably well-off," said Lady Blackburne who always knew such things about people. "I have heard her widow's portion is hers outright and need not be returned to the family coffers if she reweds."

Jack's eyes lost focus. Then, without a word of goodbye, he too left the conservatory.

Lord Hayworth struck the classic pose which denoted disgust. "What bores the next generation have become!"

"What do you mean?" asked Lady Blackburne.

Lord Hayworth grinned and shoved his hands into his pockets. "Why, only that they are a mannerless bunch, are they not? First Mrs. Haydon leaves us with nary a by-your-leave, and then Princeton behaves in exactly the same manner." He shook his head. "Boorishness is rampant, my lady. I wonder," he said, speaking judiciously, "if I might take up the fashion. Why, think! I might grab you and kiss you whenever the notion took me. I'd not be forced to ask if you wished to be kissed. I might sneak up on you—" He stalked her. "—at any time . . . like this," he finished softly, his hands reaching for her waist.

Lady Blackburne did not try so *very* hard to avoid him.

Christmas Day dawned bright and beautiful, crisp and chill, but not so icy cold as to be uncomfortable. Everyone had attended midnight services the evening before. It was a lovely service and Patricia had returned to the Lair feeling light-hearted and happier than she had for some time. Going back over their conversation in the conservatory, it had finally occurred to her that Jack might love her almost as much as she loved him.

And if they loved each other, then, somehow, she would contrive a happy ending for them, assuming he did not come to his senses and do it himself!

Sahib rose to his feet when she entered the blue salon. He stalked toward her and raised his great head to stare her in the face. She stared back. Tentatively, she stretched out a hand. Obligingly, Sahib moved until she could touch his head. She scratched him and heard that funny noise which she thought to be a tiger's purr. After a moment he moved another step nearer and pressed against her side. Then he looked up at her again. Patricia had the oddest notion Sahib was telling her to have patience, that she would attain her heart's desire.

The exhilaration grew, filling her nearly to bursting. Even when Lady Anne entered the salon, saw Sahib near to the door and, with a restrained screech, whisked herself back out of the room, it did not fade. Nor could Patricia, who truly felt sympathy for Lady Anne's fear of Sahib, repress a smile.

"Sahib, is there no way of making that woman understand you are not to be feared?" Sahib shook himself in such a way that Patricia decided it meant the same as a shake of the head. "Well, it is too bad. She will never know the pleasure of touching you." Sahib opened his mouth with that silent roar of his, nodded his head, and then returned to his place at Lord Renwick's side where he settled down, his eyes slowly opening and closing in contentment. Patricia moved forward, took the chair beside her host, and fell into conversation with him.

". . . And tomorrow neighbors drop by all afternoon to celebrate Boxing Day," he said when the weather palled and the history of how his lordship acquired Sahib had been told.

"I thought Lady Renwick seemed preoccupied. Is there any way in which I might help?"

"More decorations are to be arranged. If you would oversee the servants working in the ballroom, I know Eustacia would appreciate it very much."

"She should have asked!"

"She feels she has asked far too much of everyone as it is. All of you helped at the tenants' party, did you not? Providing yeoman service, I am told. One does not invite guests to a house party merely to have extra help at hand, you know."

"I enjoy Christmas decorating. Even when alone at Merwin Hall I have greens brought in. Some years ago I bought wide, red ribbons which I save from year to year. From them I fashion bows. The red satin and the greenery are quite a striking combination, you know. And the doing of it is great fun. The servants enjoy it too, you know."

Others entered the salon just then and the conversation became general. Only when they were ready to move in to dinner did Patricia manage to have a word with her cousin.

"Has it arrived?" she asked softly.

"Yes," he answered, equally softly. "I have studied it and believe it will work just as you hoped."

"I pray it does."

"So do we all."

The Boxing Day party wound down well before the light faded, the last of the company having no wish to drive home in the winter dark. When the Renwicks and their houseguests were alone again, all gathered in the blue salon in which Patricia had expended her greatest effort when arranging Christmas greenery and in which the Yule log burned.

Patricia sniffed. "I love the smells of Christmas."

"Yes, especially the evergreen boughs. But I also love the earlier hints of Christmas. I mean the aromas released during the Christmas baking," said Lady Anne who had, just that morning accepted Lord Bladney's latest offer of marriage. She was feeling relaxed and happy for the first time in ages and could, now that she had relinquished any notion of a marriage with Lieutenant, now Lord, Princeton, forgive Patricia for her unkind words and for pushing her patient into doing more than any sensible person would try. *Although,* the bemused thought passed through her mind, *his efforts seem to have done him no harm.* Not wishing to consider the notion further, she added, "The spices seem to permeate the whole house."

"Yes," agreed Lady Serena, "and more spices go into the

Christmas punch. There is something distinctive about the scent of a wassail bowl, is there not?"

Lord Renwick moved nearer, along with Sahib, followed by the other men in the party. Lady Anne, reminded she was threatened, turned her gaze on Lord Bladney who came quickly to her side, seated himself beside her on the sofa, and drew her protectively close.

Those who had not already done so added their gifts to the pile on a table near the fireplace. There were so many gifts, they threatened to slide down onto the large crate McMurrey placed on the floor.

There was one other gift not on the table. Patricia's gift to Jack lay in her lap, not to be given to him until after the opening of the gift from his friends.

Lord Renwick moved to a spot before the fireplace and caught everyone's attention. "I wish I could hand around the gifts as a good host should do," he said. "Since I cannot, I have asked Lord Hayworth to do the honors. My lord?"

Lord Hayworth made a ceremony of the handing out of gifts, foregoing all his usual mannerisms. But even serious and lacking in his usual clowning demeanor, his wit shone through—and soon everyone was laughing and talking back and forth, exclaiming and showing their appreciation.

Jack even managed to thank Lady Anne for the embroidered slippers without feeling wary. It was, he decided, because Lady Anne, having betrothed herself to Lord Bladney, no longer threatened his peace. Jack was fingering the satin stitches on one of the slippers when Lord Hayworth, pretending great effort, lifted the last gift. Then, grinning, he brought it to Jack who stared at it and then around the room.

"What is this?" he asked.

"Patricia's notion which we five of the Six, thought good. We arranged for it and we hope to God it does what we think it will," said Lord Merwin, the faintest of frowns drawing his brows together.

Jack, too, frowned and wariness returned. "I wonder. Do I *dare* open it?"

"It is not a jest, Jack," said Lord Wendover. "We would not do that."

"*Nor,*" rumbled McMurrey, who had arrived from Scotland only a day or two before Christmas, "would Mrs. Haydon."

Jack looked toward Patricia, who sat still as a stone, a worried look in her eyes. "What is it, Patricia?"

"In the box?" she said, pretending to misunderstand. "Open it and you will know."

"You are concerned about it."

"Now that the time has come, I fear I have erred, that it will *not* help, that you will . . . oh, I do not know!" She bit her lip, staring at Jack, her heart pounding, her growing uncertainty causing her to tremble.

"Come Jack. Do not hesitate. If we have done wrong, believe it was with the best of intentions," said Lord Renwick.

"I begin to feel as nervous as Patricia appears," said Jack, but he finally pulled the crate nearer and worked at the rather complicated latch holding it closed. The lid came up, and Jack frowned. The inside was full of something wrapped in soft, natural brown woolen fabric. Carefully he lifted the thing out and Lord Hayworth helpfully pulled the crate from under it.

Moments later the new saddle, the leather glowing with the rubbing it had received, sat before him. Jack's brows clashed together. "But . . ."

"Take a closer look, Jack," said Seward, interrupting what he feared would be a tirade.

"Ah!" Jack touched the odd feature near the front of the saddle. "I think I see," he said slowly. "This will clasp my leg firmly and hold it close as it should be held, will it not?"

"Our main concern," said McMurrey, "is that you will not be sensible and will attempt to ride in the neck or nothing fashion which is your custom. *That* we fear might be a serious error."

"*Now* I understand," said Lady Blackburne, turning to Patricia. "I apologize for having no faith in you," she said. "Had you not better give his lordship your gift to him?"

"I think she already has, since this was her notion," said Jack, his eyes glowing and his hands, trembling slightly from emotion, caressing the specially built saddle which would, pray God, allow him to ride again. Even if only at a sedate pace and over easy terrain. *He would ride!*

Patricia rose and took to him her gift, moving back as he unwrapped it. He looked up at her. "You bought this that day in Lewes?" he asked softly.

"Yes."

"Thank you," he said, his gaze, holding hers, trying to say everything he could not put into words. He rose and, limping badly, went to her. He held out his hands and Patricia put hers into them, reveling in his warmth and strength.

"I knew how very unhappy you were that you could no longer ride," she whispered. "It seemed that, perhaps, if that problem were solved, you might manage to accept the rest?"

"You have given me more than you will ever know. More than anyone will ever give me." His gaze held hers in thrall. "You have given me back my life."

Patricia's hands tightened around his. "Jack, you will be sensible, will you not?"

He threw back his head and laughed loudly and freely. "Oh, my dear, yes of course I will be sensible. Most of the time, anyway!"

"That," she said, frowning, "does not alleviate my worry!"

"Be easy. I will do no more than I can manage. On horseback, I know myself. I will discover exactly what I can and cannot do." He grinned. "As you have urged me to do again and again."

"Then it is on my head if you come a cropper," she said,

pretending a moroseness she could not truly feel in the face
of his happiness.

"No. On my head be it. You will not be responsible, Patricia. Only my own stupidity or an egotistic lack of caution
will lead me into difficulties. And I am not stupid, I hope."

"But a trifle egotistic when it comes to riding, I seem to
recall!"

"I promise to have a care. Will that do?"

Patricia discovered they still held hands. Coloring rosily,
she pulled hers free. "Yes. If you promise, then I am certain
you will keep to a sensible course."

"I promise."

"Then I may be at ease."

The Renwick butler announced that a supper had been
laid in the dining room for those who were interested. The
men, excepting Jack, left in something of a rush. The women,
excepting Patricia, followed in a more restrained fashion.

"May I have a moment," asked Jack, glancing at the open
door which allowed them to be together, alone but with propriety.

"Of course."

"Alex told me a bit more of why you urged him to come
find me. He says you have always had these strange feelings,
these premonitions. I would think it a terrible burden if you
are constantly made aware of situations when others will
find themselves in difficulty. It is no wonder you prefer to
live in the country where there are fewer people around you."

"I do not have premonitions on every and all possible
occasions, Jack. Only about those—" Very nearly she had
said, *those I love,* but changed it. "—I know very well.
Strangers and casual acquaintances haven't that effect on
me."

"But you had it for me."

"Yes." She blushed slightly. "It was an exceedingly strong
and urgent feeling."

"I see."

He eyed her and Patricia wondered if he saw more than it was proper for her to reveal. Ah! If only it *were* proper for her to beg him to wed her. If only she dared ask him when, by every convention, he must ask her.

"But," she added, "although you said it for the wrong reason, you are correct that I prefer the country. And the quiet life." He frowned slightly. "It is nothing new. For years I have felt that way," she said, wondering if he would take the hint that she would like it best of all if she were married and lived a country life with him.

Unfortunately, if he did, it did not bring him to speak the words she wished above all else to hear. She sighed. "I think," she said, "that I will forego supper and go up to bed."

Jack nodded and offered his arm. With his crutch under his other, he escorted Patricia to the foot of the stairs. He watched her climb them and, once she reached the top and disappeared, he turned into the Renwicks' hall and on to his own room.

Jack, who had tried out his new saddle in the company of his friends, entered the long hall leading to his room—and was stopped short of it when, Sahib, who lay near his door, rose to his feet. The big cat snarled. Jack paled.

"Sahib. You know me."

The tiger growled softly. Carefully Jack backed up a pace or two. The cat moved an equal space toward him. Again Jack hopped back. The tiger opened his mouth in one of those silent snarls which were exceedingly intimidating. Jack made another move toward the entry hall. The tiger lay down but when Jack didn't move again, he raised his head and gave another rumbling growl.

Jack sighed. It seemed his presence in the Renwicks' private wing was unwanted. At least, Sahib made it clear *he* did not wish it!

Jack stepped back out into the front hall where he found

Patricia contemplating the stairs, a look of satisfaction giving her face a glow. She heard Jack and looked around. "You sat down and scooted up and down the stairs on your rump!" she said, triumphantly.

He grinned. "You have guessed. And now you mean to hold me to learning how to manage stairs in a less infantile fashion? Well, you needn't. It will perhaps surprise you to know I have already done so!" Curiosity filled him. "How *did* you guess?"

"Not through logical thought," she said ruefully. "A maid was dusting. She sat on one step while she worked on what she could reach, and then she scooted down a step when she finished in order to do the next. She did the last just a moment ago and took her rags into the back of the house."

As Patricia spoke, she drifted beneath the kissing bough which Lady Renwick had hung from the chandelier. Jack, glancing up, approached.

"I have guessed," she said, "but you say you've already solved the problem? I win the skirmish but lose the war?" She frowned. "Not exactly lose, of course, if you have done what I wished you to do, but *how* do you manage?"

"My bad leg has grown far stronger. Not so strong as I'd like, but much better. I can balance on it now. For a time. So I go up side-ways. I stand on the crutch and bad leg, move the good leg up, pull the bad leg up to join it, and do it all over again. A bit slow and not exactly graceful, but, if the steps are reasonably broad, it works."

The distance between them was bridged by one more step and Jack grasped Patricia in a one-armed embrace.

"Got you," he said and leaned to steal a kiss.

It was supposed to be a light-hearted touching of lips, a teasing Christmas mistletoe kiss, but when Patricia clutched his shoulder and leaned into him, he deepened it . . .

. . . deepened it still more when he heard a faint moan and felt her pressing closer. When the kiss ended, they stared

t each other in astonishment, neither quite certain what he
r she felt, let alone what the other felt!

Patricia, blunt to a fault, had the courage—or was it the
oolhardiness?—to ask. Ever after, she was uncertain
vhether it was the one or the other.

Bemused, he repeated her question. "How do I feel?" he
sked. His devil-grin appeared. "As if I would like to try
iat again."

"You would?"

"Don't pretend you didn't enjoy it," he retorted, his eyes
arrowing, "or that I will not indulge you in as many such
isses as you like."

"But only if I likewise . . . indulge you?"

Jack sobered. "Tricia, why do you shake your head? I
*now* you liked that kiss."

She smiled. "Of course I did. It is the Tricia to which I
bject. I have never been a Tricia. A Patty, perhaps?"

"Never. Tricia."

"Nonsense." If he had not been holding her, she would
ave stamped her foot. "Someone named Tricia must be
mall and perky and nothing at all like my sturdy self."

Jack eyed her. "Very well. But not Patty. Patty is a sober
iame. I will call you . . . Trixie. As I used to do when we
vere all young together."

"You will what? You did?"

"Actually, it was Tricksy Minx, or some such thing." Ut-
erly bland of expression, he added, "When we are wed, I
vill merely call you Trixie."

*"When we wed!"*

"Yes." He nodded solemnly, although his heart was in his
hroat with the fear she'd say him nay. Or that she *should*
ay him nay. "Or perhaps *before*. Now, in fact. My Trixie
ady."

"I've played no tricks on you," she objected, half insulted
nd half laughing.

"No. But you are a very tricky lady who has made life

worthwhile when I was certain it never would be again. rode this morning. *I actually rode again!"* He hesitated "Trixie—"

His sudden descent from elation to uncertainty disarme her.

"—you will wed me, will you not? I know you shoul not, of course." Before she could respond he continued. "I'r not much of a bargain, lame and in debt to my ears, and never thought to ask you. I have wanted to, but it seemed t me that it would be unfair to you. Still . . ."

"Still you managed to kiss me silly!"

His eyes sparkled with sudden satisfaction. "Yes I did, di I not? Perhaps—" His brow quirked down in that oddly sel deriding way it had. "—we will discover I have not harme myself in any way which is, hmm, important?"

Patricia ignored his suggestive tone. "Your injury wa never important to anyone but you," she scolded.

His grin faded and he looked over her shoulder. "It is stil important to me, Trixie. What I lost because of my wound will always be lost to me and I will not pretend I will eve totally accept it. But you, my dear—" He looked her in the eye. "—convinced me life need not be utter misery, wholly lacking in interest. The thing is—" The derisive look turne to one of mock concern. "—I cannot promise to remembe it. So. Will you wed me? Lame and poor and the very bad bargain that I am? To kick me when I need kicking and help me when I need help? I don't know how it is," he continued "but I do not mind when *you* help me. I *do,* you know, wher it is anyone else."

"Perhaps you don't mind because you know I love you," she said, holding his gaze. "Love soothes a multitude o problems, you know."

"You . . . love me?"

"Dolt!" But she said it softly, lovingly. *"Of course* I love you! I have known for days now!"

"Only days." Jack sighed a lugubrious sigh. "Ah me. Now I *know* I am less a man than once I was."

Warily she eyed him. "Oh?"

"Of course." She attempted to move away but he refused to allow it. "If I were *not,* you would have fallen in love with me when first we met." He pretended a smugness he didn't truly feel and this time she escaped—although not far. He caught up her wrists together in one hand when she beat her fists against his chest. "Trixie . . ."

He released her and her palms flattened, pressed against him. "Yes?"

"You will marry me, will you not?"

"I think I *have* to." Her arms slid around his waist and again she leaned into him.

Her unexpected weight nearly upset him. He steadied them. "Why should you if you do not wish it?"

"Because one of your friends and at least two servants have been in the hall since you came." She grinned over his shoulder at her cousin but made no attempt to remove her arms from around Jack's waist. "If we do *not* wed, my reputation will be in shreds!"

He observed the twinkle in her eyes and pulled her closer. After a glance up at the mistletoe, he moved them a few inches until they were once again directly beneath it. Then he kissed her again. Thoroughly.

When they came up for air, spots of color marred his cheeks. "Listen, woman. And listen well. I don't know if I can ever admit this again."

"Yes?"

"I love you, too," he whispered and then shut his eyes tight.

"Ah. Was it truly so difficult to say the words?"

"Well, yes," he admitted. "Quite as difficult as I'd feared."

"Hmm. What *you* need is *practice.*"

"Oh?" he asked.

"Hmm. And, since we won't always have a kissing

bough as an excuse, I think perhaps I'll insist on the words before I—" The tip of her tongue appeared between her lips. "—*indulge* you," she finished.

"You will, will you?"

One side of his mouth lifted in that half-smile so characteristic of him.

"I *think* I will," she said, his look giving her pause.

"Hmm. I wonder which of us will give in first."

"What?"

"I might make the same demand, might I not?" One brow arched. "Before *I* indulge *you*."

They eyed each other. Then, simultaneously, they whispered, "I love you."


The hall was off-limits to servants and company alike for the remainder of the afternoon because Lady Renwick, passing through at just that particular moment, ordered it so.

Sahib, yawning now and again from boredom, was a more than adequate enforcer of their privacy.

## AUTHOR'S NOTE

Dear Friends,

THE CHRISTMAS GIFT is the third in the Sahib-the-ti-
ger series about the Six. The fourth involves Lord Wendover
who always assumed he'd be blessed with the sort of marriage his parents enjoy, one of love, trust, and companionship. Imagine his chagrin when he finds he has unwittingly
compromised a young lady. It is worse. The lady, hoping to
save her brother and herself from utter poverty, had chosen
another as the hero of her little plot. When she wakes in
Tony's bed she is upset to discover the wrong man occupies
the other half! Eventually she realizes Fate took a hand to
find her THE PERFECT HUSBAND—but still longer before Wendover, with Sahib's help, realizes he has just the
marriage he always thought to have. Look for it in June 2001.

Two more books complete the series. Lord Merwin, a Tory,
loves the daughter of a Whig gentleman. Winning the Whig's
respect and blessings on a marriage between Alex and his
daughter is difficult beyond belief! This novel, still untitled,
will be published in October 2001. And finally there is Miles
Seward, adventurer. *His* bride is very nearly as daring as is
he. (Miles, by the way, played a part in my novella, "Mistletoe Kisses," which is on the shelves now, October 2000,
in Zebra's STOCKING STUFFERS.)

Finally, a Mother's Day collection, A KISS FOR MAMA,
will include my novella, tentatively titled, "Happily-Ever-

After," about a blue-stocking spinster forced to accept the care of her brother's offspring. Miss Justina Dunsforth is, secretly, the author of a series of well-liked Gothic tales. Children underfoot, along with the godfather of one of them, make it difficult to finish her latest book! A KISS FOR MAMA will be published in April 2001.

Season's Greetings to all and to all Happy Reading!

Jeanne Savery

P.S. I love to hear from my readers. You may contact me at either of these addresses: P.O. Box 833, Greenacres, WA 99016-0833; e-mail: JeanneSavery@yahoo.com